"Don't you dare die, Ember Riddick."

"'Kay," she murmured, feeling her world tip and begin to go black again. "Raum?"

"What?"

"Are you my guardian angel?" she asked, and smiled at his snort, which was as much of an answer as anything.

"No," he finally said.

She dug her fingers more tightly into his shirt, and only fleetingly wondered whether her claws had retracted. Either way, he didn't flinch, didn't make a sound. And it no longer mattered because she was falling, falling, like Alice down the rabbit hole, into a darkness that even she couldn't see through.

"Save me anyway?" she asked, her voice barely a whisper. Then she was gone.

KENDRA LEIGH CASTLE

was born and raised in the far and frozen reaches of northern New York, where there was plenty of time to cultivate her love of reading thanks to the six-month-long winters. Sneaking off with selections from her mother's vast collection of romance novels came naturally and fairly early, and a lifelong love of the happily ever after was born. Her continuing love of heroes who sprout fangs, fur and/or wings, however, is something no one in her family has yet been able to explain.

After graduating from SUNY Oswego (where it also snowed a lot) with a teaching degree that she did actually plan on using at the time, Kendra ran off with a handsome young navy fighter pilot. She's still not exactly sure how, but they've managed to accumulate three children, two high-maintenance dogs and one enormous cat during their many moves. She's very happy to be able to work in her pajamas, curled up with her laptop and endless cups of coffee, and her enduring love of all things both spooky and steamy means she's always got another paranormal romance in the works. Kendra currently resides wherever the navy thinks she ought to, which is Maryland at present. She also has a home on the Web at www.kendraleighcastle.com, and loves to hear from her readers. Please stop by and say hello!

RENEGADE ANGEL

KENDRA LEIGH CASTLE

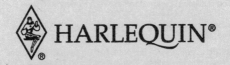

HARLEQUIN®

TORONTO • NEW YORK • LONDON
AMSTERDAM • PARIS • SYDNEY • HAMBURG
STOCKHOLM • ATHENS • TOKYO • MILAN • MADRID
PRAGUE • WARSAW • BUDAPEST • AUCKLAND

Recycling programs
for this product may
not exist in your area.

ISBN-13: 978-0-373-61842-2

RENEGADE ANGEL

Dear Reader,

Thank you for picking up *Renegade Angel*. I'm very excited to be sharing this, my very first Nocturne, with you!

I've always loved the idea of angels, especially the ornery, sword-carrying kind. This is probably partially because I was once a Catholic schoolgirl with a very active imagination, and partially because my own life has been full of wonderful, unconventional, and yes, even ornery angels. So it's small wonder that I'd eventually want to write a story featuring a hero with a sword, wings…and a less than angelic disposition. Raum, an ex-angel, is also on the run from Hell, making him for all intents and purposes an ex-*demon*, as well. So where does an ornery supernatural being with wings fit in when he's caught between angels who've hired him to do their dirty work and demons who will stop at nothing to see him reduced to soulless cinder?

You and a woman named Ember Riddick, who has quite a few problems of her own, are about to find out. I hope you enjoy watching Raum and Ember find their places in this world—and of course, in one another's arms—as much as I enjoyed writing their journey.

Happy reading!

Kendra

This one's for my Angels of Sanity—

Marie and Cheryl, for the sisterhood

Donna, Lisa, Ana, Elizabeth aka "Ms. Moonlight," Jessica, and Leslie, for all the support, cheerleading, and incredible humor, not to mention the fascinating things that continue to turn up in my inbox on a regular basis…couldn't have written this one without you!

And as always, my wonderful family. Thank you for continuing to live with, and love, my own special brand of crazy.

Prologue

He left at twilight, moving swift and silent beneath a deepening blood-red sky. Beyond the gleaming walls of the Infernal City, across the cracked and barren wasteland that rang day and night with the cries of the damned, the crow soared on sooty wings toward the gnarled shapes jutting into the acrid air just beyond.

The Gate of Souls. Freedom.

That was, if they managed to make it out.

Raum coasted on the hot currents of a smoke-filled breeze, trying to concentrate on the final barrier of the mountains as he was borne ever closer to his destination. Beneath him, small fires dotted the barren desert landscape. A quick glance, and Raum could see the lurching figures of the legions of lesser demons, the *nefari*, who had served his kind in battle since the original Fall.

Disgusting creatures, Raum thought, jerking his gaze away from the hunched and muscular beings, red-skinned with curved horns sprouting from their foreheads, gamboling around the flames. As an earl of Hell, he had twenty legions of his own to command. But even after thousands of years in the Infernal City, Raum had never really developed much of an appreciation for the ill-tempered, dimwitted foot soldiers of the damned.

If he looked hard enough, Raum knew he'd be able to make out other, smaller figures writhing in torment on the ground around the demons plying their trade out here in the wastes. Of course, that might have indicated he had an interest in the bunch of primates, thrown together with a handful of clay and some divine spit, who kept Hell in business.

And he was going to be in close contact with *those* useless creatures soon enough.

If only there were another way. But there wasn't. Raum flapped his wings once, twice, picking up speed, anxious to have the final betrayal done with. When you were a fallen angel who had been marked for death by the Infernal Council, your options became very limited. He had already walked away from Heaven, anxious to help create a paradise that had nothing to do with serving the hated humans. Even after all this time, he couldn't understand what about humanity, so inferior in every way, had merited the reward of an eternal soul. It had been the final straw, a slight he could not ignore.

But in walking away from Heaven, he'd had another option. This time, Raum still wasn't clear on what, or where, he was running to. Only that, if he wanted to survive, he must help save the humans from the rapidly encroaching darkness: a darkness he had helped create, and which now threatened to swallow him whole unless he did the unthinkable.

Curse you, Mammon, he thought. Not that such thoughts had ever done him any good.

The betrayal shouldn't have surprised him. Mammon wasn't the Prince of Avarice for nothing. Eternally jealous, eternally greedy, Mammon had long been tired of always being in Raum's shadow. Raum had simply found the other demon's constant efforts to outdo him amusing, or mildly irritating, when he'd even bothered to notice. After all, his own prowess at theft, deception and destruction had made him a legend. Mammon's singular talent for sucking up had gotten the demon lord a seat on the ruling Infernal Council and ready access to Lucifer's ear.

To each his own, Raum had always thought, and paid little attention. Until recently, that was, when some of his brethren, tired of Mammon's utter uselessness and lack of leadership, had begun encouraging Raum to make a challenge. And he, Raum thought darkly, fool that he was, had begun to consider emerging from centuries of relative seclusion to do it. Then the serpent king had arrived on his doorstep just a few nights past, bearing the news that he, Raum, would soon be charged and executed as a traitor, accused of willfully undermining Hell's cause by his obvious and egregious lack of support.

He would have been destroyed for nothing more than

his own indifference to the games of the Council and life at Court, his own solitary nature all the evidence Lucifer needed to finally succumb to the venom Mammon had spewed for years. Raum had to give Mammon some small amount of credit: though he himself had never spoken publicly of his intention to challenge for Mammon's position on the Council, his old rival knew a threat to his position when he saw it.

So now here he was, forced to choose between the eternal darkness of a demon's death, or living by doing things he would once have considered even worse than such a death.

The irony wasn't lost on him.

The sky began to darken as he approached the far edge of the underworld, and Raum's heartbeat accelerated no matter how hard he tried to force calm. Condemned or no, the finality of his decision had only just begun to penetrate.

He could sense Leviathan as he drew near the mountains, and the gate beyond. Leviathan, and the five others who would be accompanying them, now traitors below just as they had been above. Raum didn't know all of their stories, nor did he care. All that mattered was that they were united in their refusal to die quietly. He could feel his brothers' power drifting upward like hot sparks carried on a desert breeze, surrounding an unmistakable shard of deathly cold that cut like a knife through the heat.

Leviathan. Only a fool would have felt safe under the gaze of those unusual, oceanic eyes. Raum was no fool. He wondered if he would ever understand what had driven the serpent king to this, leading a ragtag collection of marked nobles out of Hell and into the employ of the white-winged control freaks they'd all spent so long either fighting, infuriating or avoiding. What did Leviathan care if the balance between good and evil on Earth was tipping into darkness? And even more confounding to Raum was the question of how Lucifer's prized pet had known that the highest ranks of angels, the seraphim, would be desperate enough to want the help of a bunch of Hellish exiles in righting the Balance.

Of course, if he hadn't been so desperate himself, he wouldn't have touched this with a ten-foot pole, and he was in no position to be asking questions. The pay was good. The prospect of continuing to exist was even better. And dirty work was, after all, his specialty, no matter who he was doing it for. He was Raum, Destroyer of Dignities and Robber of Kings.

At least, he had been. Now, he was no longer sure what he was. But with luck, he would have more time to figure it out.

The mountains rising ahead were stunted, blackened things, the grotesque monotony of the ring they created around the kingdom broken only by the places where the five rivers sliced through on their way to the endless Stygian sea. Raum soared higher, clearing the peaks with rapid, graceful movements, and then dipped to descend into the roiling black mists that eternally blanketed the Borderlands, and the Gate of Souls.

Anticipation rushed through Raum's blood. He was about to have a purpose again. And for the first time, it appeared that his former brethren needed *him*. It was incredibly satisfying…perplexing, weird and almost deviant, but satisfying.

The Infernal Council was right about one thing: he'd never given a damn for them. They'd now given him the perfect excuse to be an eternal thorn in their sides. Raum looked forward to it…and to the day when he could confront the Prince of Avarice on his own terms, when there would be no one for the insidious coward to hide behind. *If* that day came, that was. If he saw tomorrow.

But no matter what, it was time to find out. Raum took a deep breath of the sulfur-tinged air, and dived into the eternal night surrounding the gates of Hell.

Chapter 1

Johnstown, Vermont
Six months later

If darkness had a voice, Ember Riddick thought, his would be it.

"Excuse me, miss...I was told that if I wanted cologne, you were the woman to see?"

Her hand stilled in midair. She'd been diligently restocking essential oils—and truth be told, zoning out—and her back was to whoever had just blown in with the crisp fall air. The owner of that dark, delicious, decadent *voice*.

Her stomach sank as awareness prickled over her skin, responding to the new electricity in the air that she'd sensed the moment the little silver bell had rung above the door.

Had to be today, she thought. In the year since she'd come to this quaint, upscale little town in Vermont, there had been no slipups, no accidents. She'd made sure of it, even when her nerves felt worn nearly to their breaking point. Like today. Ember closed her eyes and inhaled deeply, trying to concentrate on the soothing scents of vanilla and lavender rising from the candles she'd lit.

Didn't work. Then she laid eyes on him.

Hell.

She would have run, if she could have moved.

"You were told right," she heard Ginni say, her voice taking on the honeyed tones it only did when she was in the presence of someone interesting of the male persuasion. "What exactly were you looking for?"

"I'm looking for something…unusual," the stranger replied, his deep and smoky voice sending a delicious shiver from the top of Ember's head to the very tips of her toes. Ginni's answering giggle, on the other hand, had her curling her lip, though she fought it. To push it back, she had no choice but to refocus on *him*.

The pagan god of Lust, come to finish her off completely.

Ember shivered again, and not from the chill air that had wafted in from the open door. Her eyes roamed over a man who should, by rights, be way too beautiful to exist in real life. He was dark as sin itself, with curly raven hair worn long enough for it to coil loosely around his face. His features, in profile, were sharp, almost hawkish, though they were softened just a little by a full, expressive mouth that still looked disinclined to smile.

He wore only black, she noticed: jeans, boots, T-shirt, leather jacket.

A bad boy. He would have to be, Ember thought ruefully. And the severe color showcased his vampiric beauty perfectly.

Her nails began to bite into her palms, and she realized she'd clenched her fists. She also realized that those nails had suddenly become awfully sharp. Ember forced them open, alarm rising almost as quickly as the strange fire in her blood. Sure enough, there were angry red crescents where her nails had been, though even as she watched, they began to disappear.

If normal men healed as quickly, her life would have been a whole lot less lonely.

"You're Ember Riddick, then? The owner?" the stranger asked, his gaze still fixed on Ginni, who looked pretty close to overheating herself. Though Ember kind of doubted her employee would sprout fangs and claws no matter how lust-fuzzed her brain got.

Unlike some people.

The sound of her name on his lips had her licking her own. Ember found herself stepping forward before she could think too hard about what she was doing. Then he turned to look at her, and she had no choice but to follow through with what was no doubt one of her patented Extremely Bad Ideas. She was normal, she told herself. *I can do this.* It echoed in her head, her mantra.

I'm normal. Normal, normal, normal...

This was her place now, and her shop, damn it. She might be weird, possibly even possessed, but she could keep her tongue in her mouth and off the floor long enough to make a sale.

"Actually, I'm Ember," she said, trying to ignore the way Ginni still stared at him, her eyes slightly glazed. And there was nothing *normal* about the possessive snarl that welled in her throat, designed to drive away any female stupid enough to think of competing. Defiantly, she forced a smile, and hoped it didn't just look as if she was baring her teeth.

"Welcome to Lotions and Potions. What can I help you with?"

She'd wanted his attention, and now she had it. The most unusual and beautiful pair of eyes she'd ever seen locked with hers. They were a pale green, like sea glass, a stunning contrast against his black hair. And though Ember knew it was just a trick of all the inner circuits he was busy frying, she'd swear those eyes began to glow a little, the light in them intensifying as he looked at her.

"*You're* Ember Riddick?" he asked, and the thorough appraisal he gave her was anything but shy. Wicked delight surged through her, even as all of her warning bells began to go off inside. It occurred to her that she was, in all likelihood, the only woman on Earth who would be conflicted about flirting with Mr. Tall, Dark and Smoking Hot.

Usually the thick—and unnecessary—glasses and severe ponytail were enough to prevent her from getting a second look. Unobtrusive, she'd decided since her arrival here, was key. This guy, however, seemed unsettlingly oblivious to the superficial defenses she'd thrown up. He could really see her, Ember was suddenly certain. It *was* nice to let herself be admired again, she had to admit. As long as that was as far as it went. But the longer he stayed here, the less certain that got.

She forced herself to form words, halting though they were. She was at least pretty sure they made sense, which was good. And they weren't "Hi, I want you," which was even better.

"I am. And you are?" She held out her hand out of habit, and regretted it instantly when he took it, enveloping her small hand in his impossibly large one. It was a casual gesture, but Ember sucked in a breath at that first bit of contact. The smooth, silken skin of his palm was warm, almost hot, and that intangible sense of power that seemed to surround him flooded her instantly.

She would have thought it odd that he dropped her hand so quickly, as if she'd burned him, except that Ember was sure her facade of control was slipping. God knew what her eyes must look like…. Ember looked away quickly, grateful that at least the blood roaring in her ears had quieted the instant his hand left hers.

"Raum. I'm Raum," he said in that delicious voice, like chocolate for the ears. He sounded as puzzled as she felt. It wasn't like her to react so strongly, not this fast, anyway. He was no doubt just wondering what sort of drugs she was on. It was only the last shreds of her pride that had her lifting her chin and pressing on.

"Raum…" She trailed off, waiting for him to offer a last name, wondering if it would be as strange as the first. When he only looked back silently, however, Ember decided to let it drop. The sooner she got through this and sent him on his way, the better. And if he really did go by only one name, then he was probably a complete weirdo, which made getting him out of here an even better idea.

"Raum, hi. We, um…we have lots of unusual things here. What were you looking for specifically? Cologne for yourself? Perfume for your…your girlfriend, maybe?" God, she hoped she'd said that last part without gagging too much on the word. Or growling. That would send things from bad to worse in a hurry.

Fortunately, her question seemed to have been the right one. At least it got him to reply.

"I'd like to buy…" He looked around, frowning, as though not quite sure of where he was. "For myself. Cologne would be fine."

"Raum, I doubt there's anything on earth that would get your natural stench out. Still, it can't hurt to try. What do you think, beautiful? Up to the task?" It was only then, at the sound of another throaty, musical voice, that Ember finally noticed he hadn't come in alone. For the second time in minutes, she was stopped in her tracks. At least this time she managed to keep her chin off the floor.

A quick glance told her that for Ginni, not so much.

Good God, could the invasion of Mount Olympus have come at a worse time? This one was a blond, with a face that could have been carved by Michelangelo and eyes such a vibrant green, not sea glass but more like emeralds, that Ember had to assume they were contacts.

And when his eyes dropped to give her an appreciative once-over, it was either look away or make an utter fool of herself.

These men, the devil and the angel both, were sex incarnate.

And she was in big, big trouble.

"I'm sure we have something that will work for you," she said, deliberately ignoring the sarcastic blond, who had a nasty edge to his voice she didn't much care for despite his beauty. She headed for the shelves of essences, but not before she caught Raum's eyes again for a moment. Ember averted her gaze quickly, but it was too late. Those eyes, so intense, sent another blast of heat through her that then coiled and spiraled outward, until she was suffused with it. Ember could already feel her walk changing, becoming sinuous, suggestive, knew that the alluring scent she wore was intensifying as her body chemistry changed. Deep inside, the saner half of her moaned in despair and covered her eyes.

And the part of her that had finally slipped all the way out of its well-locked cage did exactly what it always did: prepared to get in trouble. Ember wanted to lock it down again…really, she did. But it got so hard to behave when there was so much power always fighting to get out. And she felt so *good*….

"Here," she purred, her voice going low and throaty. Ember plucked a fragrance blend from the shelves as she approached, her lips curving in an inviting smile. There was no apprehension now, no fear of what was coming. That was always the good thing about giving in. The bad things, unfortunately, always seemed to outnumber that one considerably.

Ember only stopped moving when she was inches from Raum, never looking away as she unscrewed the small black cap from the bottle.

"I think I have just the thing. Try this," she coaxed, moving in even closer, her body almost touching his. She lifted the delicate amber bottle to just beneath the beautiful stranger's nose. "I think this would suit you perfectly."

He inhaled gently, and as Ember had hoped, heat flashed in his luminescent gaze. Good. That was good, to be wanted.

No, it's bad. And I have serious impulse-control problems. And claws. And fangs...

"Interesting. This is a cologne?" he asked, his voice a velvety rumble. He lowered his head to her when he spoke, his large body curving around her small one until she felt they were the only two people in the room.

For the first time, rather than enjoying the knowledge of her own dominance, something in her recognized a stronger power than her own. Ember's fascination rendered her strangely helpless.

"It's a blend of essential oils," she replied, tilting her head just a little as she looked up at him, startled again at just how fathomless his eyes seemed. "You could let me blend it into something for you...lotion, bath salts, that sort of thing. I could dilute it, make it more subtle. *Or,*" she continued, tipping the little bottle against her finger, "you could just wear it the way it is. Strong," she breathed, hesitating only for a moment before daring to reach up and trail the finger down his throat, from Adam's apple to the warm, intriguing hollow right at the base of it. "Elemental."

Ember heard his sharp intake of breath, saw his pupils dilate. His lips, sculpted perfection, parted slightly as he dipped his head toward her.

"You're a clever little demon, aren't you?" he whispered, his breath feathering her ear.

It was a strange thing to say, but she hardly spared a thought for it. Instead, Ember gladly fell under the thrall of whatever strange magic this man carried with him, her surroundings fading until there was nothing for her but his scent, the steady sound of his breathing, and the intense heat that radiated from him and made her feel as though she'd gotten too close to the sun. She let her eyes drop shut, skimming her cheek against his, tipping her head back to allow him access to her waiting lips.

After so long, such a relief, to give in. Maybe this one would be strong enough to take all she had to give....

Come to me. Mine.

But when he was just a breath away, her beleaguered nuisance of a conscience managed to get in one final word.

I can't believe you're going to make out with this guy right now. In front of everybody. In the STORE!

That was what yanked her back, with an agonizing jolt, to herself—and to the reality of a strange man (albeit a stunningly gorgeous strange man) moving in for a very public lip-lock. Ember gasped as she realized what she'd been about to do, and the bottle of fragrance slipped from her fingers to shatter on the wooden floor.

The mess, and the now overwhelming smell of too much fragrance in one place, helped her hang on to sanity, even as shame flooded her and set her cheeks aflame.

"I'm so sorry," she said, stumbling backward two steps, her eyes wide. Her heart pounded in her chest, and her body was racked with flashes of both intense heat and brutal cold. She didn't know what the hell was wrong with her, but she had to get out of here, and away from the man who watched her with a steady gaze that was less human than it was pure predator.

She watched in horror as he reached for her, a frown creasing his dark brow.

"Ember," he said. "It's all right, wait—"

"I'm just…c-clumsy today, I guess!" She backed away from him so quickly that she banged her hip on the sharp edge of one of the small tables that were scattered about the shop. She barely felt it through the adrenaline, though the display of decorative glass perfume bottles wobbled precariously. Ember forced out a sharp, nervous laugh. The unnatural sound of it made her wince, but she kept backing up, wrapping her arms protectively around herself.

"I'll go get something to clean that right up. Watch out for the glass." She started to go, then turned, suffused with a helpless misery she'd sworn she was done with. But of course, she would never be done with it.

Not as long as she lived.

Why couldn't she just be like everyone else?

Unable to resist, she took one last look at Raum. He really was magnificent. And because of it, one of the most frightening things she'd ever encountered. She knew she'd never be able to get him out of her mind… but since that, at least, would be safe, Ember knew she would welcome the dreams.

There was just no way they could ever be her reality.

"Ember, are you okay?" she heard Ginni ask, though it sounded far away. All she could see were the two men watching her with eyes that suddenly seemed to flare and burn, everything around them going dark. She had seen eyes like that before. No matter how she tried to block it out, she remembered.

"I'm just…I'm sorry," she said softly. And though she knew it was madness, she turned and fled. But she knew now that she would never be able to run far enough.

There was no way to run from herself.

Chapter 2

"So. Our first she-demon. This one's going to be interesting."

Raum slouched over his beer and glared at Gadreel, whose infernally good mood was improving with each passing second. He shot a quick look at Leviathan, but the serpent was as impassive as ever. He had a sudden urge to throw a punch that would knock him out of the chair. Maybe *that* would elicit a reaction.

"You think anything with a vagina is interesting," he said instead, and took a long pull of his beer.

Gadreel's grin widened, and the sudden burst of feminine giggling from the direction of the kitchen door told Raum that the waitresses in this little sports bar had already formed their own Gadreel fan club. Disgusting. Raum frowned more deeply, and hoped it would keep any admirers away. Since his glory days, during which

he'd earned his one great claim to fame of having se-
duced Eve into partaking of a certain forbidden fruit in
the Garden, Gadreel had moved on to the seduction of
every female, be it lovely and lethal she-demon or soft
and yielding human, that he could get his hands on.

The show was getting old.

And like every day since he'd drawn the short straw
and had to accompany Gadreel on this mission, Raum
wished that just once the stupid idiot had ignored the
useless piece of flesh between his legs and thought
better of laying so much as a finger on Lucifer's favorite
concubine. That would have improved his own existence
greatly.

But no. Another little nothing of a human town, another homicidal half-breed demon to take out, per the
orders of the white-winged powers-that-be. He'd had no
idea how overrun Earth had become with such things,
or how difficult it was making life for the angels who
actually gave a damn about protecting humans. Too
many half-breeds, not enough white wings who could
devote all their time to slaughtering them. Enter the
demon assassins with nothing but time on their hands.
It really was the perfect solution.

Raum might have found it amusing, in a sick sort of
way, had it not meant that he now got to be graced with
Gadreel's golden presence all day. Every day. Forever.

Or until one of them finally got fed up enough to go
after him with a blowtorch.

Raum growled as another burst of feminine giggling
erupted, turning his head to look out through the window.
He now had a fine view directly into the large glass

window of Lotions and Potions, even though Ember had not come into view again. He also had decent beer, though the company left a lot to be desired. For once, he wished for a few of his brethren to appear. As annoying as they were, he much preferred their company to what he'd ended up with on this mission: the underworld's most notorious narcissist, and an unsympathetic sea monster.

Raum slumped further into his chair and glared at the bottle in front of him. He did not, as a rule, bed she-demons. He liked control, which the succubi delighted in wresting from any man brave, or foolish, enough to succumb to their many charms. But Ember Riddick had affected him…differently. He was intrigued, and not just because she was by far the most beautiful creature he'd seen in ages.

Raum didn't want to be interested. It pissed him off. Like a lot of things these days.

"Oh, stop brooding, Raum," Gadreel sniffed, motioning to the waitress to bring him another beer. "You're so *boring*. Be happy, will you? We found the half-breed, which means all we have to do now is wait for some asshole to descend from on high to tell us to send her back where she belongs. Then I can go work with someone who appreciates my talent, and you can do…" He trailed off for a moment, then waved his hand dismissively. "Well, you can do whatever it is you like to do. Sit in the dark. Write bad adolescent poetry. Buy more black shirts. Whatever."

Savoring the image of slamming that pretty golden head into the nearest wall, Raum took a deliberate swig of his beer, middle finger extended. Then he looked to Leviathan, who was toying with one of the small electronic devices he himself wanted nothing to do with.

"You're quiet," Raum finally remarked. After punching a few more buttons, Levi raised eyes that were a pale, icy blue to look at him. His hair was as black as Raum's own, but hung straight to the middle of his back. Today he wore it pulled back with a simple leather thong, exposing high cheekbones and elegant, angular features that drew human women like flies. Not, Raum had noticed, that Levi really seemed to care. About much of anything, actually. But he was wickedly clever, which was what truly counted. Leviathan was ancient, possibly even older than the demons themselves. He had been in the underworld long before Lucifer had claimed it for his own, that was certain. But the sea monster had been tamed by Lucifer's hand, and had come to be a prized pet of the King of Hell. Leviathan had certainly wreaked his share of havoc on Hell's behalf, Raum thought, considering the enigma sitting across from him. But after all these thousands of years, it seemed as though they had all made a mistake when they'd assumed that Levi felt any loyalty to what they had created…and that a monster like him must necessarily be pure evil.

In fact, since leaving Hell, Raum had come to realize that he didn't know anything at all about Leviathan. And the serpent shifter, for his part, seemed happy to keep it that way.

"I don't like it," Levi said, trading the BlackBerry-thing for the glass of water he'd opted for instead of the beer. "Too many Reapers hanging around. Too many *nefari* skulking around in one place, for that matter. It's not like this is anything like a big city, and this half-breed hasn't killed anyone."

"Yeah, I'd say killing is pretty far down on her list," Gadreel snorted, trailing a finger absently down the waitress's arm as he accepted his beer. Raum saw her quiver before she headed back to the bar, and knew that Gadreel, at least, would have plenty of company to distract him later. For once, Raum envied him that.

He thought again of Ember's eyes, the way they'd turned from warm honey to hot gold when he'd touched her. She was a luscious little creature, though she was trying rather badly to hide it behind those ridiculous glasses: small but perfectly curved, and with pointed little features and a rosebud mouth that made her look like a sexy faerie. It fascinated him, that she would run a shop devoted to scent when she wore none but her own natural one. The heady combination of sweetness and spice that poured from her creamy skin had made him want to tug the band out of her wild tangle of fiery curls and plunge his hands into it, holding her still while he ran his tongue over every inch of her to see if she tasted as good as she smelled.

Stupid. It didn't matter. *She* didn't matter. She was a job, nothing more.

"Do you think the Reapers are here just because of all the extra *nefari?*" Raum asked, frowning. "I haven't seen anything like this before."

"Don't think so," Levi replied with a small shake of

his head. Then he indicated the window. "Look at them. It makes no sense. They're all just *waiting*."

Raum followed Levi's gaze and watched a black-robed man, slim and pale and dark, flicker into existence across the street, walk past several shops, glance his way and vanish once more. Around him, humans walked and drove on the bustling main street, enjoying the crisp fall day. Raum wondered how complacent they'd be if they could see what he saw...if they knew their sleepy little town was now a hotbed of supernatural activity of a rather dark kind.

He wished they could. It would at least make for some entertainment.

The bell above the door rang again, but Raum didn't bother to look. Not until Gadreel growled several colorful curse words with venom that was uncharacteristic even for him. Then Raum knew who it was, even before he heard the creak and groan of the vacant seat at the table as another, very large, body settled into it.

"Well," said a familiar voice. "This is cozy."

Reluctantly, Raum turned his attention to the new-comer. His white wings, tipped in gold, were hidden away, but everything about him still bespoke his exalted status. Light gleamed from his short, wavy cap of golden hair, from his gold-dusted skin, keeping him in a nimbus of light that even human eyes would be able to see faintly. Hard, intelligent blue eyes swept the three demons, and from the expression on the angel's face, he didn't much care for what he saw. As usual.

"Hello, Uriel," said Raum, not bothering to disguise his lack of excitement. "To what do we owe the pleasure?" Levi was normally the only one who had to deal with the seraphim running the little operation they had going, and that suited everyone just fine. But every once in a while, the highest rank of angels stuck their nose in a little deeper than their demonic recruits would prefer. And because Raum's existence had turned into one epic failure after another, it seemed like every time this happened, they sent Uriel.

"I wouldn't think another half-breed would merit so much attention from someone of your…elevated status," Gadreel added. "We are but your lowly exterminators. Isn't that about right?"

Uriel shot him a look. "Shove it."

"It's not just the half-breed," Levi said coolly, drawing a surprised look from the angel and demons alike. "Maybe you should tell us what exactly is going on here, Uriel, before we go any further."

Uriel snorted, but Raum caught the quick flash of something one rarely saw in an angel's eyes: fear. It only validated his own suspicions about this mission. There was something very off about this place, even beyond his odd reaction to Ember Riddick.

"I'm not sure what you think you're entitled to," Uriel said with a hard smile.

"We're entitled to some small amount of courtesy, considering we put our asses on the line for you on a regular basis."

"You're paid well for it," Uriel replied. The light around him contracted and turned a deeper gold, a sure sign of his rising anger.

"As we should be, considering your kind has turned

a blind eye to demonkind for so long that you can't see what you need to anymore. Levi's right," Raum said flatly, his own temper flaring. "This place has the stench of death all over it, and it's not coming from the woman."

Uriel shoved a hand through his cap of golden hair, agitated. "No, we thought not." He shook his head and gave a mirthless little laugh. "I shouldn't be surprised. It's so much like last time. Come on, Raum," he said. "You were there. Don't tell me you don't remember." Again, that hint of bitterness in his voice. "You seemed to be enjoying yourself quite a bit that day."

The door opened and shut as the bar's one remaining patron left, sending a gentle rush of chilled air past the table. Again, Raum caught the faintest hint of brimstone, and this time the memory rushed to the surface so quickly that he wondered at having missed the signs before. Of course he remembered. Even now in Hell, they sang songs about that glorious day.

The witch had been the key. Young, untried, with power it would take years to hone, she'd drawn the handsome lust-demon to her like a moth to the flame. She had caught him, bound him to her, loved him…while the incubus had twisted her into the most deadly weapon that humankind had yet seen.

On a cold day in November, she had stood in the center of her little English village, in the place where worlds touched, and for a few dark hours thrown open the gates of Hell.

"You're thinking Hellhole," Raum murmured, his mind fogged once again with the smoke that poured from the flaming thatched roofs, from the massive chasm that had opened straight down into the bowels of the earth and beyond. The air had been thick with screams of terror, the wild screeches and howls of the *nefari,* the shouts of Fallen and angel as the two engaged in bloody battle. Raum remembered the harsh music of clashing swords, the taunts and catcalls that had risen above the destruction as the angels had slowly fought the demon horde back into the ground.

Not soon enough, though. Not before the horseman called Plague had ridden off into the night.

"This is one of the thin places," Uriel said softly, looking directly at him. "And I have no doubt there is an actual Nexus point here, where Hell touches Earth."

"You think the woman is the key," Levi said, threading long, elegant fingers together on the table. "How?"

"I wish I knew," Uriel growled furiously, fists clenching reflexively on the table. "I can't seem to *see* their kind like I used to be able to. The half-breeds are like the rest of the Lost Ones, without hope, without Light. What reason was there for us to watch them destroy themselves? Except…now I can't seem to see like I should…and the Balance is precarious enough as it is…"

"Oh, come on, Uriel," Gadreel groaned, rolling his eyes. "You can whip yourself later, in private. I may be a demon, but that's not really my thing."

Raum just watched Uriel's impotent fury with interest, and no small amount of trepidation. Right now, the Balance, the natural equilibrium between Light and

Dark here on Earth, was the only thing standing between him and a permanent swim in a flaming river. And it was hard enough to maintain without a seven-on-one fight against the demon horde. He couldn't really count the angels as allies, though they'd be fighting, too; he was pretty sure that most of them would be happy to use him and his fellow exiles as shields.

He tapped his fingers impatiently against the side of his beer bottle and tried to focus. It fit right in with his current run of miserable luck that he'd find himself up against one of the only things he had absolutely no control over. The natural Balance on Earth was a thing that neither the Dark nor the Light truly understood. One side fought it, the other accepted it, but nothing changed the fact that there were only ever as many demons allowed to walk in the Above as there were angels. The mysterious safeguard, however, could be affected by Earth's natural magic and the humans with the ability to wield it. Even a small fluctuation in the Balance could have big consequences…the summoning of a demon noble, for instance, which occasionally ended badly for the demon and almost always ended badly for the Summoner, as well as almost everyone within a ten-mile radius.

At least the humans themselves had weeded out the Summoner bloodline. The ability to call and enslave demons had been one of his least-favorite facets of Earth magic.

But in any case, opening a Hellhole was a hundred thousand times worse.

"Fine. If Ember Riddick is the key, then we'll just take

her out. Boom. Done. End of problem," said Gadreel, making a slashing motion across his throat with an unrepentant smile.

Raum and Uriel spoke in unison.

"No."

He could feel Gadreel and Levi staring at him, but there was no going back now. He thrust his chin up defiantly and glared at Uriel.

"She's not a normal half-breed," he said. "I don't know why, but Ember Riddick is…different. Not violent. Not stupid. Definitely not insane."

"She liked *you*," Gadreel muttered, "so that last part's debatable."

"Hmm," Uriel said, his dark eyes searching Raum's face. His expression turned thoughtful, softening features that seemed to have been chiseled from stone. Raum watched him think, dreading what he would come up with. He knew better than to underestimate the seraphim, little as he cared for their company. They weren't the greatest of the warrior-angels for nothing.

"Let me try to understand this. You think we're sitting on top of a Nexus point, you're fairly sure that a local half-breed is about to blow it wide-open, and… your solution is to do *nothing?*" Gadreel whipped his head around to glare at Raum. "And *you*…she's just a sexy little slice of evil, Raum, nothing more. I've had twists of tail just as enticing a thousand times over! If you're that hard up, screw her before we send her back to Hell, but don't be an idiot!"

"You will not touch the woman," Uriel said, that deep golden glow beginning to pulse from him once again.

"There will be no murdering of innocents, Gadreel, and this woman has hurt no one. It may be that she has enough Light in her to stand against the darkness… though I've never seen such a thing from her kind…but she will not be harmed by you, or our arrangement is at an end and you can damn well fend for yourself. Is that understood?"

Gadreel glared at him, seething. "Whatever you say, *boss*," he finally hissed, his eyes the vibrant green of the snake within. "But don't think I'm babysitting her."

"Fortunately, that's one area where we agree," Uriel said, still pulsing with furious light, though his expression was neutral. Raum knew the tone of voice well, though. It was the one the angel used when he was trying, very hard, to refrain from shouting.

"What do you need from us?" Levi asked, and Raum saw him give Gadreel a sidelong glance that promised bloodshed if he didn't keep his mouth shut.

"I need the Nexus found, the exact location of the touch point. I don't want to flood the town with my legions until we know for certain where it is, because I'm afraid that's just going to push things along that much faster. At that point, there are certain things that can be done…" He trailed off, looking troubled. "Well. We've done it before. I don't want this place to end up like Hiraeth."

Raum had been back once, to the location of the tiny village where Hell had broken loose, and found nothing but a patch of scorched earth where nothing would grow, where animals came to die and where men, if they lingered overlong, went mad. It was a desecrated place. Perhaps it would always be.

He looked out the window again, at the oblivious humans, and wondered whether that would happen here. And oddly, his thoughts went immediately to Ember, the sadness in her eyes right before she'd run away from him. How would she feel about causing such destruction? Would she break free of her humanity in triumph? Or would she just…break?

He felt a strange pull of something that felt almost like melancholy at the thought. Which was ridiculous. He'd sworn off feelings long ago. And why the hell did he care anyway? Maybe Gadreel was right, for once. He needed to get his head out of his ass…or his pants.

Uriel was still blathering on, puffed up, Raum thought irritably, with his own seraphic importance.

"In the meantime, I think it would be best for me to assign the woman a temporary Guardian to watch over her—"

"Fine," Raum said, cutting him off. "I'll do it."

Uriel stopped short, staring at Raum as though he'd just grown another head. The look alone was worth the immediate shock to his own system. Had he actually said that? Out *loud?*

"I…appreciate the offer, Raum. But I was more thinking of someone who would appeal to her *better* nature," Uriel said slowly.

"Won't work," Raum said with a shake of his head. "She'll have to make peace with her worse nature if she wants to live. Gadreel is perfectly capable of finding the Nexus. I'll be her Guardian."

The seraph frowned. "I didn't ask. Last time I checked, you were the opposite of a Guardian Angel."

"And yet I'll be watching over her anyway," Raum replied, crossing his arms over his chest, fully prepared to argue…and win. "Imagine that."

"Raum." Uriel's tone was warning, but Raum's mind was made up.

"She's mine. Deal with it."

The words came out strangely, giving him pause. Still, he meant them, if only in the most temporary sense. He'd brought out the demon in Ember once, and easily. He'd no doubt see quickly that she really was no different from every other stinking half-breed on the planet. When she broke, which she would, he could handle whatever she threw at him until the damned cavalry arrived to save the day. He'd get over this stupid *thing* about the woman, she'd get shuttled off to Hell that much sooner, and best of all, Uriel would be pissed off the whole time.

It was the perfect solution.

Uriel's jaw tightened to the point Raum thought it might crack…and wouldn't *that* have been satisfying… but finally, he rose stiffly and fixed Raum with eyes that were full of warring emotions. Raum himself felt nothing but disgust. Uriel was everything that was wrong with the angels, letting his heart rule alongside his mind, placing some misguided idea of right and wrong above cold logic. He had grown past him.

Then how do you explain what you're doing right now?

The whisper in his mind was soft, insidious, the

shadow of the demon who had been celebrated as the
Destroyer of Dignities before being brought low. The
demon, he thought with a furious sort of determination,
he still was. Still, the voice made his blood run cold.

Uriel's eyes narrowed, but he turned to Levi. "Let me
know," was all he said. Then he was gone, slamming
out of the bar with such force that the door frame
cracked.

They sat in silence, the three of them, the faint sound
of music from the jukebox the only sound in the nearly
empty bar. Finally, Gadreel broke the silence.

"Well," he said with a humorless flash of his teeth.
"That was fun. Now if you'll excuse me, before I dash
off to find the Nexus and save the world, I believe there
are several deadly sins that require my immediate attention."

He stood, pushed in his chair and strode off in the
direction of the waitresses, who were still huddled by
the kitchen door and watching him hungrily.

Raum watched him go, forcing himself to relax his
grip on the bottle before it shattered in his hand. He
felt Leviathan's eyes on him, but ignored that searching
stare. He wasn't in the mood. He hated talking, and he
hated company. And he particularly hated Gadreel.

His gaze drifted back to the little shop across the
street, and just for an instant, his eyes met Ember's.
There was a hot rush of awareness, like being caught in
a sudden blast of desert wind, and the hair on his arms,
the back of his neck, rose at the electricity that seemed
to snap through the air between them.

He watched her flush and turn away, retreating farther

into the store where he couldn't see her. All he was left with was a toxic combination of fury at his want of her and utterly reckless, overwhelming desire.

Chapter 3

Ember woke in a cold sweat, thrashing her way to the surface until she realized that all she was fighting were her sheets, twisted around her body.

She'd had the nightmare again: a red desert. A gaping hole in the sand full of living, writhing horrors...a hole *she* had created. And all the while, the beautiful, terrifying man with the wings looking on approvingly. He had given her the words, though by now she knew them by heart...and as it always did, power had poured out of her like rain in a summer storm.

Not like when she was awake, living life as an undercover mutant without a cause. Though she didn't think she would ever want that sort of power in her real life.

She'd had dreams like that off and on since she was a kid, an awkward little redhead with few friends, a dad whom she'd never met and who was only ever referred to as "that good-for-nothing scumbag," and a mother who alternated between ignoring her and hating her. They were always scary. But in a way, they'd been kind of comforting. At least the man with the wings, the Bad Angel, as she'd always thought of him, hadn't judged her so harshly as everyone else. He'd *liked* the things that made her different.

Too bad he was just as unreal as her stupid dreams. Then again, she wasn't completely sure she wanted to meet that guy in real life. Not that he'd ever hurt her, but she'd never been able to shake the impression that he'd be a much nastier customer in person than she could ever be in her worst moments.

A soft, tapping sound jerked Ember from her jumbled waking thoughts, bringing her crashing back to the dark silence of her room. Or near silence. Ember lay utterly still, warm beneath her covers, hearing nothing but the faintly ragged sound of her own breathing. Moonlight poured in her window, the wind making the shadows of trees dance across her wall.

Ember exhaled slowly.

Calm down, she told herself. It was just her frayed nerves playing tricks on her, that was all. There was no doubt that her week had been one of the weirdest in recent memory, and she could pinpoint exactly when it had started: the second the tall, dark and strangely irresistible man had wandered into her shop and sent her sex drive into nuclear territory. She hadn't had a reaction like that since puberty had hit her like an oncoming train, but even so, this time had been different. She'd never felt called to a man like that.

Of course, Ember was pretty sure she'd never seen a man quite like that. Period. But still...

She'd just begun to relax, accepting that she was only freaking herself out, when she heard it again.

Ember blinked the sleep from her eyes, and everything in the dark room came into sharp relief. As annoying as her weirdness could be, being able to see in the dark occasionally came in handy. She slowly sat up, telling herself that it was nothing, even as adrenaline began to pump through her system.

Then she saw them, twin red coals watching her unblinkingly from right outside her window. Her heart stuttered in her chest, and Ember barely stifled a small scream as her hand went to her mouth. The red pinpoints bored into her, unblinking...

Then it fluttered its wings, and the illusion was broken. Moonlight glinted in eyes that were no longer red. Wind lifted shadows that became feathers.

"You've got to be kidding me."

Ember found herself fending off a fit of nervous laughter. It was a crow. Not a demon, not Poe's ominous raven, but a common crow, probably cold and taking a breather from the tempestuous night wind. Except...

Ember narrowed her eyes, taking a good look at it. It couldn't be the same bird, but damn it, it looked just like the enormous crow that had taken up residence at her shop. It had been there all week, perched on the sign, or the windowsill or the tree planted in the sidewalk just down from her door. *Weird,* she thought with an involuntary little shiver. Even weirder was that she hadn't been able to shake the sensation that the bird wasn't just hanging around, but watching her. Which made no sense. As little sense, in fact, as her continuing obsession with the fact that the crow had arrived on Monday afternoon, not long after she'd seen Raum in Mick's, the bar across the street. And he *had* been watching her then.

She'd broken three more bottles of essence after that.

"Not thinking about it. Not going there," Ember said aloud, hoping the sound of her own voice would add a little more reality to the decidedly surreal night. Bolstered, if only a little, she addressed the bird on the sill.

"Fly away, birdie. Go home. No vacancy."

It really was a beautiful bird, Ember thought as it watched her unblinkingly, the largest crow she'd ever seen, at least up close. She knew they were scavengers, but they were supposed to be really smart, too. This one certainly looked as if it had its wits about it. But enough to follow her home from work?

As she watched, it held her gaze, leaned forward. Then:

Tap tap tap.

It wanted in.

"No *way*," Ember murmured, amazed. She'd sure as hell never seen a bird wanting to visit inside someone's house before. Obviously, all it would do if she opened the window would be to either fly off into the night, or worse, to come in and then freak out about what it had thought it wanted. But…what if it was tame? Someone's escaped pet, caught in the oncoming storm? What if it wasn't used to being outside and would wind up dead if she left it in the cold?

What if it *needed* her?

That was the sweet spot, right there. The one she couldn't resist indulging.

"Oh, honestly," she muttered. "Fine. Let's be stupid."

She got out of bed and padded to the window, the moonlight painting dappled images on her bare skin. It was probably idiocy, but she was never going to feel right about it if she just let the poor crow sit there. And anyway, she had few enough friends. That was one of the overarching themes of her life: *alone.* Who was she to shun a fellow creature based solely on species?

Her fingers had just flipped the latches when there was a flurry of motion behind her, a rapid scuttling noise, *clickity-clickity-click,* like a small animal scurrying across her floor. The window slammed up of its own accord just as the claws sank into her shoulders.

Ember had only a vague impression of something huge and black exploding into her room from the night, just before she was hurled across the room as though she weighed no more than a doll. For a moment, she was weightless. Then, in a lightning-quick burst of instinct that came out of nowhere, she tucked herself into a ball, rolling rather than slamming into the floor or wall and ending quickly in a defensive crouch on the far side of her bed.

There was a split second of recognition that, under

other circumstances, she would have thought her move had been pretty damn cool. Then she heard an inhuman, outraged shriek, and something deep inside her roared in response. A sudden wave of bloodlust crashed through her like a tidal wave. All her carefully constructed barriers crumbled in an instant, and the daylight creature she fought to be evaporated in the face of the night creature she truly was.

There was a crash, the sound of shattering glass. And a fierce growl that stirred Ember in ways that had nothing to do with violence. So familiar...she had to see, to know. In a single, nimble leap, Ember cleared the bed and immediately found herself confronted with a sight straight out of a horror movie.

The two creatures grappled by the window, reduced to shadows where they fought, backlit by the moon. One of them, the one she knew immediately had drawn the blood that had already dried on her shoulders, was truly the most hideous thing she'd ever seen. Its skin was a deep and angry red even in the darkness, and its squat and muscular body strained as blood poured from a gash across its head. And that head...stubby, curved horns protruded from the forehead, and its snout pulled back to reveal a maw full of dagger-sharp teeth.

As Ember watched, the creature drew back its arm and slashed its claws across the cheek of its opponent, earning, amazingly, no more than a pained grunt for its trouble.

"You'll pay for that, you *nefari* piece of shit," snarled a voice that she recognized the second she heard it. She would know that voice anywhere. The wings, however, sprouting from his back with a kind of strange majesty, took her utterly aback.

Just like in my dreams.

His blazing eyes, a hot and angry green, connected with hers for only a split second, sending a jolt through her that seemed to set every nerve ending she had aflame at once. Stripped of her inhibitions, Ember let the connection between them ripple through her, the siren song of pleasure promised far greater for her than the interest in the fight.

Sensing it, the horned creature's attention moved completely to her. It quickly forgot Raum in favor of its initial prey and shoved away from him to stalk toward her, gleaming red eyes full of blind hatred and a terrible hunger.

This time, the warning growl that filled the air was Ember's. Her body felt loose, agile, and she realized that all her fear had evaporated. It had been replaced by a sort of breathless anticipation. That, and a complete confidence that when she and this creature went for one another's throats, she would win. Which was good, because Raum's presence had her blood singing. If she had to tear through this thing to get to him, so be it.

Ember growled louder, her claws extended, her long and deadly incisors bared.

Come and get me, you son of a bitch.

It leaped, and Ember propelled herself into the air, ready to clash, to meet it in a biting, tearing frenzy. All of her passion, her pent-up energy, sizzled through her veins in anticipation. She would make her kill. She would teach this *thing* a lesson.

And then it was gone, stolen from her out of midair as Raum swooped out of nowhere and slammed it against the wall. Ember had the wind knocked out of her in one harsh breath, one swift blow to her gut sending her hurtling back to the floor. There was an almost piglike squeal, followed quickly by an ear-piercing shriek of pain so intense her ears throbbed with it.

Then, silence, except for the blood still rushing in her ears. Ember gasped as her lungs shuddered back to life, dragging herself to a sitting position while she grappled with a barrage of coughing. Her eyes darted around the room as she tried to brace herself for another attack.

Raum rose to his feet on the other side of the room, over the crumpled form of the creature that had attacked her. Without even glancing at her, he pulled a small pouch from his pocket and sprinkled something over the body, murmuring words she could barely hear. She began to make her way over to him, slowly, deliberately, maintaining her crouch and silent as a ghost. She'd take him down first and ask questions after, she decided, trying to keep in mind that he'd come tearing into her house uninvited and ready to fight.

But it was the prospect of having him pinned beneath her as she straddled him that moved her forward, silent as a cat in the dark. The body of the dead creature began to smoke, then vanished in a burst of orange flame. Ember's mouth fell open, her eyes rounding in disbelief as she stopped short.

This had to be more of her nightmare. Had to be. Except it all felt terribly real. She shuddered in a breath, pinched herself with claws that drew blood with sharp little pinpricks of pain and made her hiss. But it couldn't be real, Ember thought. Because if it was…

"Raum?"

Raum turned to stare at her with green eyes that glowed brightly in the dark. All at once his scent flooded her nostrils, an exotic musk that reminded her of candles and incense. The scent of dark places, of mysteries undiscoverable. She could hear him now, his slow, steady breathing, the thudding rhythm of his heart soothing the erratic beat of her own. Ember started to get to her feet, then staggered as an unexpected wave of dizziness knocked her off balance.

Immediately, his arms were around her, pressing her into a chest that felt like hot stone. Ember shivered from the warmth, leaning into his heat even as she fought off the escalating light-headedness.

"Don't," she protested weakly, knowing full well that she was already an active participant in this little embrace. She was going to get herself killed. He could be getting ready to shred her even now. All her stupid instincts demanded she get as close to him as humanly possible. Her head was so foggy all of a sudden… Why couldn't she *think?*

"I'm not going to hurt you, Ember," Raum said, making no move to let her go. "You have plenty to worry about, but not that."

His voice was stern, but somehow that was a comfort. Especially because she was suddenly having a hard time keeping her feet under her.

"Raum," she murmured, her speech going slurry. "I feel kinda funny."

In response, he ran his hands over her shoulders, and Ember was surprised at the dull and throbbing pain at his touch.

"Ow," she complained, jerking her shoulders so that his hands returned to her back.

"Your wounds are deep," he said, and the anger in his voice made her shiver again.

"It's only a flesh wound," she informed him, then giggled foolishly. The laughter made the dizziness worse, though, and Ember brought her arms up to wrap around Raum's waist. She groaned as her stomach gave a sudden, violent lurch.

"I'm going to be sick," she announced, and her knees began to buckle beneath her.

He sighed, taking on more of her weight. "You're going to be a lot worse than that if we don't get you some help. Stupid demon. I don't know who sent him, but he seems to have forgotten his orders. If I hadn't killed him, his master would have…" He trailed off, squeezing her tighter. Concern darkened his voice.

"Ember? Stay with me. Okay?"

"Hmm? You have the nicest voice," she said, darkness beginning to encroach on her vision. "I could listen to you talk forever. Would you tell me a story?" Sleep was barreling toward her, though, and Ember frowned at the injustice. "Whassa matter with me, Raum?"

He bent, and in one quick motion caught her behind the knees and scooped her into his arms, cradling her like the child she suddenly felt like. The world spun nauseatingly, and she buried her face against the soft cotton of his shirt.

"Ohh," she groaned. "Not good."

"No," he agreed, "it isn't." That undercurrent of anger in his voice had grown stronger. "Listen to me, Ember. That demon stuck his claws in you, and it looks like he was poisonous. You've got to try to stay awake, all right? I have to find someone who can help. So just… No, look, don't do that," he said as her head lolled back. He shoved it back against his chest and gave it a little shake for good measure. It didn't feel great, but it pushed the darkness back a little.

"Are we flying?" she asked, remembering the wings.

"Mmm-hmm," he replied, jostling her, and she realized, albeit dimly, that he was swinging a leg out the open window.

"Do you have an airsick bag, then?"

"Don't even think about it," he said. His voice was strained, and Ember thought he was probably imagining what might happen to his clothes in the absence of that airsick bag. Then she felt a rush of air, and clung more tightly to his chest as her stomach threatened to do exactly what he had just commanded it not to do.

"This is a hell of a way to start," she heard him growl. "Don't you dare die, Ember Riddick."

"'Kay," she murmured, feeling her world tip and begin to go black again. "Raum?"

"What?"

"Are you my Guardian Angel?" she asked, and smiled at his snort, which was as much of an answer as anything.

"No," he finally said.

She dug her fingers more tightly into his shirt,

and only fleetingly wondered whether her claws had retracted. Either way, he didn't flinch, didn't make a sound. And it no longer mattered, because she was falling, falling, like Alice down the rabbit hole, into a darkness that even she couldn't see through.

"Save me anyway?" she asked, her voice barely a whisper. Then she was gone.

Chapter 4

Raum soared into the night sky on ebony wings, a blur invisible to the human eye as he cradled his unconscious cargo close to his chest. The death smell mingled unpleasantly with the autumn spice of the night air, fueling his urgency as he headed for a place where it would be safe to call upon the power he would need. How, Raum asked himself, had he managed to get himself into the position of playing not only Guardian, but *hero?* It was utterly disgusting.

He glanced quickly down at the woman in his arms, noted how pale she had become, the shallowness of each breath. Even her natural warmth, higher than that of an average human, was growing cold. Her jerked his head up and flew faster, swallowing his rising panic.

Damn whoever had chosen the cataclysmically stupid, poisonous *nefari* to send after him, he thought angrily.

And damn him for his utter lack of sense where the woman was concerned. He should have known she'd be watched. Hell, he shouldn't even be here.

In seconds, the mountains were all around him, the dark shapes of the trees beckoning him into their safe haven. When he found a likely spot, Raum dropped lightly from the sky and landed in a secluded clearing. This was a cool, dark, soothing place, and rife with both the rich scent of decaying leaves and the wintry promise of pine in every frigid breath. A good place. He needed privacy for this.

Raum strode to the center of the clearing, bathed in the light of a moon that was nearly full. In his arms, Ember began to shiver uncontrollably. He could actually feel the life force ebbing from her, could feel the final spark of warmth, her soul, preparing to take flight.

It would, he knew, make Gadreel happy. The rest would just see it as an easier way out of the situation and think nothing more of it. But if the Nexus had drawn Ember to it, it would eventually draw another with the ability to open it. That was the way of the old magic of Earth: it called to those who could hear it.

But beyond that, something about Ember Riddick intrigued him. Pulled at him, even more than her beauty. All week, he had watched her, solitary even as she interacted with those around her. She kept much to herself because she had to, Raum assumed. Perhaps, probably, she'd been hurt for being what she was. At first, he'd wondered if maybe the cycle was repeating itself completely and she had a *nefari* lover already. He'd been far too relieved to discover that wasn't the case.

He just hoped he remembered what he was doing, because it had been an awfully long time since he'd called upon this ability. Actually, he wasn't certain he'd even retained it after his Fall.

Nothing like having to find out under duress.

"All right. Let's get this over with," he said, rolling his shoulders and neck as he planted himself firmly in the middle of the clearing, legs slightly apart. He adjusted Ember in his arms, exposing her small form to the pale light of the moon. Then, with a deep breath, Raum closed his eyes. Cleared his mind. And after a moment's hesitation, called the Light.

He arched his back and spread his wings wide, waiting. Slowly, he could feel it filling him, the white light of healing using him as a conduit to suffuse the woman he held. It started slowly, then strengthened, filling him until it pulsed right along with his heart. The power flowed faster, brighter, rushing through him and from him with such strength that the air around him began to whip and pull at him. And now it was Raum shuddering, fighting not to recoil as something wild and sweet flooded him, something he had forgotten long ago.

Beauty. Joy. Love…

Means to an end, he insisted to himself, even as the Light began to illuminate even the darkest places within him, invading. Awakening. *Just a means to an end. I do not care. I will NEVER care. I am darkness. I am sin. I am the enemy of love.*

That was about the time his hands, pressed against Ember, began to sting. Then throb.

Then smoke.

Raum's eyes flew open in horror, and he let Ember fall to the ground just as they burst into flame.

"Son of a bitch!" he roared. Everything fled his thoughts but white-hot pain. Raum mashed his flaming hands against his chest and collapsed onto the ground, smothering the flames with both his weight and the damp soil and leaves beneath him. He closed his eyes tightly, though nothing on Earth, in the Above or the Below, could have taken him far enough away from the blinding pain in his hands.

Through gritted teeth, he began to recite some of his favorite human expletives.

His fury was rudely interrupted by a soft moan, and his anger vanished as he realized Ember was still sprawled on the ground where he'd dropped her. Raum scrambled over to where she lay, keeping his wounded hands close to his body.

She was still, so still, her face half in shadow as he knelt over her. She was still far too pale, even for one with her light complexion. But her breathing appeared to have steadied, her lips parted slightly as her breath sent small puffs of mist into the cold night air. The thin T-shirt she wore was covered in blood, still wet, and so close to her, Raum's nose was filled with the coppery scent of it. Despite his pain, he fumbled at her shirt with red, raw hands, rending the material in two down the front of her and pulling it away where the fabric had adhered to the small, deep puncture wounds around her shoulders.

Ember moaned again, a soft, thick sound in the back

of her throat that twisted like a knife in his chest. Raum tentatively brushed his hands against her skin, examining the way the blood flow had stopped, frowning as he realized the skin was knitting itself back together even as he watched. It was incredibly rare for a half-breed to be able to self-heal so quickly. But the wounds were vanishing, leaving unbroken skin beneath a thin and tacky film of Ember's blood. Her soft skin warmed beneath his hands.

His gamble had worked. But Raum realized too late that in his haste, he hadn't thoroughly considered the possible consequences: he hadn't dreamed that touching her would become so addictive so quickly. But even as he willed himself to stop, his hands stroked and soothed with a gentleness he had thought was long forgotten.

This time when she shivered, he knew it was from the deepening chill in the air and not because she was leaving him. He gathered her up again, eyes skimming down her exposed torso as he did and lingering on her full, rounded breasts, the nipples taut in reaction to the cold. The intriguing indent of her navel in her long, lean waist.

Raum jerked his gaze away and pulled her into his chest, wrapping his wings around her as he got to his feet. The pain in his hands had lessened to a dull ache, smoke still coiling lazily from the raw skin, but concentrating on holding Ember pushed it to the back of his mind and made it more bearable. They would have been healed already, had it been anything but fire. *That* fire, in particular. Still, the damage should be gone by morning, though they'd be misery for a while yet.

Ember hadn't yet wakened, but she curled into him, nuzzling her face into his chest. She sighed softly, and Raum felt a strange tug somewhere in the dark and blackened vicinity that supposedly held a heart. He had a sudden, overwhelming desire to protect her, to keep her close….

"Well," said a voice, "this is a new one, even for me."

Raum hunched his shoulders defensively in reaction. He wasn't at all in the frame of mind he liked to be in when confronting the almost always unhelpful Reapers. And this one, Jarrod by name, had thwarted him before. Raum made sure his hands were well-hidden beneath his wings along with most of Ember, determined not to let the Reaper see the damage he'd inflicted on himself. Then he might ask questions, and Raum was in no mood to answer them.

"What are you doing here, Jarrod?" Raum grumbled. "Your services aren't needed."

"Apparently not," Jarrod replied, quirking a brow. The Reaper was clad as the rest of his kind always were, all in black, and with a long coat that had been known, on occasion, to hold wonders. Not that they shared, Raum thought, glowering.

The Reaper stretched his neck, trying to get a better look at what Raum was holding on to. "What have you got there?"

"None of your business," Raum snapped, wrapping his wings more tightly around himself. Why, after millennia of Reapers avoiding him like the plague, did this one have to show up now?

"Well, I was minding my business, now that you mention it," Jarrod said. His fair skin shimmered faintly in the darkness, a marked contrast to his severe clothes. "But see, then I was called by a woman's departing soul, so here I am, ready to guide her into the beyond, and instead, I find a Fallen angel who thinks I don't realize he's hiding her under his wings. Right. There. In front of me." He cocked his head, amusement and curiosity glittering in his dark eyes.

"You're not needed here, Jarrod. Go away." Raum pulled an arm free and waved him off with an irritated jerk, then remembered his hands.

Shit.

"You're burned," Jarrod said softly, his surprise evident. "Did you…?"

The question, only half-finished, hung in the air between them. Raum considered denying it, but though he was adept at lying, anything he said was going to sound ridiculous. All he could hope for was that the truth got rid of the Reaper faster. He fixed Jarrod with a steely glare that greater beings had withered beneath.

"What if I did? It's no business of yours."

Jarrod looked nothing short of stunned, an expression Raum didn't think he'd ever seen on a Reaper's face before. The other man was silent a long moment, though he made no move to leave. Then he said, "I'd heard you were one of the defectors, you know. But I didn't actually believe it was true." His dark eyes narrowed slightly, considering him with unnerving intensity when Raum said nothing, which he knew the Reaper would take as confirmation enough.

Then, Jarrod said softly, "This is not the place for you right now, Raum of the Fallen."

Raum stared. It was the first time he had ever received any information that might be remotely construed as helpful from a Reaper, who were stubbornly neutral. Jarrod's face betrayed no emotion, though he continued to watch Raum with that look of frank assessment.

Finally, Raum said, "I know about the Nexus. We're not going to let it happen."

Jarrod's smile was thin. "That's a switch. But you're up against more than you know." Then he walked toward him, his stride purposeful. Raum took a step back, glaring.

"Don't be greedy, Raum. Let me see the woman."

"Piss off."

Jarrod stopped and folded his arms across his chest. "She's not so far from the borders of death yet, Raum. I want to see if you've done your job right." He shook his head. "At least, I'm assuming that saving innocent humans is part of your job now?"

"Not really," Raum grumbled, unable to let it go. He had no interest in word getting around that he was trying to get back into the white-winged contingent when it was so entirely untrue.

Jarrod stepped forward again. "Then all the more reason for me to have a look. You probably screwed it up and I'll have to take her anyway."

Raum bared his teeth. "Try it and lose an arm." But he relented at last, parting his wings to reveal Ember's unconscious form. He remembered that she was naked from the waist up, and turned her into him so that Jarrod couldn't get a good look, gripped by another wave of unreasonable possessiveness. He could tell from the odd look the Reaper gave him that he'd noticed, but for once, Jarrod kept his opinion to himself.

Instead, he leaned over her, eyes intense. He reached out one long-fingered hand and brushed a lock of gleaming hair away from the side of Ember's face, and Raum felt his fists clench. That was followed by a wave of nauseating pain, payment for moving his abused hands without thinking.

"Well?" he gritted out when the Reaper continued to examine her silently. Jarrod raised his gaze to him, and it was as black as a starless night.

"Why did you save her?"

Raum blinked. "What?"

"Why did you save this woman?" Jarrod repeated. "Because that's what you've done. And considering what, and who, she is, I'm a little confused. I don't know what it cost you, exactly," he continued, his voice dropping, and Raum saw his eyes go to his smoking hands. "But I'm going to guess it was quite a bit."

Raum paused, torn between the truth and keeping up appearances, though the latter would mean the end of this bizarre conversation with the Reaper. He'd never looked at the agents of Death as much more than a necessary nuisance, sometimes entertaining to bother, completely useless when it came to information. But Jarrod, with whom he'd engaged in the occasional war of words with over this soul or that, seemed to want to tell him something. And the days when he could afford to blow such an impression off were gone.

"It…she was guarded. Stupid *nefari* was meant to protect her and turned on her as soon as it got excited." He shrugged. "I should have been more careful. She's important to this Nexus business, and…Uriel doesn't want her hurt." It was as close as he would come to the truth, to his own interest in protecting her.

"But why *you?*" Jarrod asked, and he seemed genuinely perplexed.

"Because I said I would. Because this is the sorry state my existence has been reduced to." A muscle in his jaw twitched. "Because it's my fault she got hurt. Why does it matter to you anyway, Jarrod?" The words sounded foreign to his own ears, rolling strangely off his tongue. When was the last time he had admitted to anything resembling guilt? And yet it was true, all true.

He suddenly felt ill.

Jarrod seemed to sense this, and his gaze softened, though Raum didn't appreciate it. He had no use for pity, and wanted none. Still, the truth got him what he'd wanted.

Or thought he wanted.

"You really don't know, do you?" Jarrod asked, still looking puzzled. Then he shook his head, seeming to accept the situation. "It's ironic, that you've unwittingly given a part of yourself to the daughter of your enemy. A noble gift I wouldn't have expected you to give in a million years, don't get me wrong. But this is going to infuriate him. You may want to get out of here until you can muster some backup. Otherwise…" he trailed off for a moment, his gaze dropping to Ember's face with a look of sympathy, "there's no way you'll stand between him and what he wants. Not alone."

Raum's eyes narrowed as he grappled with Jarrod's words, trying to discern any meaning but the one he feared. But his longstanding feud was well known even to midworlders like the Reapers, and he knew, in his gut, exactly what Jarrod had meant.

"Mammon?"

Jarrod gave a single nod. "He watches his daughter, and waits for the right time to unleash her power. The darkness is growing thicker here. Don't you sense it? The Nexus is ripe for breaking." He lifted his head to scan the sky, breathing in deeply, as though he could scent the gathering evil in this place. Raum could only stare.

"Mammon's daughter," he said, struggling to reconcile the warm creature in his arms with the foul, grinning, glad-handing demon who had engineered his downfall. But it was so obvious, now that he looked: her unusual strength of mind, her power…she even had her father's red hair, and the rare beauty that could only mark her as high demon. There was no *nefari* in her. Ember carried the blood of the Fallen…and it made her far more dangerous than Raum had ever thought.

"Why are you telling me this?" Raum asked hoarsely, his thoughts hopelessly tangled in the wake of this news. His kind rarely impregnated human women, who were almost always too fragile for such a thing to be possible. And yet of all the Fallen to have produced a creature with beauty, power and a coveted, indestructible *soul*…

Mammon. His mortal enemy. Her father…

"I told you because you treated a human life as though it had value. It seems only right that I help you retain yours." Jarrod took two steps back, then offered a lopsided smile. "You surprise me, Raum. Do yourself a favor and get the seraphim here, then take Ember Riddick where Mammon can't find her until Nexus has been sealed. Leave the fighting to the angels and demons."

"But I *am* a demon," Raum protested.

Jarrod cocked his head at him, still wearing his half smile. "Are you?"

"Wait," Raum began, holding out one still-smoking hand to stop him. But it was no use.

In the irritating manner of all ethereal beings, the Reaper had already gone.

And Raum was left in the darkness with nothing but the steady sound of Ember's beating heart.

Chapter 5

When it hit, the goblet shattered the looking glass into a thousand pieces.

"Hellfire!"

Mammon's roar filled the Chamber of Glass, echoing off the infinite mirrors of all shapes and sizes that covered walls soaring upward into infinity and beyond sight. He hovered in the air for a moment longer, the enormous black wings that sprang from his back holding him steady, and stared at the shattered glass where only a moment before his daughter's face had been.

He had come here to gloat over his progress with her, to toast himself with the finest wine Hell could offer. A handful of the Fallen nobility had sired children with humans over the centuries, but half-breeds truly of the blood were rare. And none, Mammon knew, compared to his Ember. She was a beauty, of course, with his fiery hair, his perfect features. But more importantly, she had such potential, such power, and with the strength to keep it from driving her mad.

An unexpected gift, a key to tear open the Nexus and wreak Hell on the unsuspecting human world. It had been far too long. But he and the Council had had years to plan their next, greatest assault. And with him, the perfect guide to stoke the darkness within her, Ember would soon be commanding legions of her own.

Mammon had never seen her equal in an eternity littered with insane half-breed offspring whose violent natures had little intellect to hone them. Ember was the fruit of a one-night dalliance born of boredom, with a pregnancy as the surprising result. Even more surprising was that Dina Riddick, judgmental whore that she'd been, had managed to carry the tempestuous little brat to term. From a distance he'd watched, interested despite himself in the only child he had ever sired. Still, Mammon had expected little Ember—a name he himself had selected and pushed into Dina's mind, though the woman still hated it—to be nothing more than a tool, a toy to be quickly used up and thrown away. Good for a single burst of horrific violence, perhaps. But Ember had surprised him as he'd visited her dreams, watched her grow.

So in her sleep, he began to train her. Even now, unsure as she was, his daughter had a great deal more ability than she was consciously aware of. And one day, he decided, when Hell on Earth became a reality, she would sit at his side. His demon child, made immortal. And she with a soul, that precious gift that could never be destroyed, not even in the fiery river Phlegethon that would turn angel and demon alike into nothing but dust. She was perfection. The perfect embodiment, as he was, of beauty and death. No she-demon had ever risen so high. And she was his.

Until that wretched traitor had swept in and run off with her, that was. He had seen it, watched with impotent fury as the *nefari* set to guard Ember had turned on her as soon as Raum had burst in. Raum, with his precious Ember in his arms, vanishing into the night, cloaked in the protection of his kind that made it impossible for Mammon to see where he had taken her...*his* daughter, with the bastard's unworthy hands on her!

Filthy traitor, fit only to burn.

The Prince of Avarice gave one more furious snarl before he descended to the ground, his boots touching down gently on the marble floor. He folded his wings behind him, then whirled and stalked from the room.

"No," he growled, heading for the Throne Room. "I will not have it. I will not *allow* it. She is *mine.*"

As he walked, his scattered thoughts of vengeance began to coalesce into a plan of attack. A thin smile curved Mammon's lips, and with great relish, he began to plot in earnest. The wheels for the final triumph had finally been set in motion. Ember, his Ember, was only the beginning. He would get her back, he soothed himself. She would break the Nexus wide-open, and this invasion would make the last one seem like child's play. The Balance would never recover.

But first, it seemed he would have to show one foolish

prodigal Fallen angel what happened when you tried to steal from one of your own.

It was always better to rule in Hell, even if that rule ended with the soulless death that awaited them all, than to serve the Light. Raum had forgotten that lesson, it seemed.

It would be a pleasure to refresh his memory.

Chapter 6

Ember awakened to find herself strapped into the passenger seat of a sexy black Corvette, slumped to the side and with her mouth wide-open. Since that was her usual mode of travel sleeping, it wouldn't have been a really big deal, just kind of embarrassing.

Except that she also felt as if a truck had driven over her recently. And she didn't normally travel in mismatched pajamas with strange men who sometimes turned into birds.

She swallowed hard as she tried to sort through the hazy, fun-house memories of the night before, and the adrenaline began to pump again through her sluggish, sleep-addled system. Seemed as if there was plenty to be afraid of, all of a sudden. And that was a switch, since she was usually the scariest thing in any given place.

At least, that was what she'd always thought. Now,

Ember wasn't so sure. About anything. And there was only one person available to ask. She cleared her throat softly, and hoped that her rapidly beating heart wouldn't be given away by a shaking voice.

"Wh-where am I?"

Raum looked frighteningly intense with his hands on the wheel, piloting the sports car smoothly along at well over eighty miles an hour. She didn't know what he'd been thinking about…wasn't actually sure she wanted to know. He jumped a little at the sound of her voice, though, as if he'd forgotten she was even there.

Then his eyes met hers, just for a quick instant, and Ember felt a hot sizzle of connection that had nothing to do with fear. Her heartbeat slowed a little, but the fear was replaced by an angry tug of possessiveness that was disconcerting in its strength.

Mine, she thought, and remembered thinking it right before she'd fallen into his arms. When the poison had begun to work on her. And his touch had been so much gentler than she'd expected. She knew she should be afraid. But knowing that this man, supernatural creature, or whatever he was, had saved her life prevented her from being much but grateful that he'd been around when she'd needed him to be.

"You're awake," he said, and there was a slight edge to his voice, as though he wasn't quite sure what to do with her, either. To have at least that in common was oddly soothing to her.

"Awake," she agreed, trying a small smile. "And alive. Thanks to you."

Ember fully expected that this would be the opening

to a detailed conversation about why, exactly, her house had been invaded by something that looked to have come from the seventh circle of Hell, not to mention why Raum had been looking out for her.

She did not expect that he would continue to drive, silently and way too fast. Or that he would look kind of pissed off, which she thought was an inappropriate reaction to her continued existence, at best.

"You don't need to thank me," Raum finally said, and the surly tone of his voice told her that yes, he was in fact kind of pissed off.

"Okay, I'll be angry that you saved my life," Ember said with a frown. "Would that suit you better?"

"You could just forget about it. That would be my preference." His rich, warm voice slid through her, waking up nerve endings that had no business being awake right now. Her eyes drifted for a moment, and Ember noted for the first time that his hands, gripping the steering wheel, looked red and raw. Painful.

The old and familiar guilt flooded her immediately.

"I didn't do that, did I?" she blurted out, and without thinking she reached out to brush her hand against his. It was her greatest fear, hurting people. Especially when they had done nothing to warrant it. It seemed she hurt anyone she got too close to; God knew her own mother had gotten scars from her when she was too young to know better, only one reason why the woman wanted next to nothing to do with her only child. And a big reason, despite the widely recognized fact that Dina Riddick had never wanted and still did not want responsibility for anyone other than herself, that Ember had let it go. Let *her* go.

But every once in a while, that deep and denied need for a bit of human contact got the better of Ember's common sense. She felt it only for a moment when their hands touched, that hot and tingling rush when their skin connected, before Raum jerked his hand away with a furious glare. Ember let her own hand linger in midair for a moment, staring at it as it continued to tingle with tiny aftershocks.

"No," Raum growled. "You didn't do this. Now, sit still. We have a ways to go yet, and you don't need to be crawling all over the car. You already know I'm not going to hurt you."

Ember pulled her hand back and looked away, angry and embarrassed all at the same time. She knew what he'd meant: *crawling all over ME,* he might as well have said. But she knew he'd felt it, too. She just didn't know why he found it so repulsive, when to her it held the promise of something like Heaven.

Ember ran a hand through the unruly tangles of her hair, winced as she pulled through innumerable snags. Then she sighed and again looked over at her big, grim-faced chauffeur. Her reaction to him was no less powerful than it had been last night, but this time it was tempered with annoyance. It didn't stop her from wanting to crawl into his lap, but it did allow her to hang on to her wits this time. Or maybe her body was adjusting to a new, erotically charged baseline.

"Raum, if that really is your name," she said, and saw by the slight turn of his head that he was listening.

"I really don't feel like I should have to ask, but what the hell is going on?"

He paused. And at least this time, when he answered her, he didn't sound as if he wanted to fight. It was progress, of a sort.

"I've been trying to figure out a way to explain this that doesn't end with you throwing yourself out of the car," he said. "So I'll tell you what. Why don't you just ask me the things you want to know? And start small."

She nodded, inadvertently amused. He really did seem to be a man of few words. But as long as he was answering, she could work with it. "Okay," she said. "Agreed."

"Good." He took a deep breath, and Ember realized, suddenly, that Raum was as knotted up as she was. Somehow, knowing that made it easier to start.

"What are you?" she asked.

He considered this for a moment. "Start somewhere else."

Ember blew out an irritated breath. "Okay, fine. What am *I*? I'm assuming you're not unaware of the fact that I was growling and snarling right along with everyone else last night."

"At least you have a sense of humor about it," he said. When she just glared at him, waiting for a response, he relented.

"You're a half-breed, Ember Riddick. Half human, half demon. And I'm going to guess, since you seem like an intelligent woman, that you've considered that to be a possibility already." His eyebrow quirked slightly as he slid her a look. "I doubt that's the first time you've dealt with the growling and snarling."

He was right. It wasn't. And if he'd explored her house at all, Raum would doubtless have discovered no less than twenty books on mythical creatures, magic and most of all, types of demons. She had known...but she still hadn't quite wanted to believe it. Hearing the truth was far more of a body blow than she'd ever imagined it would be. Ember could only stare helplessly at Raum, searching for any sign that he wasn't completely serious. But "deadly serious" seemed to be the only way this man, or whatever he was, operated. It would have been so much easier to believe he was lying if last night had never happened...and if he hadn't just been giving voice to what she had suspected all along. Her stomach knotted painfully. One word filled her head, the thing she'd researched most extensively over time. The one that fit best, even though she didn't want it to.

"Oh, God," Ember said hoarsely. "I'm a succubus." She cringed as she said it. Ember knew way more than she wanted to about the supposed habits of the female demon who was compelled to both sex and violence. Still, it had always made the most sense. And her human half would temper that, she supposed.

Or not. A memory surfaced from high school, of awakening from an erotic dream to find herself hovering a full two feet above the bed. And her friends wondered why she couldn't watch that scene in *Ghostbusters,* when the Zuul-possessed Dana did the same thing. She didn't think an ancient Sumerian god was her problem, but still, it just wasn't as funny as it should have been. And then there was her ill-fated first make-out session, which had ended abruptly with Ty Richmond freaked out over his shredded Pearl Jam T-shirt.

At least he hadn't told anyone, though she knew it was more because it sounded nuts than out of any kind of compassion for her. And at least it had been his shirt, not his skin, which it easily could have been. But he had avoided her for the rest of high school. And the other boys had made it clear they were only interested in one thing where she was concerned. The girls, on the other hand, had avoided her like the plague. Too pretty. Too quiet. Too damned weird.

Good times, she thought, smarting a little at the memory. She had always been alone.

"You aren't a succubus," Raum said, drawing her out of the unpleasant reverie. "That would be the case if your blood was common demon, what we call *nefari.* Like the creature in your room last night. But your *father,*" he continued, his lip curling a little at the word, "is placed a little higher than that in the scheme of things. You are a she-demon, though. There are…certain things you'd have in common with the average succubus."

His mouth tightened a little when he said it, and Ember was sure he was thinking of the way she'd nearly mauled him in her store. Great. And his qualified definition didn't make her feel the least bit better.

"Can I fix that?" Ember asked, only half joking while she tried not to sound as bleak as she felt.

"Fix what?" he asked, his brow creasing slightly.

"The succubus stuff. I'd really like to get rid of it."

She supposed she wasn't actually joking after all. But Raum wasn't in the mood to humor her, it seemed.

"No. But that's really the least of your problems right now, Ember."

"No kidding." She sighed, and when he stayed silent, guessed he expected her to continue with the questioning. Right now, it seemed only marginally better than thinking quietly.

"Okay, next question, then. If you had to name my biggest problem at the moment, what would it be?"

He thought about it, longer than she was really comfortable with.

Finally, he said, "We're going to have most of Hell hunting us down. That's a big one."

Ember's mouth dropped open, and she was gripped by a sudden urge to just throttle the rest of it out of him.

"Hell."

"Yes."

"After *me*."

He didn't even bother to look at her. "Yes."

"As in, biblical Hell, with flames and torment and the devil."

"It's a little different than that, but pretty much. Yes."

"Damn it, Raum," Ember snapped, floored at the utter lack of concern he seemed to have about this. She began to hope, fervently, that she was dreaming. "I'm sitting in a car going I don't know where, I'm in pajamas I did not put on last night, and you can sprout wings. Oh, and by the way, Hell is real, and the things that live there are after me." She threw her hands up in complete exasperation. "I really appreciate you saving my life and everything, but seriously, would you please just quit screwing around and tell me why I would be attacked by a demon if I *am* one? Also, and I know I'm repeating myself here, but *what are you* and why me?"

He looked a little startled by her outburst, and there was another flash of those incredible green eyes as he glanced at her. Still, she didn't think he was really going to answer her. But just as she was about to start after him again, he decided to give it a shot.

"There are places," he said slowly, "where the ethereal border between Hell and Earth are very thin. These come and go, changing with the ebb and flow of the natural energies and shifting of both places, but it happens. When one of these spots occurs, when it's thin enough that a break is possible, we call it a Nexus."

"Great," she said, thinking that it was weird, but at least she could follow it so far. "And what does this have to do with anything I just asked you?"

"When there's a Nexus, it tends to draw humans to it who are still attuned to the old magic, the inherent powers of Light and Dark that Earth has always had, but that most humans have forgotten," he replied. "When the conditions are right, one of these humans, with the right direction, can break a Nexus wide-open."

She closed her eyes the instant she realized where he was going with this. "I don't think I want to hear this."

His voice was calm, steady. Relentless. "You need

to. Because you have this ability. You're what is known as a Breaker. And Hell knows it."

Ember's eyes opened, widened as she tried to absorb this.

Raum's expression was calm, and he might have been discussing the weather for all the excitement in his voice. "If I hadn't gotten you out of there, it was only a matter of time until you threw open one of the Gates of Hell."

"I'm not sure I buy that." Ember was beginning to feel slightly ill. "I would never have done that."

"You would have," Raum said. "When a demon wants something from a human, or a half human, they tend to get it. And don't tell me you haven't struggled with your impulses before." He tilted his head at her, and Ember felt herself flushing when she realized he'd had a front-row seat for her most recent slipup. Did he know about the other times? How could he possibly know?

Common sense told her he couldn't. But her common sense didn't seem to be holding up very well right now. And besides, Ember thought with new unease, she'd done exactly what she was told in those strange dreams she'd had off and on throughout her life. Even though those were only dreams. The powers she'd flexed and honed in her sleep had always been too wild to believe, even for her.

Except suddenly, she wasn't so sure. Flustered, wishing she had some space and time in which to sort through her jumbled thoughts, Ember shifted the subject slightly.

"So a Nexus breaks, and the place is overrun with

demons. Can you fix it when something like that happens?"

Raum shrugged. "The angels always manage it after a while, but the effects can be felt for hundreds of years. Thousands, if it's bad enough. But there is always a battle. And it's always bloody."

Outside, the world rushed by in a blur, and Ember wondered in passing how Raum managed not to either crash them or get tagged by the cops. Which brought her back around to her initial question. He seemed to know quite a bit about her. How?

"I asked you last night if you were my Guardian Angel, and you said no," she said slowly. "I saw the wings... Are you an angel at all? Or something else?"

He glanced at her, and his expression was guarded. "I freelance. We'll leave it at that for now. But I'm no angel," he continued, his voice hard. "Don't ever mistake me for one."

Noted, Ember thought, feeling her pulse quicken at the darkness in his gaze. She knew she should be repelled by it, that he wanted her to be. And part of her was. But even more of her was completely ensnared by him, and his strange combination of consideration and danger. Her fingers itched to reach out and skim over the skin like marble, to feel the power and heat that pulsed just beneath the surface again. Ember flexed her fingers and struggled to turn her attention back to the matter at hand.

"You think Johnstown is a Nexus," Ember said hollowly. "Right? That's why we're taking off. Because you were afraid I was going to...to..." She couldn't finish.

It was one thing to have struggled with relationships, with the line between sex and violence. It was another to deal with the possibility that she was some kind of key to the underworld, a real-life hell-raiser.

"Johnstown *is* a Nexus," Raum replied. "The Infernal Council has had a watch on you your entire life, I'm sure. But especially since you were drawn to the Nexus, waiting for the barrier to get thin enough for you to be used to break through it. That's why the demon was in your room last night. To guard you." His lip curled. "Whoever chose that one did a very poor job of it."

Ember stared at him in horror. She'd figured it would be bad, but this…this was a lot worse. Instinctively, she tried to find a way around it. But…hadn't she always dreamed of the green mountains of Vermont? Hadn't she been amazed to drive through Johnstown and find it exactly like a little town she'd always pictured herself in? It had felt so *right*.

"No," she said softly. "Johnstown is a good place. I've been…happy there." And she had, Ember thought, or at least as happy as she got. She'd felt as if she was finally building a life for herself. At the very least, she'd been content. But even as she thought it, she knew that was a lie. Her innate restlessness had been bothering her again lately. And despite the fact that her business was successful, any attempts to make real friends had been subtly rebuffed. People always seemed to sense an otherness about her and steer clear.

And once again, she had stopped trying and accepted it, staying as she had always been: alone. On some level, it was a relief to finally have an explanation, even if she wasn't entirely convinced. But then, there was something about Raum that called to that solitary part of her. She knew nothing about him, but Ember felt with deep certainty that he was someone who would at least understand what it was to be alone.

Maybe that was the continuing pull she felt toward him. Beyond his sheer physical beauty, she felt like this, at last, was someone who might sort of understand her. Still, the thought that she'd had so little control over her life so far, that every decision she'd made had all been somehow manipulated, rankled.

"I don't believe it," she said. "This is insane."

Raum simply shrugged, not even bothering to glance at her. He seemed to have expected this reaction. "You can believe it or not. You're still not leaving my sight until the Nexus is sealed. Unless, of course, you want to run the risk of being responsible for the deaths of thousands of people."

His words had the intended effect, Ember thought ruefully, as guilt flooded her.

"That's a cheap shot."

"That's the truth. Whether or not you accept it as such changes nothing." He sounded so sure, almost bored. There was no attempt to convince her, no cajoling or coddling or working to smooth her ruffled fathers. And oddly, it was that, more than anything, that told her he wasn't lying. But if that were true, it threw everything she'd struggled for her entire life into doubt. All her hard-won stability and control meant nothing in the end. But she couldn't think about it. Not yet. It made her sick to the very depths of her soul…if, indeed, she even had one.

"This is all just because I'm a half-breed?" she asked hollowly.

"No," Raum said, seeming to hesitate. "You're unusual even for them, because your father isn't a common, low demon. He's one of the ruling lords of Hell, a fallen angel." He paused. "As am I."

Ember's mouth went dry as she thought of those beautiful black wings, of the power he wore like a second skin. A fallen angel…a *demon*. And she realized, too late, that he had never actually said whom he was working for. Which meant that this car was exactly the last place she ought to be.

"I…thought you said…you freelanced…" Ember stammered, wondering if her healing ability would extend to throwing herself out of a speeding car. Not just a half demon, a half fallen angel. Well, that explained everything. No wonder she was so screwed up. Her fingers curled around the door handle.

His eyes flicked to her hand. "Ember. Don't do anything stupid. I don't work for Hell anymore."

Ember gave a high, trilling laugh that sounded very off-balance to her own ears. "Don't do anything *stupid?* Are you serious? Why did you even bother to save me last night, if all I am is some…some evil *thing* that's going to blow a hole in Hell? I went to freaking Sunday school, Raum! If you're a fallen angel, you're sure not taking me somewhere *safe!* How can you expect me to trust anything you've said?"

He pushed a button, and the doors locked. Panic rose

like bile in her throat and Ember began to pry at the lock with her fingertips, tugging fruitlessly at the door handle with the other.

"Damn it, Raum, just dump me off somewhere, let me out of here! Wherever you're taking me, I don't want to go!"

"Ember, would you… Hey, quit pulling on that!" he demanded, and Ember was gratified that there was finally some emotion in his voice, even if he only sounded pissed off again. She tugged harder.

He jerked the wheel hard enough that her head smacked against the window and pulled to the side of the highway, slamming on the brakes before turning to shout at her.

"Damn it, Ember, I got thrown out of Hell! Hell is the *last* place I want to go! Heaven hired me to *protect* you!"

Ember rubbed the sore spot on her forehead and turned to stare at him. A curly lock of hair had fallen over one eye, and he was breathing heavily, eyes glowing with a light of their own. She could barely see the tips of two sharp, pointed incisors between his parted lips… like hers when she got worked up.

"Angels, demons," she spat, furious at him for destroying the illusion of any hint of control over her life. "What difference does it make? I don't want anything to do with this. And I sure as hell don't want anything to do with you!"

It happened so fast, she didn't even see him move. In the blink of an eye, she'd been hauled into his lap and was plastered awkwardly against the front of him. Not that the "awkward" did anything to diminish the heat that flared the instant he touched her. His face was only inches from hers, and she could see now that he wasn't just angry, he was furious. His eyes were all but spitting sparks.

"Yes, you do," he snarled.

Her eyes widened in outrage…in part because he was right. "How dare—"

But she never finished. His mouth was on hers, his arms crushing her to him and preventing any escape as he proved his point. Instantly, Ember's simmering attraction caught fire. She found herself drowning in a kiss that was nothing but heady, liquid sin as his mouth plundered hers ruthlessly. There was no gentleness to him, nothing but inhuman strength and aggression and raw, unvarnished desire. And yet Ember found her fingers sliding into the dark silk of his hair to pull him even closer. This was what she had sensed from him, what she had always wanted and never found. Whatever else he was, in matters of the physical, Raum was more than her match. His mouth was hard, demanding, taking her captive with every thrust of his tongue. She matched his rhythm with her own, wordlessly demanding more.

Her sensual nature, too long ignored, had now brutally awakened in a single impulsive heartbeat. Ember moaned into his mouth as his hand cupped the full mound of her breast and gave it a rough squeeze. Her claws sharpened and begin to dig into his broad shoulders, and when she pulled his bottom lip with her teeth, she tasted blood. She waited for the inevitable, for him to pull away in pain, or disgust.

Instead, Raum gave a ragged growl. She felt his hands grab her ass as he shifted so she was straddling him, and the feel of his rock-hard shaft between her legs told her he liked how she was just fine.

Her heartbeat accelerated, and her system flooded with heat as her core went liquid. He rocked his hips up into her, and the crush of pleasure was intense, immediate. Ember cried out hoarsely, her head falling back. She felt his teeth graze her neck, and he made a guttural sound of raw pleasure that had her quivering on the edge of the release her body begged for every time he was near.

The blast of a horn directly behind them reminded Ember where she was, and she jerked her head up with a gasp. From her vantage point on Raum's lap, she could see the flame-red sports car that had pulled up nearly to their bumper. She could also see the gorgeous blond from the first time she'd met Raum was behind the wheel, and her cheeks flooded with heat that had nothing to do with the blind passion that had gripped her only moments before. She couldn't remember his name…something even stranger than Raum's…but he dropped a saucy wink at her before laying on the horn again.

And she was still very much on Raum's lap, on the side of the highway in broad daylight. Ember closed her eyes and tried to pluck some sort of coherent thought from the whirlwind that was her current state of mind. She'd wanted to fight him. How had she ended up trying to devour him? He'd knocked her entire world out of whack. He was very quickly ruining the life he'd saved.

And all she could think of right this second was drowning in another of his kisses.

"Son of a bitch," Raum growled, and she pushed back slightly to look at him, sanity returning in small increments. He was completely disheveled, his ebony curls tousled, his mouth slightly swollen from the force of their kisses. He looked at her with a mixture of annoyance and a boyish chagrin she would never have expected to see on his regal features.

"I, ah…I didn't know he was coming," she said. "The other one."

"I've been trying to forget," Raum replied as the horn went off again in a series of short, irritable blasts. "Gadreel isn't needed, which I tried to tell him. But arguing with him is pointless. He's determined you're going to instigate a bloodbath at some point, and I didn't want to waste time arguing with him."

Ember stared at Raum, aghast. "He's coming to protect people from *me?*"

"Actually, I think he just wants to watch," Raum said flatly. "He'll be sent back to Johnstown soon enough, which is where he's supposed to be. Just ignore him." His mouth hardened. "And stay away from him if at all possible."

"I still don't get why you expect me to believe you're working with angels if you're that dangerous," Ember muttered, and clambered off him, gingerly avoiding the shifter. "I suppose he's a fallen angel, too, right? What are you guys trying to do, switch back?"

It was, she saw immediately, the exact wrong thing to say.

"No." Just a one-word answer, but it dripped with ice. "And as I said…you can believe whatever you like. It changes nothing."

His green eyes flashed at her, hot and violent, before he looked away, his expression quickly schooling itself back into stony intensity. Raum leaned his head back against the headrest, staring ahead as she fastened herself back into her seat. He seemed to be deep in thought. After a few seconds, he put the 'Vette into gear and pulled back onto the highway.

They rode in silence, each of them lost in their thoughts. Ember watched the world fly by outside, heart slowly sinking as she digested what she'd gotten herself into. What her mother's lousy taste in men had gotten her into, Ember mentally corrected herself. This was all about genetics. Fallen angels, holes in Hell… Obviously, her father hadn't been the absentee drunk she'd spent her formative years hearing about.

It wasn't the first time she'd felt as if her life had been specially designed without any real choices. And Raum's deep rumble of a voice did nothing to make her feel any better. It was simply a variation on a theme she'd heard from members of the opposite sex since she'd been old enough to be rejected by them.

"That can't happen again. I'm only here to guard you. And I need to be able to focus."

It's not you, it's me. It's not me, it's you. Whatever.

"Of course," Ember said stiffly. "Not a problem." What else could she say? Apparently, she wasn't even fit for her own kind. All she was made for was destruction. It was a lesson she should have learned that night on the beach in Florida two years ago. The night that had, eventually, sent her running here. Had even that terrifying encounter been orchestrated, she wondered? Had it all been a setup to get her here?

Her stomach knotted painfully as it occurred to her, not for the first time in her life, that she, and the world at large, might have been better off if no one had ever bothered to save her.

As though he'd sensed her thoughts, Raum said, "I'm not going to let anything happen to you, Ember. I'll keep you safe."

It sounded almost sweet, until he added, "It's what Heaven is paying me for."

Chapter 7

It was called Benny's Hideaway Heaven, and it was the nicest motel in the area. This was according to Benny himself, a good-natured, heavyset man who manned the front desk in a flowered shirt that looked as if it could have made an adequate sail for a small boat.

Of course, it was also the only motel in the area. But it was as good a place as any to stop, consider his options. As far as he knew, there weren't any contingency plans for situations like this, and he certainly hadn't planned on ever skipping town with a beautiful she-demon whose father was his worst enemy. None of which changed his situation, or the fact that he had no idea what to do next. Or his growing certainty that any more time alone with Ember Riddick would cause him to simply burst into flames, saving Hell the trouble.

Raum left Gadreel to entertain Ember while he

checked them in, and then headed out to direct them to two adjoining rooms in the long, low, sagging building tucked into the trees of rural Pennsylvania.

It irritated him to find Ember laughing at whatever ridiculous thing Gadreel was telling her. Particularly because the silence that fell when he reached them told him he'd been Gadreel's target. He told himself that Ember's mood had lifted simply because Gadreel was good at putting women at ease. After all, that was what the demon *did*. Still, that didn't quite smother his annoyance that Ember was already more comfortable with his erstwhile partner than she was with him.

It shouldn't matter. It *didn't* matter. After all, hadn't he insisted to her that he was only her guard, nothing more? And yet the sight of Gadreel's easy, suggestive smile was more than he could bear.

"Here's your key," Raum said, shoving it in Gadreel's smug face. "Now do something useful and go find us some food."

Gadreel accepted the proffered key with a sigh. "See?" he asked Ember. "I told you what a pain in the ass he is." Raum didn't miss the nasty glint in Gadreel's eye, however, as he stalked away. He didn't like being dismissed. Raum had to assume that his hunger, at this point in the day without stopping, had just been great enough to supersede his annoyance.

It might not have mattered. But Raum found himself smirking at Gadreel's retreating back anyway.

"Come on," he said, heading for the car once Gadreel had peeled out. Ember followed him quietly, the tension between them returning as quickly as the silence had.

It was better this way, Raum thought as he hoisted two bags out of the car. Even with the tension, he hadn't been able to keep his hands off her. Getting friendly would lead to worse. And he was already concerned over the woman's softness. Ember Riddick was going to be difficult enough to keep alive without someone like him pawing at her.

He was not fit for softness, for sweetness. He had known it most of his long life.

But it had been a long time since the thought had produced the strange ache that he now felt, the touch of shame that he had long ago thought he'd buried.

Hellfire, he thought, disgusted with himself. All this time above was turning him into a fool. Gritting his teeth, he dumped a small duffel on the ground at Ember's bare feet and glared at her, willing her to be offended.

She simply looked at it and raised her eyebrows.

"You packed for me?" she asked, sounding a lot more grateful than he would have liked. "When did you do that?"

"It's just a few things," he muttered. "I took you back to your house...after...because of all the blood." *Because I wasn't going to have Gadreel seeing you as you were. Naked. Perfect.* "Since I was already there anyway, I figured you might want to change out of the pajamas at some point, so I threw a couple of things in a bag." He wouldn't tell her that just getting his hands in the frothy, lacy treasure chest of her underwear drawer had given him a hard-on that had lasted for an excruciating hour, and threatened to return at the slightest thought of it.

Or rather, of her wearing any of it. And that was after he had dressed her, carefully cleaning the dried blood from her bare skin. His hands had been shaking.

Damn her.

"Thanks," Ember said, giving him a small, uncertain smile. He ignored it, stalking to the room and fumbling it open with the key. It would be better if she looked at him as nothing more than a bodyguard, he knew. And better for him to behave like one. It wasn't as though he was ever friendly, anyway.

He just wished he didn't have to keep reminding himself of that around her.

Raum felt her step into the darkened, musty room behind him. The light cinnamon scent of her wafted to him, and he had to grit his teeth against it. His instincts where she was concerned seemed to run along two very clear lines: Protect and Devour.

She flipped on the light, and though Raum had seen what they were going to be dealing with perfectly well in the darkness, it managed to look even worse lit up.

The room was mostly taken up by a single bed, which purported to be king-sized but was in reality a queen-size with delusions of grandeur. This was covered in an ancient comforter decked out in the most hideous brown paisley Raum had ever seen. Beside the bed was a single nightstand with a phone, and in front of it was a television, topped with a folded ad for low-price adult viewing.

The thought of watching something like that with her around was all it took to have his shaft at full attention.

Raum bit back a groan. He thought he'd left Hell, but it had found him anyway.

"I'm going to change," Ember said, her tone slightly uncertain, as though she thought he might argue with her. That or demand to watch.

If only.

"Make it quick," was what he said, and he saw her eyebrows draw together, a hint of the temper that had up until now been buried beneath her understandable fear and confusion.

"No problem," she said, and her voice crackled with her irritation as she spun on one heel and headed into the bathroom with her duffel bag while he busied himself thinking about demons with flatulence problems, demons with partially eaten faces, anything that might have a dampening effect on his ardor. He rummaged around in his bag, found his stupid cell phone and stared at it. He needed to consult with Levi, little as he wanted to. Because after this little stop, he had absolutely no clue where to take Ember that they wouldn't be followed to, before long.

Leaving had been logical, instinctive. Johnstown wouldn't be safe for her anymore, and chances were good that the Infernal Council had figured out Levi's little club of exiles was involved. But where to go from here? Hell, he knew quite well, had eyes everywhere. And Mammon was, to give him some small amount of credit, doggedly determined when he wanted something.

"Forget demons," Ember said, heading quickly out of the bathroom with a wrinkled nose. "I just found something way scarier, and it has a lot more legs. To say nothing of the shower mold it's living in."

Raum grunted by way of a reply. She sighed heavily at him—she seemed to have been doing a lot of that today—and then went back to looking resigned.

"Can I use your phone?" she asked, looking at the duct-taped cell phone in his hand with no small amount of trepidation. "I have to do damage control. Do you have any idea how long it's going to be before I can go back?" He saw the hope written plain in her eyes, on her open, lovely face, that this would somehow be fixed quickly. He also saw, with some consternation, that she might be nervous around him, but that she wasn't exactly afraid of him, either. A little fear would have been helpful. Raum's eyes narrowed as he wondered what exactly Gadreel had said about him.

"Phone? Please? I have to let everyone know that the shop is closed. I'm sure you don't have these problems," Ember said, a definite edge creeping into her voice, "but I can't just walk out of my life without a word."

He shrugged and said nothing because he knew it would irritate her. Sure enough, Ember pursed her lips into a small *moue* of distaste, propped one hand on her hip and held out the other. Fighting back a smirk, Raum handed over the phone, and she looked at it like he imagined she'd probably looked at whatever bug was lurking in the bathroom, before opening it and starting to punch in numbers.

"Thanks," she said, in a tone that was anything but thankful. Then she turned away, and Raum felt free to let his eyes roam over the jeans that hugged her ass in exactly the right way, the sweater that clung to her ample curves and accentuated the long, slim waist he'd gotten a good look at the night before.

"I think I'd rather room with Gadreel," Ember muttered as she punched in numbers. "At least he talks."

"Over my dead and rotting carcass," he shot back, eyeing the size of the bed and imagining what Gadreel would get up to in no time at all. "You stay with me. I told you, you're my responsibility."

She arched one slim red brow, her mouth set in a hard, irritable line. *No,* Raum thought, *she definitely isn't afraid of me. And that's going to be a problem.*

"I can take care of myself," Ember said flatly. "But I'm glad to see you've regained your powers of speech." Then someone picked up on the other line, and she began to talk about managerial duties, imaginary family emergencies and other things he had no interest in.

Raum gritted his teeth and dug in his bag for the tattered paperback he planned to pretend to read for the rest of the afternoon, all while staring at Ember. She'd known right where to hit him, after all. Maybe she had more of her father in her than he'd thought.

In any case, it was going to be a long night.

Somehow, Ember had dozed off.

Her tired body had demanded it, and it might have done her some good, but for the angry jumble of half-remembered dreams. Had the Bad Angel been there? She really thought he might have. Especially since she felt a hazy certainty that she'd given something away that she shouldn't have. Dreams were dreams…but after the events of the past twenty-four hours, Ember had to wonder if maybe, after all these years of thinking she was only dreaming, there might be a lot more to it than that.

In fact, she thought it was likely.

She wasn't ready to discuss it yet. Not with Raum, whom she barely knew and certainly didn't trust. But if the dreams continued, and all of this insanity was proven true, Ember knew she was going to have to tell *someone*.

To steady herself, she watched Raum through her lashes, concentrating on the deep and steady sound of his breathing, savoring the occasional whiff of air scented with his own singular combination of spice and wildness. He sat by the door, legs propped on the small TV table, reading a battered paperback mystery.

There was, she thought, no better distraction than watching a man like him.

God, but he was gorgeous. Ember's secretive gaze slid up one hard, muscular thigh encased in black denim, over the bicep that stretched the limits of the fitted T-shirt he wore. A warm knot tightened low in her belly and began to ache, and she shifted uncomfortably in the bed. Instead of making the problem better, her nipples pebbled as the soft cotton of her shirt dragged across them.

Okay, so watching him had been a bad idea after all.

She sucked her lower lip into her mouth and bit back a frustrated moan. She didn't know what it was like, for a normal girl to look at a man and get worked up. But for her, it could get excruciating. And this was worse, far worse, than usual. Or, in fact, ever.

Ember's core went to pulsing, liquid heat as she silently willed herself to think of something, anything but sex. Of his skin against hers. Of his tongue tracing a hot path down her stomach…

"Stop," he said, and his voice was rough, fingernails against velvet. Giving up pretense, Ember opened her eyes fully and found Raum looking at her the way she imagined the big bad wolf might have regarded Little Red. His eyes glowed faintly in the dim light of the shabby room, and she realized, all of a sudden, that he hadn't actually turned a page in quite a while.

"Stop what?" she asked, daring him to answer, her own voice dropping to the husky come-hither tones it always did when she was in this state. It drew men like flies. Well, all but Raum, who remained stubbornly in his chair, which looked as if it might give up under his weight at any time. And she'd be damned if she'd beg him for something she was fairly sure was a bad idea, no matter how much she wanted it.

"Stop thinking about it. I told you, it won't be happening again. It's a bad idea."

"How do you know what I'm thinking about?" she asked irritably, rising up on one elbow to glare at him. She caught the way his eyes went to her breasts, to the tight buds of her nipples pressing against the thin fabric of the shirt. It was petty, but she savored that small triumph. He wasn't as unaffected as he claimed to be.

Raum's jaw tightened, and he looked resolutely at the wall. "I just know."

"You don't know anything," she snapped, annoyed that he seemed to have all of the discipline she lacked. She knew he wanted her. And because he was the first man she'd ever encountered whom she wasn't worried about breaking, maiming or mauling, his refusal to at least acknowledge it was beyond infuriating.

Ember shifted again, trying to ignore the answering throb between her tightly clenched thighs.

"I was thinking about inventory," she lied, thrusting up her chin. "And about all the income I'm losing from this little adventure."

"No, you weren't," Raum shot back. "But you'd be better off thinking about inventory."

Ember gave a frustrated growl and kicked off the covers, flopping over on her other side to face away from him. Maybe if she quit looking at him it would help.

"You suck," she told him. "You're a high-handed, overbearing jerk with zero personality. I do *not* want you."

"You could have fooled me earlier." His eyes narrowed into dangerous slits, but all that warning did was provoke her.

"I didn't start it," she snapped, her temper sparking at the implication that somehow she had been the one to blame for his reaction to her. She might have enjoyed it, but she sure as hell hadn't asked for it.

"I didn't hear you complaining," Raum replied with a flash of his now-lengthened incisors. According to the oh-so-helpful Gadreel, Raum was never exactly Mr. Sunshine. So far, it looked as if the other fallen angel hadn't been exaggerating.

"Whatever, Raum," Ember bit out, trying to hold very still so that nothing else would create any friction against her highly sensitized skin. "You said yourself I'm half demon. Maybe I just like sex. That doesn't make you special. And believe me, I'm not interested on a personal level *at all*." She said it to cut him, not because it was true. Unfortunately, his pigheadedness prevented him from feeling any sort of sting.

"Good," Raum said, and his voice dropped to a dark, sexual rumble that vibrated straight through her. "But it's the physical interest that's the problem. I can smell it all over you. It's cinnamon, and clove and honey. You smell *delicious*." His voice hardened, not complimentary, but accusatory.

"That's why you need to stop thinking about it."

But she couldn't. Not now, when everything inside of her was so tightly coiled she could barely think. How could he say these things and not expect her to react? She whipped her head to the side to glare at him, but whatever snide retort she'd planned to throw back at him died in her throat the instant she got a look at him. Raum was a man right on the edge of his control. His chest rose and fell quickly, and his eyes glowed brightly now. With his head lowered the way it was, he looked like some wild jungle cat about to pounce.

Ember closed her eyes and prayed for some discipline, though all things considered, she doubted anyone was listening.

"Just. Go. Away," she bit out, not looking at him. "Go sleep with your buddy. I need space."

There was silence, which told her he hadn't gone

anywhere. She was about to start hurling expletives at him when she heard him mutter one of his own beneath his breath. And when the bed dipped beneath his weight, she wasn't sure whether to cry out in triumph or despair. It was a bad idea. She was intimately familiar with bad ideas. But of all the ones she'd ever been tempted to indulge, this was by far the most difficult to resist. If she even decided to.

Ember opened her eyes to find him crawling toward her on hands and knees, dark intent in his eyes. Only the shred of her pride that was left allowed Ember the strength to hold out her hand to stop him.

"Don't do me any favors, Raum," she said firmly, and noticed with dismay that her well-manicured nails had gone sharp and black. "I don't need to grovel for sex, especially not from men who've made it very clear they don't want me. I'm used to not getting what I want. I'll live."

He swatted her hand away as easily as he would have a fly, his eyes burning with intent. "That's no guarantee that I will. Now shut up and let me…"

She didn't know quite what he wanted her to let him do, but when she opened her mouth to ask, he covered it with his own.

A startled gasp tore from her throat as his tongue swept into her mouth, hard, brutal…hot. Then she was pressed against him as he lowered himself to her, pinning her to the bed and wedging one of his thighs between her own. Her gasp became a broken moan as Ember surged upward against him, the simmering attraction between them bursting into flames, burning through her at every point of contact. She couldn't breathe, didn't even want to move for fear that all of Raum's heat, hers at last, might be torn away. But he was insistent, his wicked mouth urging her, tempting her to let her demon out to play. She slid her hands into his hair, the dark and coiling silk of it, as she lifted her hips into him, once, then again, until the two of them were locked in a primal rhythm, writhing against one another.

One of Raum's hands cupped her breast and gave the nipple a hard pinch, an action that sent shock waves of pleasure rippling through her. Her claws dug into his shirt, and she heard the soft tearing as the fabric gave beneath them. She was trembling, her breath coming in hard pants as she rode the slowly cresting wave that the delicious friction was building within her.

Ember could feel him, the hot length of him, pressing insistently against her. It wasn't enough, not nearly enough. She wanted to feel him inside her, was almost desperate to join with him fully. It didn't matter that it was unexplored territory for her.

He was all she wanted.

"Let go," he whispered in her ear.

Ember's power surged with her need, and this time, she embraced it. With a growl, she tore Raum's shredded shirt the rest of the way off him, enjoying the rough groan that elicited from him. He slid his own hands up the length of her torso, and she could feel the tips of his own claws as he did, not quite gentle, but not painful.

Like me…he's like me…

It was arousing in a way she had never before experienced. Maybe that was just as well, because right now, caught in the throes of sensation, Ember wasn't at all sure she would survive their coupling. She also found she didn't much care.

Her shirt hit the floor, followed by her pants. But when she began to breathlessly fumble with the fly of his jeans, Raum grabbed her wrist.

"Told you," he breathed, a thin sheen of perspiration on his brow. "It's a bad idea."

Ember bared her fangs at him, even as she continued to move beneath him.

"This isn't really the time to be telling me that," she gasped, then gave a sharper gasp as his hand slipped between her legs. Rational thought fled instantly.

Ember's head fell back on a moan of pure, unadulterated pleasure. She wanted to tell him that it wasn't enough. She wanted to flip him, tear the rest of his clothes off and ride him until both of them were shattered. But she was so tight, so slick with the need for release at this point, that the promise of it wouldn't allow her to do anything but accept what Raum had to give.

"Let go for me, Ember. Come for me," he breathed, dropping his head against her neck as his finger slipped between her folds to find the tight, swollen nub they concealed. His breath was hot on her neck, and his lips trailed down the side of her throat. Then his teeth were on her, the twin points of his incisors scraping against her sensitive skin.

In an instant Ember was right at the edge of blinding climax. She heard herself faintly gasping his name, telling him in raw, explicit terms all the things she wanted him to do to her.

Then his teeth were in her, and the bright flash of pain was followed by a hot rush of pleasure that finally pushed her over the edge. She gave a hoarse cry as her hips slammed upward and all her quivering tension imploded in wave after wave of bliss.

When the tremors finally began to subside, Ember realized that though Raum had removed his fangs from her neck, he was still tight against her, his face hidden from view. His heart pounded so hard that she could feel it, pressed together as they were, and through the satisfied haze of her own fulfillment, Ember realized that what he had given her had come at some cost to himself. She could feel how hard he still was, how he throbbed against her in time with his heart.

Slightly dazed, very sated, she stroked her hand up Raum's bare back. He shuddered.

"Ember," he groaned. "Don't. I didn't realize… don't."

"Let me," she purred, wanting to give him the same pleasure he'd given her, wanting him to find his release, as well. She turned her head slightly, placed a gentle kiss on his ear. "It's the least I can do."

Her hand stroked down his back again, and slid between them to find where he still ached for her.

"We've already done too much," he protested, but he made no move to stop her as her fingers wrapped around his shaft. "It's— Hellfire," he snarled, and his head snapped up at the same instant as a crash sounded from the next room. Instantly he was off the bed, sparing her only a single, accusing look that seared her.

This is your fault. He might as well have said it, Ember thought, all of her pleasure evaporating. It was a look she'd seen often enough to know what it meant.

God, she was a fool.

The doorknob to their room began to turn back and forth, followed by a solid *thump* that made the walls shake as whatever it was threw its weight behind breaking the door down.

"Get in the damn bathroom," Raum growled, not sparing her another look as he prepared to meet whatever was coming in.

"No way," Ember shot back, leaping from the bed and landing lightly on her feet beside him. He'd wounded her pride, but there was no way she was going to let him see it, much less play the helpless female when that was one thing Ember was very sure she was not.

"I'm not hiding while you do the hard stuff. I told you, I can take care of myself."

He started to argue with her, but the next blow to the door snapped the lock and splintered the wood as it slammed open to bounce against the wall. The muscular demon behind it stormed in with a deafening shriek, and another leaped over the top of it directly at her.

For once in her life, Ember willingly let her fury get the better of her. These pieces of shit had ruined her evening. While Raum caught the first demon quickly and snapped his neck with a sickening sound that Ember knew she would never forget, she made short work of the other, catching him in midair with a quick and furious slash of her claws across his throat, then stepping nimbly aside to let him fall. She had never been a killer, had only really come close to killing once before. But the ability to destroy, the will to do it, came back to her as though she had taken thousands of lives.

Ember heard the warning grunt from outside the door, knew there was at least one more and let the blood now coursing hot through her veins dictate her action. Ignoring Raum's angry command to stay put, she was outside in another leap, welcoming the attack of the two *nefari* who seemed to have been stationed outside because they were far too big to fit through the door.

"Don't hurt the woman," she heard one grunt. "Kill the others."

"Not a chance in Hell," she hissed.

She caught only a glimpse of one demon's piggy black eyes widening in surprise as she sprang at him, claws and teeth bared. The one she landed on gave a high-pitched squeal, and the unexpected fury of her assault seemed to throw both creatures off.

Ember fought like a woman possessed, taking the few hard blows the demons managed to get in as though they were nothing more than taps. To her consternation, however, she couldn't seem to take them down. Their skin was as tough as rawhide, and though they were large and slow in battle, they seemed to be creatures of immense strength.

Dimly, she became aware that Raum and Gadreel had joined her, sending one of the two crashing to the ground with what seemed to her to be very little work. There was obviously a trick to this she didn't know.

She'd just decided to get out of the way when one meaty arm the size of a tree trunk wrapped around her waist and began to squeeze.

All the air left her lungs in a rush, to be replaced with a burning, suffocating sensation that made her eyes feel as though they were bulging out of her head. She felt a rib crack, then another, but was unable to even scream the excruciating pain. Despite her own substantial strength, Ember found herself outmatched. She looked wildly around for Raum, but blackness was encroaching rapidly on her vision. There was a rush of wind beside her cheek, a roar of pain, and she was released, slamming to the ground as a fit of coughing took her. Somehow, she managed to get air back into her battered lungs, but moving away was out of the question.

She felt herself lifted by an unfamiliar pair of arms, and Gadreel's honeyed voice murmured in her ear as he carried her away from where it sounded as if the remaining demon was in the throes of a rather violent defeat.

"Those are cave demons, sweet. Like trolls. You have to get their underbelly just so, or they'll go ahead and crunch you up. Classic mistake, but you fight very well. And I love a woman who fights in the nude. Very Celtic of you."

The pain ebbed, then vanished as her body restored itself, and Ember was left feeling nothing worse than slightly tired and extremely humiliated. So much for taking care of herself. She couldn't even avoid the "classic mistake" with the cave demon. And never mind that she'd never even heard of a cave demon before.

That was about the time she realized she was covered in black, viscous fluid that stunk like roadkill that had been baking in the sun for a few days. Her stomach lurched.

"You'd better put me down, Gadreel."

"Why? I think this is pretty cozy, myself." She heard the smile in his voice, but her feet hit the ground barely a second after she told him exactly why.

Ember raced into the bathroom of her ruined motel room, and managed to completely ignore the hairy-legged company in the shower as her stomach gave up the pizza Gadreel had brought back earlier.

Outside, Raum joined Gadreel in pouring salt over the bodies, making them vanish with the standard incantation as Benny, not exactly the picture of stealth, stumbled out of the office and raced off into the night. His heartbeat was still uneven. But he was well aware it had nothing to do with the fight.

"Shit. We'll have to get cleaned up elsewhere," Raum muttered, watching the man move faster than he'd thought a man of his size would be capable of. Then he looked down at himself and sighed. "This is going to mess up my car."

"Yeah. Cave demons are always a good choice in a pinch," Gadreel said, looking down at his blood-spattered chest with distaste. "Must have been some in the area. It'll be worse next time, though. This was just a shot across the bow, something thrown together as soon as they found us." He looked up, green eyes gleaming in the darkness. "How *do* you think they found us so quickly? There's no one here. And I hadn't so much as smelled a *nefari*."

Raum looked uneasily at the doorless room where Ember was currently retching. "I think he can sense her, somehow. It's a problem."

Gadreel followed his gaze. "She held her own. Hell of a fighter…and a lover, from what I could hear above my own private showing of Girls Running Wild Volume Forty-Eight."

"She's not my lover," Raum growled.

"Then you're a fool. But I already knew that," Gadreel said.

Raum refused to meet Gadreel's eyes, worried about what the demon would see if he did. For the love of all that was blighted, he was still concerned his knees might just give out from under him every time he thought of the way she'd taken out one *nefari* and then rushed off after more without a single thought that she might be in over her head. Which she had been. His first reaction had been fury at her that she'd distracted him so completely. But he was still amazed how quickly that had become fear for her safety.

He'd been wrong, though, to think she'd gotten nothing from Mammon. He'd been as impressed by her natural skill as Gadreel, though horrified about the way she'd decided to use it.

But for all of that, the woman was now throwing up

her dinner because at her heart, Ember was no fighter. She was made for gentler, more pleasurable things, though he doubted she'd appreciate it if he told her that. A good woman. He had never touched anything good that hadn't become blighted, stunted. Once, that truth had pleased him. Now, it provoked in him a sort of slow-growing terror. Did she have any idea how many times he'd wanted to laugh at her barbed comments today? How he could barely take his eyes off her?

How close he had come to losing himself in her, even though he knew that his darkness would corrupt the very things he found beguiling about her?

Most importantly, though, why did he suddenly care if it did?

"So where do we go from here?" Gadreel asked, providing a welcome distraction from the insidious tendrils of guilt winding themselves around Raum's thoughts as the final *nefari* carcass burst into flame and vanished.

"I'd say a tropical island, but you know what sort of things might come out of the water after us. That is, if you're right about Mammon being able to sense her. She *is* his daughter. But the whole Fallen/child connection isn't one I'm familiar with, thankfully."

He hesitated. It was madness. Then he looked at their ruined hotel room, and accepted that there was really no choice.

"There's one place the Fallen can't see," Raum said, finally giving voice to the idea he'd been toying with all day. It made sense, even if it was likely to end as badly as Gadreel's island idea. But he hadn't been able to shake it. And his gut instinct rarely failed him. It was time to focus on his strengths, and push aside this unhealthy fascination with the woman.

The other demon stared at him. "I hope you're not serious."

He was, even though Gadreel was looking like a mutiny risk. "Think about it. Where better to hide than among creatures who can't stand the sight of us?"

"Raum, we don't even know where the city is anymore," Gadreel said, his voice perilously close to a whine. "They threw us out almost a thousand years ago, remember? They moved it so often, it could be under Eastern Siberia. It could be *gone*."

He shook his head. "I don't think so. I've seen a few here, Gadreel, in the cities especially. And knowing Justinian, America would be just his style. I'll put a call in to Levi. He'll know."

"Probably," Gadreel agreed, and he didn't look happy about it. "Scary bastard knows everything he's not supposed to. Fine, Raum. We'll give it a shot, but only because I can't think of anything better right now. Levi's just going to send my ass back to Johnstown anyway, since seraphim don't know a Nexus from a hole in the ground until it's too late. Then you can deal with the bloodsuckers on your own."

"Works for me," Raum said, feeling more centered already. He preferred to work with a plan. Logic over emotion. Not that he had emotions of any sort for Ember.

Raum headed into the room to get Ember as sirens

began to wail in the distance, wondering how she'd feel about their new destination.

He was sure of one thing, though: if Ember could handle demon attacks and fallen angels, a vampire city wouldn't phase her a bit.

Chapter 8

She was going into hiding with a bunch of vampires.

Ember shifted her weight from one foot to the other and looked up at the place Raum insisted, after several very grouchy phone conversations with people she assumed were the rest of the demons he worked with, was the entrance to an ancient underground city full of nocturnal blood drinkers. A city that, according to her companions, had been moved everywhere from ancient Rome to turn-of-the-century Paris using magic she still wasn't quite sure she believed in. In theory, she'd found the idea of a magically protected bastion of legendary creatures fascinating, even darkly romantic.

In reality, it was…kind of underwhelming.

"This is ridiculous," Gadreel said, glowering at Raum while he vocalized exactly what she'd been thinking. Ember watched him as his golden hair gleamed in the sunlight like a halo. He was certainly no worse for wear after fighting with demons and winding up covered in stinking goo. A hurried trip through some truck-stop showers had taken care of the grime for all of them, though Ember's stomach was still not right. Having had to sleep in the car again hadn't helped.

Nor had the new certainty that her dream had been the thing that had led the *nefari* to them. She was deeply conflicted about sharing it, though. It came as a shock, but there was a large part of her, larger than she'd realized, that was protective of the dream creature who had been, in her youth, the only thing remotely resembling a caring parental figure in her life. Her father, the fallen angel.

Would she really be able to stand back and let him be killed, if it came down to it?

The demons he sent could have killed you, whispered a soft and reasonable voice in her mind. *If he really cared, he would have been more careful.*

Maybe. But try as she might, Ember had a hard time believing she was in any real danger from the red-haired demon who had often haunted her dreams. Raum, on the other hand, was in very serious danger. And she knew that at some point, she would have to decide who mattered more to her.

Troubled, and trying to push it from her mind, she turned her attention back to Gadreel and was met with a glittering green gaze that was as suggestive as anything she'd ever seen. Any other time she might have been interested. But next to Raum's dark, smoldering beauty, Gadreel seemed slightly faded to her. And though she actually found Gadreel pretty amusing, she could kind of see why Raum kept lobbing verbal spitballs at him. At least the two men had driven here in their own separate cars, providing a few hours of relative peace. But they'd arrived in this shabby suburb of Washington, D.C., in darkness, and the time spent waiting for the sun to rise had been spent at a Denny's. Ember had wanted to eat, but she'd spent more time refereeing. That, and wondering if she really wanted to meet a group of vampires who were best approached at a time when they couldn't chase her past the borders of their own city.

She had a nasty suspicion that Raum and Gadreel weren't expecting a warm welcome.

"Which part is more ridiculous?" Raum asked, glancing at Gadreel before returning his attention to the building they now stood in front of. "That the entrance to Terra Noctem is apparently in a house in the suburbs, or that we're here at all?"

"Both." Gadreel shook his head. "Though I guess I can understand the house. It's so obvious that it isn't at all. But they were always clever about concealing themselves when they had to." He paused. "Still. Did it have to be quite so ugly? I remember columns. Not cheap wood siding."

Ember stood with them at the front door of the ugly little split-level ranch, looking around with as much interest as trepidation. However she'd imagined the entrance to an underground vampire city would look, this was not it. Though it was kind of funny, in a Brady-Bunch-Goes-to-Hell sort of way. The place was a little on the seedy side, but so was the rest of the neighborhood. Not great, not awful. The lawn needed mowing, but not terribly. There seemed to be a few scrappy plants still living in the flower beds, and a fresh pot of cheery yellow mums sat at the edge of the front stoop.

She raised her eyebrows at Raum. "You're sure this is it?"

His pale green eyes glowed a little even in the sunlight when he looked at her. And the look was, apparently, all the answer she was going to get, though it was pretty clear. Gadreel chuckled.

"Oh, this is it, all right. Take a whiff, Ember. I'll bet you can smell them if you really try."

Curious, she did, closing her eyes to concentrate. He was right: after just a few seconds, breathing deeply, Ember caught a strange scent she'd never encountered before. Not quite like this, at any rate. And since she dealt with scent for a living, that was saying something.

"Smells a little like…sandalwood. Except there's a funny edge to it." She opened her eyes to find Gadreel watching her expectantly.

"Blood, right? That coppery tang is blood." She inhaled again and wrinkled her nose. "Yeah. That's kind of gross. Thanks."

"Good girl. You've won the grand prize." He gave her a lazy smile that Ember imagined had turned plenty of women's knees to jelly.

"What's that?" she asked. "Painful death by dismemberment?"

"I was thinking more along the lines of a kiss from

me, but take your pick." He grinned at her, and she couldn't help but return it.

Raum, on the other hand, seemed to have decided to pretend Gadreel hadn't spoken at all. Instead, he focused all his attention on her.

"When we go in, stay close," he said. "I haven't been to Terra Noctem in ages, but I doubt the rules have changed. Human blood means dinner. They're not going to like that you're off-limits."

"They're not going to like that we're here—period," Gadreel muttered, leaning over to slam his finger against the doorbell. "And wait until the rest of our merry men show up. That should go over well." The sound of the bell echoed inside the house, but nothing stirred. The stillness of the place was eerie.

Raum snorted. "If they demand a sacrifice, we'll just use you."

Ember stifled a laugh at the expletive Gadreel fired back at Raum. It was as much at their snotty interplay as it was the utter insanity of her situation. She kept expecting some guy with a camera to pop out of nowhere and announce that she'd just made an ass of herself on national television.

If it weren't for the fact that she might react by sprouting fangs and snapping at the cameraman, she'd be expecting it anytime. As it was, she had to admit that Raum's prediction, that she would feel better once away from Johnstown, had been right. She hadn't noticed while she was living in it, but there was a weightiness to the air there that was absent here, and a strange and dark layer of grime seemed to have been peeled off everything around her.

All effects of the Nexus. She knew it now. But even here in the sweeter air, she felt drawn back toward it, and all the darkness it contained. Ember focused on Raum's broad back, determined to shake it off. They couldn't help protect her if she decided not to protect herself. And whether or not her father gave a damn about her as a daughter, something she was determined to find out, there was no way she would ever willingly open the Nexus.

Ember exhaled heavily and watched Raum look into windows. He'd been cool ever since they'd escaped from the motel. Annoyed, she figured, that he had allowed himself to succumb to her again. And no doubt more determined than ever that it wouldn't happen again. All things considered, that was probably the better course of action, Ember knew. The problem was logic didn't seem to have any place in her continuing fascination with the surly fallen angel. She was fascinated by his flashes of humor, by his intellect, by the emotions that occasionally bled through the wall he'd so obviously erected against them. What made him tick, this being who had saved her life and was busily—if irritably—protecting her from harm? She didn't think it was just money, no matter what he said.

But she didn't know whether she would have either the time or the opportunity to find out.

"Well, I guess nobody's home at this time of day," Raum finally said, oblivious to her stewing about him. "No surprise. Not even a spare minion to be found. Oh, well." He reached out and pushed the door open as easily as if it had never been locked, though Ember heard the snapping noise that several metal bolts made as they gave way all at once. Then he stepped in.

"Coming?" he asked over his shoulder.

She nodded, though the hair on her arms prickled and stood up as soon as she entered the cool, still air of the house. It was like walking into a crypt. Gadreel followed her and closed the door behind them.

"I really don't know about this," she murmured, more to herself than anyone.

"Scared, little one?"

Gadreel's voice was a warm puff of air on her ear, and she started at his nearness. He and Raum were both unnervingly quiet when they wanted to be. She turned her head to look at him, but Gadreel didn't look particularly concerned. She had a suspicion he was enjoying her discomfort, too, and frowned at him. His eyes shone like a wild animal's in the half-dark.

"Not exactly," she replied, keeping her voice low while Raum craned his neck to look around. "But it's been kind of a rough couple of days. I think I'm hitting my tolerance limit for new legendary creatures."

He smirked. "You seem to like fallen angels well enough. Or so a very thin motel wall told me."

Damn it. She'd known he was going to bring it up. Ember colored and looked away, determined to ignore Gadreel and his mouth. Instead, she focused on the oddity that was supposed to be the entrance to an underground city of the undead. Terra Noctem, Earth by Night.

The smell was heavier in here, Ember thought, though still not overpowering. And the furniture she could see from the landing, which had probably been the height of fashion in the late seventies, was obviously nothing more than window dressing. A thin layer of dust covered the wrought-iron banister. The stairs from the landing went both up and down, and it was down they headed, past faded bamboo-print wallpaper that was strangely sinister in the way it reached all the way to the ceiling, like bars.

Below was a cavelike room, shades drawn to the outside, done up like a game room with brown shag carpeting, an ancient television set and a dilapidated dart cabinet that hung slightly askew on the wall. Ember had always liked the dark, the warm mystery of it. This dark, however, was cold, and not at all comforting.

She shivered slightly and moved closer to Raum, who was examining the door behind the small bar. Gadreel, meanwhile, had found the swizzle sticks cut in the silhouette of well-endowed naked women and seemed far more interested in examining those.

"Seems sort of obvious," Raum murmured, more to himself than to her, "but then again, as long as they're paying the mortgage and mowing the lawn, who's going to wander in here?"

"I'm assuming anyone who did would be sorry," Ember said as he turned the shabby brass knob and the door swung open. She would never admit it, but she didn't think this was an obvious setup for a bunch of vampires at all. Though in her world, at least up until a couple of nights ago, she'd barely had room in her belief system for her own weirdness, much less for the existence of things which she'd only ever seen in horror movies.

Of which she was one, she supposed.

Pushing the thoughts from her mind, Ember craned her neck so that she could see between the two massive men who were peering into the closet. It was, unfortunately, about as unnerving as she worried it might be. Rather than revealing mops, broom and maybe a hot-water heater, instead there was a blast of clammy, cold air and stone steps that descended into pitch blackness.

"Hellfire." Gadreel sighed, obviously unimpressed. "Do they always have to be so damned creepy about everything? Come on, you two, let's get this over with. I could use a drink, if they let us in, and if they don't, it'll at least be fun to knock a few bloodsuckers' heads together. I'm going to complain about the theatrics first, though." He shook his head and looked at her meaningfully. "Just because you're a soulless monster doesn't mean you have to be a freak."

Ember watched, startled, as Gadreel stalked past her and thundered down the steps so loudly that she was sure there would be hisses and screeches and whatever other sorts of noises an actual vampire might make before long. Instead, all she heard was the sound of his boot heels clicking against the stone down into the blackness.

She glanced at Raum, who was watching her intensely. He'd been doing that off and on all morning, and she didn't know what to make of it. Except that it made her nervous, and tangled her stomach in a series of far more pleasurable knots…and that it was a reminder that despite their undeniable connection, she didn't really know him at all.

"You really think they won't let us in?" she asked, needing to break the silence.

Raum glanced down the steps. "The rift happened a long time ago. But Justinian was always a reasonable man. He's had a few centuries to cool off. I believe he'll hear us out, at least. Especially since we're no longer really…affiliated."

"Oh. Great," Ember said, trying to feel it. "And we have to hide underground with a bunch of demons and vamps because why, again?" she asked, wrapping her arms around herself as the clammy chill coiled around her ankles and began to seep into her skin.

"They're not demons. Their kind was created long ago, by humans willfully tainted with dark magic. But they're purely of the Earth, and they don't really act like demons most of the time." He looked into the darkness again, and murmured, "That was really most of the problem. Regardless, there are protections on this place that even the Fallen can't break through. If they let us in, you'll be safe. There are no other demons here."

Relief flooded her. *Safe*. She was safe, for now, despite those unnerving dreams. And so was Raum. It was enough to make her want to run down into the clammy darkness.

"So…do I need to worry about getting bitten, or anything?"

He grinned, a rare flash of mirth that transformed his

face. She couldn't help but smile back, nervous though she suddenly was.

"Relax, Ember," he said as she looked skeptically down into darkness. "They're as human as you are, and this is one place you don't have to worry about being yourself. If you decide to shred any of the Lost Ones, they'll just heal themselves, give you the finger and go on their merry way. In fact, if I remember correctly, doing that can be rather therapeutic."

She turned her head to reply to his outrageous statement and found herself almost nose to nose with him. Immediately the cloying smell of the dank darkness was replaced with Raum's singular scent, a sensual spice that flooded her senses. Her thoughts tried to scatter once again in favor of sheer heat, and she felt herself flush. She really needed to get used to him being this close without losing her mind. Except that every time he got this close, she'd ended up wrapped around him. Which she couldn't quite make herself believe was a bad thing, no matter what he said.

"Not funny, Raum. And what are Lost Ones?" she asked, her voice sounding breathless to her own ears.

This is so, so not the place for this, she instructed herself. It was a little tough, though, with Raum directly in front of her face.

"I'm not trying to be. And that's what we call them. They're no longer human, not quite demon, but devoid of souls. Lost to all worlds. So they created their own, down here, and are careful enough when they venture up to yours that they've stayed the stuff of legend instead of winding up on the news." He tipped his head slightly, a smirk playing at the corners of his lips. "They never liked the name much."

Ember felt her own lips curving in response. "Which explains why you keep using it," she said. Maybe she was beginning to understand him a little after all.

There was another quick flash of white teeth in the dim light as the clammy air swirling around them warmed. She could actually feel him relent, just a little, in his stubborn isolation. And the intimacy of their sudden, unexpected connection gave her a little shiver of pleasure.

"Maybe," Raum said, humor flickering in his strange eyes. "Come on."

Then he was gone, winding down the steps after Gadreel. Ember had little choice but to follow, though it went against every instinct. Down they went, for what seemed like hours, no sound but their feet tapping endlessly against the cold stone. There were no further jokes or complaints from Gadreel, and Ember thought she understood why. The house, while creepy, was still just an aboveground prop. Now, however, they were well underground, and there was an oppressive quality to the air that set her nerves on edge. She didn't know what they would find at the bottom…and she had a sneaking suspicion that her companions weren't entirely sure either. They'd both admitted it had been a really long time, and things hadn't been left well.

Nothing in her life made any sense anymore. Angels, demons, vampires, *half* demons…an entire world she'd never known about. But there was a small seed of resentment at the core of her amazement, because really, she belonged more in this world than she did in the one she'd grown up in. And no one had ever bothered with her, until she became a threat to it. She thought again of the dream demon, her father. Raum was a fallen angel, she reasoned, but he wasn't at all the horrifying, evil thing she would have expected. So couldn't it be that her father might be the same? That she might at least have one parent who was capable of caring...of loving her, even?

Ember sighed and tried to think of something else. She knew she should tell Raum about the dreams. But she was very sure that there was plenty he wasn't telling her. At least now she had some time to sort it all out.

I'm scarier than anything down here, she told herself, an odd mantra, but one she tried to believe. It was tough, though. She was still trying to grapple with the truth that she was half demon, and her abilities were by and large a mystery to her. These vampires probably had no such doubts.

Finally, there were glimmers of light in the depths. She could see Gadreel waiting for them at the bottom, and he looked fairly bored, which she supposed was a good sign. But then, even if it was warranted, she doubted fallen angels were ever really afraid of anything.

When they reached the bottom of the stairs, Ember found herself in a massive, domed antechamber lit by torches that glowed with blue flame that danced across the walls, turning the cave into a place almost oceanic. It was eerily beautiful, and dead silent but for the faint crackling of the fires. Before them was a set of heavy iron doors, dark with age, and adorned with a number of figures raised in relief: a wolf, head down, that appeared ready to leap from the one door, a large bat superimposed over the moon on the other and a long, sinuous feline that stretched across both doors beneath each.

"It's so quiet," Ember whispered, feeling strange about disturbing the stillness.

"It's daytime," Raum replied. "Most of them will be asleep."

"Lazy asses," Gadreel added. Then, to Ember's horror, he raised a fist and banged on the door.

"Rise and shine, bloodsuckers! Your masters have returned, and we'd like a word!"

For a lingering moment, there was only silence. Then there was a series of heavy, thudding sounds as whatever locks existed on the other side of the door were unbolted. Ember noticed, with some irritation, that Raum looked as amused in his own way as Gadreel seemed to be.

The doors swung open, and Ember had to blink several times before she was positive her eyes weren't messed up in some fundamental way. Beyond the doors was a wide street, flanked on either side by beautiful, gothic buildings carved entirely out of the rock of the caves. There was no roof in sight within, no sign of the top of what Ember knew must be a massive chamber now shrouded in shadow. The entire place was lit by the same strange blue light that surrounded them in the antechamber, and Ember could see plenty of the torches mounted on the fronts of the buildings. She saw sweeping lines and spiraling parapets, the picture spread out before her that of a faerie-tale underworld.

The figure that stood at the threshold, however, didn't look inclined to let them come in to explore further.

A tall, lanky man regarded them with eyes that shone red in the near darkness. Unlike Raum and Gadreel, with their warrior's builds, this one seemed imbued with a lean, wiry strength that was probably, Ember figured, fairly formidable. He had thick, shaggy brown hair that was in danger of falling into his eyes, and sharp, foxlike features that were more striking than truly handsome. His skin was pale, though not unattractively so, and he was clad simply in jeans and a plain white T-shirt. His feet were bare. Actually, Ember thought, he looked as if he'd just been rousted out of bed and had thrown on the nearest things at hand.

"Rayne," Raum said with a nod. "We need to see Justinian."

Whatever Ember expected, a fight, a shouting match or just having the door shut in their faces, it was nothing like what actually happened. Rayne looked them all over, his eyes lingering on her for a moment longer than the others. Then he nodded and gave what sounded to her like a resigned sigh.

"Raum. Gadreel. Come on in. We've been expecting you."

Chapter 9

The streets of Terra Noctem were deserted, and the windows hewn into the pale stone were dark. There were only the four of them walking through the silence. Considering what she'd been told about the relationship between the fallen angels and these "Lost Ones," Ember was grateful for it. This way, at least for now, there was no battle...though the arrogant swagger of Raum and Gadreel told her they would have welcomed it.

She pursed her lips. She was never going to understand men, immortal or otherwise.

They walked down the main street, following Rayne. All three of them seemed surprised that they'd been expected. She could only hope that meant something good, though the chances of that, she figured, were pretty much nil. Just ahead of her, Rayne's lope never slowed, and Ember found herself nearly jogging to keep up. At last, another set of ornately carved doors came into view, set into the wall of the cavern itself at the outer perimeter of the city.

"I'm surprised by how little has changed here," Raum murmured beside her.

Rayne turned, having heard him. "It's changed more than you think, Raum of the Fallen." He gave a single hard knock on one of the doors, and they swung open to reveal a chamber full of flickering light, warm gold now rather than blue.

He beckoned them forward, letting Raum and Gadreel pass him. But when Ember stepped over the threshold, she felt a hand at the small of her back as he guided her in. When she turned her head to look at him, Rayne's strange eyes were unexpectedly kind.

"Don't be afraid of any of this," he said softly, his voice carrying more than a hint of a British accent. "It may look intimidating at first, but you get used to it. I did, anyway."

"It's beautiful," she replied, and meant it. Strange it was, but Terra Noctem, at least what she'd seen of it, was singularly amazing. She'd obviously said the right thing, as Rayne smiled, baring a pair of pointed incisors.

"You belong with us," he said. "Not with those two. I knew when I saw you. We haven't seen your sort in a long time."

The comment intrigued her. Raum, who'd noticed she was lagging behind, turn to look, and she watched his gaze sharpen as he took in the sight of her and Rayne with their heads together. The look of raw possessiveness on his face gave Ember a dark little thrill.

Rayne apparently saw it, too. Instead of answering her question, he watched Raum approach. "Be careful," he said. "Justinian may be wavering, but none of the Fallen can be trusted. And this lot just wants back into Lucifer's good graces, I'd wager."

The words sent a chill through her, even as Rayne's hand left her back and Raum's replaced it, as her dark-haired Guardian gave the vampire a look that would have sent most men screaming. Raum hadn't yet told her why he was no longer a part of Hell. And Rayne's words, spoken with such conviction, left her unsettled.

Ember straightened, tossed her hair back behind her shoulders and quickened her pace so that Raum's touch fell away. She felt a small pang at that, but pushed it aside. If she was going to make it through this, she was going to have to be able to stand on her own two feet whether or not she had protection. Her father was a powerful demon, she obviously had enough of that power to warrant being chased around and having her life dismantled, and it was about time she started figuring out how to use what she had. Whatever that was, apart from the claws and fangs. And the supercharged libido.

She strode up the length of crimson carpet that made a red slash down the middle of the chamber, heading for the figure that waited for them at the end of it. All around her was a silence so thick she might have been in a tomb, and in fact, the soaring marble arches and painted frescoes reminded her very much of a church. Before her was a raised pedestal, with two large thrones that were as black as night. Only one was occupied.

Her nerves coiled insidiously in the pit of her stomach, but Ember managed not to falter through sheer force of will. She'd already met one vampire, and he'd been... well, a lot more human, really, than she'd expected. Friendly, even. She'd just have to focus on that and hope for the best.

No matter how intimidating this new vampire was even at a distance.

He sat ramrod straight in a throne that glittered in the glow of the torches, watching her with dark, unblinking eyes. His hair was as black as Raum's, but clipped short into what she thought of as a Caesar cut. His skin was even lighter than Rayne's, alabaster that was unmistakably inhuman but compellingly beautiful. With his strong nose and chiseled features, he might have been a Roman god holding court.

And he didn't look happy.

Great, Ember thought. But she was too far along to turn tail and run now. She stopped just a few feet from him, felt the presence of the others as Raum and Gadreel came to flank her. Rayne moved off to one side, watching with undisguised interest. Probably, Ember thought, he was hoping for some sort of epic throwdown between the fallen angels and his king. She was just hoping to make it out of here in one piece.

"So," the man finally said. "I'll admit, I'd really hoped neither of you would darken our doorstep again. Though I was sure you'd show up eventually anyway." He sighed then and slumped a little in his seat, running a hand through his hair. Ember could see, then, how agitated he was, and it was finally that which let her relax a little in his presence. He was obviously important here, but he was no god. His next words only reinforced that impression.

"A thousand years wasn't nearly enough of a break," he said.

"The feeling is mutual, if it makes you feel any better," Raum offered.

"Not really."

"Justinian," Raum began, but the king held up one hand immediately.

"It's only Justin now, Raum. The Roman empire fell a long time ago, and their names along with it. I'm dated enough as it is."

"Well, you ditched the toga, at least," Gadreel said with a snort.

Justin pinned the fallen angel with a glare. "I can see *you* haven't changed. I wish I could say it was refreshing, but at least I know what to expect." Then he turned his attention to Ember.

"I'm guessing you've come seeking sanctuary. You and your…" He trailed off for a moment, raising an eyebrow at Raum and Gadreel. "Appendages," he finally finished, and a surprised laugh escaped her before she could stop it. She swore she could actually feel Raum's dirty look. Justin, on the other hand, offered her a small smile.

She decided to answer before one of the others did and the verbal fencing match turned into a bloodbath.

"I'm not sure I understand everything yet," she confessed. "But yes, if it's all right with you, that sanctuary would be greatly appreciated."

"Maybe," Justin said, and her heart sank at the calculating glint that came into his blood-red eyes. She was beginning to think that all of these supernatural creatures just liked to make things hard on purpose.

"No games, Justinian." Raum's snarl was feral as he took a threatening step forward. "Who's been here? Who told you we were coming?"

Justin leaned forward, steepling his long fingers beneath his chin. "It was an educated guess. You aren't the first demons who've visited me today, Raum. I had the dubious pleasure of having this pretty creature's father rant at me for over an hour this morning. Obscenities. Death threats. The usual. He's not happy she's run away from home. Which wouldn't surprise you."

"Mammon was here?"

Ember watched as Raum's beautiful face was contorted into a mask of rage, and suddenly she had no problem picturing him as a highly ranked demon. She felt the hair at the back of her neck rise in a strange mixture of fear and, though she didn't want it right now, arousal at the power that poured from him in waves.

But beneath that was the traitorous thought: *my father was here looking for me. Mammon.* She realized it was the first time she had ever heard his name.

"You let him in?" Raum continued, his fury radiating from him. "You let in that sniveling, conniving—"

"Don't worry," Justin said, cutting him off neatly. "I'm not interested in dealing with the Prince of Avarice. But letting him in shows I have nothing to hide. And be grateful, Raum…he doesn't think you'd be stupid enough to show up here in person. Mammon was more interested in securing my people's help in tracking you down and returning his property to him. He didn't seem very pleased with the job those damned *nefari* have done for him. Big surprise."

Ember's jaw tightened. "I'm not anyone's property, thank you."

Justin smiled thinly. "Believe me, Ember, I sympathize. The Fallen treated my people as pets for a very long time. Not that your companions would have told you that, I'm sure."

Rather than denying it, which Ember found telling, Gadreel just crossed his arms over his massive chest and stared menacingly. Gone was the playful miscreant, replaced by a warrior every bit as intimidating as Raum.

"If you feel like that, then just stay out of it," Gadreel snapped. "We'll leave."

"I would like nothing better," Justin replied. "But I now have a problem. Mammon, as you might imagine, promised to annihilate all of Terra Noctem if he finds we've been less than forthcoming with any information on his daughter's, and your, whereabouts. And though I wish it were otherwise, he can certainly do it if he really sets his mind to it."

"There are more of us. Leviathan, Meresin, Murmur, Caim and Phenex." Raum looked as though he'd rather punch someone than be speaking, but he got the words out. "We would offer you our protection in exchange for your help."

Justin snorted. "Hmm, six wayward demons and an

overgrown eel versus all the powers of Hell. Sounds like an even match to me."

"Do you really want to risk this Nexus thing happening?" Ember asked incredulously, amazed that the vampire could be so unconcerned with the welfare of his people. "I'll admit, this is all new to me, but it seems like you'd want to keep Hell out of your territory—period. If they hurt humanity, they're hurting your blood supply, right?"

Justin's considering gaze returned to her. "Why do you think we're having this conversation?"

"Then what do you want, Justin?" Raum asked, stepping up to stand beside her.

"I want what I have always wanted." He cocked his head, his expression inscrutable. "But that would require what you weren't willing to give us back when we threw you out the last time. I can say that *we've* done just fine since then. Those with wings, not as much."

Ember looked between the men, fallen angels and vampire, now glaring at one another with barely disguised hostility. *Men,* she thought irritably. Immortality didn't seem to affect testosterone. Determined to defuse the tension that was thickening by the second, she spoke up.

"I'm at the center of this. Whatever I can do to get you on our side, I'll do."

Justin chuckled then, and Ember realized too late how her words might have come off.

"Anything, little demoness?" Justin asked, and when his lips curved in a mocking smile, Ember realized that

Justin was, in his own way, almost as handsome as Raum and Gadreel. Almost.

"Don't even think about it," Raum snapped, and Justin chuckled again.

"I think the lady has already mentioned that she isn't anyone's property, Raum of the Fallen. That would, I assume, include you. But don't worry about it. Much. Now," he said, returning his attention to Raum, "I won't deny that we could use you back at the table, especially since you seem to have shed Hell. But this time," he continued, his eyes going utterly black, "it will be as equals, or not at all. How does it feel, I wonder, to finally need us more than we need you?"

Ember could see, from the look that Raum and Gadreel shared, that it didn't feel very good at all. But if they wanted to be here, there didn't seem to be any choice but to do what Justin wanted. Whatever that was.

Raum exhaled loudly through his nose. "How soon are you going to want to convene?"

Justin grinned, baring incisors that gleamed. "As a matter of fact, your little visit has coincided with our quarterly meeting."

"What a stunning coincidence," said Gadreel blandly. "And I suppose our seats are still there, covered in dust and cobwebs and the remains of the rotten tomatoes that were thrown at us on our way out of here the last time."

"I'll have someone clean them off."

Raum nodded slowly. "I'm willing, though I can't understand why you'd want a handful of exiles."

Justin's gaze was frank. "The abilities of the Fallen were highly valued, Raum. But Hell's overriding interest in having the Earth all to itself was always going to be a problem. Believe me, we can use you, and I think…no, I *know*…you need us. It's past time the Necromancium was whole again. Not having the Infernal Council's sticky fingers in everything is a welcome bonus."

"I'll have to talk to the others," Raum cautioned, and it was only then that Ember remembered there were others like Raum and Gadreel, and headed this way from what she'd heard this morning. She'd heard one of them called a serpent a few times, as well, though maybe that was some kind of demonic term of endearment or something. The thought of meeting them was more than a little unnerving, but she was intensely curious.

"Gadreel? Are you in?" asked Justin.

Ember expected some snide retort, but Gadreel only shrugged. "Well, if I'm wanted that badly," he said. Then his gaze sharpened with sudden interest. "Speaking of wanting, do cat shifters still come around these parts?"

"Done, then," Justin said, rising from the throne and looking pleased. He ignored Gadreel's question…but Ember figured that whatever cat shifters the fallen angel was asking about, they had to be female. For the first time, Ember noticed Justin wasn't in the robes she would have expected, but a dark, well-tailored suit. She had a feeling this place would be full of odd little surprises like that.

"Have a drink with me, both of you," Justin said. "We have some catching up to do."

"As inviting as that sounds, I think I'll let Raum keep you company," Gadreel replied, ignoring the look Raum was giving him for his rudeness. "I'll touch base with the others, and then I plan to get readjusted to vampire time and go to sleep for the rest of the day." He yawned dramatically. "Fighting *nefari* and then not getting any sleep has done me in for the day."

Justin, Ember thought, looked more relieved than anything at Gadreel's refusal to stay.

"That's fine, then. I've already had one of the guest apartments prepared for the three of you. Rayne will show you the way."

"Perfect. I'll just step out and make that call," Gadreel replied, gave an arrogant little bow and then smirked at Ember as he headed past her.

"A few hours alone, sweet. What *will* we do with ourselves?"

Raum gave her a hard look. "I want you to lock yourself in the bedroom. I mean it," he said through gritted teeth. Ember met his gaze, glaring into his eyes defiantly.

"That's about as likely to happen as it is for you to stop ordering me around."

Justin cleared his throat, and the sound sliced through the palpable tension crackling through the air between her and Raum. It was, Ember noted with some small amount of triumph, Raum who finally dragged his gaze away to look at the waiting vampire king. Justin looked bemused.

"Come on, then, Raum. We've got quite a bit to discuss, I can see. Ember, Rayne will also escort you."

Ember's eyes narrowed at Justin's tone. She knew she had just been dismissed. It was, she assumed, so that he and Raum could all talk about her without the added burden of having her around to listen. And though she was already on Weird Information Overload, the obvious exclusion still pissed her off. She'd done just fine running her life up until now, with only a few major snags. Turning it over to a bunch of overbearing alpha males just for the hell of it didn't sit well with her at all.

She wondered if "Necromancium" was just vampire for "penis party."

"I'm sorry, but I think, considering I'm the center of this problem, that I should get to be involved with any discussions about how to fix it," she said, settling a hand on her hip and not bothering to hide her pique. She caught Raum's frown out of the corner of her eye, but she ignored him, preferring to glare at the vampire king. It was less distracting.

Justin met her gaze, his eyes going pitch-black and seeming to expand, expand, until they were all she could see. Ember suddenly realized, with a dim sort of awareness, that she was unable to look away. A word she'd encountered in various vampire books and movies drifted through her mind: *thralled*. That was the hypnotic power vamps exerted on humans, usually so they could get the latter to hold still long enough to sink their teeth in. She was pretty sure Raum would kick his ass if he tried it, but it was still a strange, unnerving sensation. Ember knew she would have been afraid, if she could think straight, but everything seemed all warm and fuzzy all of a sudden.

Though Justin's lips didn't move, her head was suddenly filled with his voice.

Your problems are very much ours, little demon. The Necromancium is far older than you, as is my association with your Guardian, and there are things to discuss that aren't for you to know. But I can promise you, your voice will be heard, and valued, here. Be at ease.

Ember blinked rapidly when Justin looked away from her and strode down the steps to join them. It was an odd sensation, having someone speak directly into your mind, and she wasn't sure she liked it much. But his words had settled her a little. She was still going to give Raum a piece of her mind about it, though, when she saw him again.

At that, she felt the slightest tickle of panic. When exactly was she going to see him again?

As though he could hear her worrying, Justin said, "I won't keep your Guardian long, Ember. But in the meantime, you may want to get some sleep, before the city begins to waken. Also, when you feel up to a visitor, my sister lives in that building. She's offered to help you settle in, if you like."

Relieved despite the fact that she felt foolish for her sudden burst of separation anxiety, Ember considered it, then nodded. It might be nice to meet a woman she actually had something in common with. And God knew she could really use another female to bitch about all of these men with. Justin seemed, for the most part, all right. Hopefully his sister would be, too. It couldn't hurt to find out.

Rayne appeared from the shadows, materializing from the darkness as though he'd been a part of it. "Come on, then. Did you bring anything with you?"

"It's all back in the car," Ember said, thinking of the bag full of randomly grabbed things Raum had tossed in the Corvette sitting in the driveway of the hideous house so far up above.

"Ah. Well, we'll take care of that, and the cars, once the sun goes down. But I'm sure Dru will be happy to take you shopping anyway, once the night gets going."

"What are you going to do to my car?" Raum asked with a frown. "I *like* my car. Even if it needs a good cleaning now."

Rayne rolled his eyes and took Ember's arm companionably. "Whiny, isn't he?" he asked her in a conspiratorial whisper. Ember grinned. Rayne, she definitely liked.

"You three came in the back door, actually. We barely ever use that entrance anymore," Justin said as she and Rayne strolled away. "And there's better parking up by the club on the other end."

"Club?" Raum asked.

Justin's laugh echoed through the high-ceilinged chamber. "Yes, club. Did I mention the Necromancium went into business about five hundred years ago? Welcome to the life of the twenty-first-century nightcrawler, Raum. You may just enjoy your stay."

Ember glanced back once at them as she crossed the threshold back into the sleeping vampire city. Raum's eyes connected with hers, watchful, wary, looking like twin green flames at a distance. His jaw was tight, and Ember knew he was probably all up in arms about having to let her out of his sight.

Knowing that felt…good.

It took more effort than it should have, but Ember turned away and headed out, ignoring her own urge to head back to his side. She wanted him. But she needed to accept that his presence in her life was not going to be permanent. An immortal demon and a half human was a match that was never going to work out long-term, even if she lived through whatever was coming. At least, she consoled herself, she was finally in a place where she could sort out what she was, and where she might actually be accepted as normal.

Ember shared a friendly smile with Rayne and looked around with new wonder at the city of eternal night, hoping that this place, finally, would hold all the answers she'd spent her life looking for.

Chapter 10

Raum watched the doors to the great hall shut, taking Ember from his sight, and only barely resisted the urge to go after her. He hadn't changed his opinion that this was the safest place for her, but that didn't mean he had any intention of letting Justin take over responsibility for her. It shouldn't have surprised him, that Justin would demand what he had. But deep down, Raum had believed that the Necromancium would crumble as soon as the Fallen left the alliance.

Instead, it seemed that the dark races of Earth had managed just fine in their absence. The knowledge stung, though that was coupled with a grudging admiration. In hindsight, while his kind had added to the collective power of the group, the interests of the Necromancium had never really meshed with the desires of Hell. The vampires, and the others, had been determined to coexist with humanity, even to benefit from it. The demons had only ever wanted control.

The last breach of a Nexus had marked the final breach between the Fallen and everyone else.

And now here he was, in a place he had never thought to stand again. Raum studied Justinian, or Justin, as he apparently now called himself. The flickering light of the many torches that lined the walls played over Justin's features, turning his face into a mask of shadow and light. His eyes, a deep, deep red, were impossible to read.

"We need to talk."

"I suppose we do," Raum allowed. He'd expected to have a conversation with the head vampire. He just hadn't expected it to be under quite these circumstances.

"Come on, then. It's more comfortable back in my chambers. Honestly, I haven't sat on this throne in years," he said with a quick grin. "It's so archaic. But seeing how long it's been, it seemed appropriate."

Raum snorted. "You wanted us to sweat a little."

"Did it work?"

He must have seen how Raum's eyes went back to the closed doors, because he added, "She'll be fine. Dru will watch over her."

Raum had little memory of Drusilla, Justin's sister, though he had a lingering impression of a pretty, pale-haired woman. Not enough to settle his mind about leaving Ember at her mercy…or, more importantly, Gadreel's, little as she seemed to be interested in him. Being with Ember…rattled him. But being without her, at this point, was at least as bad. And that also rattled him.

He'd taken a big gamble by coming here. But this was the only place where the dislike of his kind was so ingrained that he felt that Ember would be in no imminent danger of betrayal. Taking her underground would let the angels do what they needed to about the Nexus. Raum was sure they'd take care of it… It wasn't in their natures to leave a thing like that alone. And as an added bonus, Terra Noctem was one of the only places on Earth where angels feared—or maybe just refused—to tread. As long as he had Ember here, she was away from the interfering eyes of Uriel and the seraphim, and out of the immediate danger the Nexus, and her father, posed to her.

She would be, as he had sworn to keep her, safe.

At least, he'd thought so. Mammon having been here first was the curveball he hadn't seen coming. That was just one of the things he was sure Justin wanted to discuss.

They exited the great hall through a small door to the right of the dais and headed down a wide hallway, walking in silence through a winding labyrinth of corridors until they reached a set of heavy double doors, hewn of metal and heavily inlaid with gold. With a careless pass of Justin's hand, they swung open, revealing a sitting room bathed in the light of a crackling fire in a large hearth. Once they'd crossed the threshold, the doors swung shut, and Raum moved to settle himself in one of the plush chairs arranged in the middle of the room.

These, he knew, were Justin's private chambers, and he had to appreciate the luxury. Shelves carved of dark wood dominated the walls, and those shelves were teeming with books, making this a sort of library. The rugs on the floor were rich and ornate, but not ostentatious. It reminded him, powerfully, of his manor in the Infernal City, the place he had painstakingly constructed as a retreat. However he had grown to feel about his demon brothers, that had been home for a very long time.

The sudden wave of homesickness surprised him. It was probably too much to hope that he would find such a place again. And never, for him, amounted to a very long time. He would still be searching long after Ember was nothing but dust.

Hellfire, he must be tired... For a moment, he'd actually felt a touch of sorrow. He pushed it away, but a trace of it lingered stubbornly, coloring everything with a thin layer of melancholy.

Justin headed for a small table, on which was set a decanter of deep red liquid and several glasses. He began to pour for himself, then turned his head and cocked an eyebrow at Raum.

"I don't suppose you'd care to indulge?"

Raum waved his hand dismissively. "Blood has never been my preference, Justin. You go ahead, though."

Justin smirked. "I planned on it, but thanks." He finished up, then brought the glass over and sank into the chair opposite Raum. He drank deeply, draining half the glass, then tipped his head back with a sigh.

"I appreciate you not having us thrown out immediately. Gadreel still talks about where you threatened to stuff his wings should he ever show his face here again."

"I thought about it the second I saw him, but no." Justin chuckled. "I have to say, I'm surprised to see the two of you together."

Raum scrubbed a hand through his hair and slouched into his seat, relieved that at least one of his sources of constant stress had been removed for a while. "So am I," he replied, prompting another laugh from the vampire.

"Some things haven't changed. And some have changed almost beyond recognition." Justin shook his dark head. "I have to say, I never thought I would see the mighty Raum so protective of a human woman. Though that's probably secondary to hearing about you hanging around with the white wings without inciting some kind of violence. What, by the Above and Below, are you thinking, Raum of the Fallen?"

Raum frowned and wished for a stiff drink of the nonbloody variety. It had been easy before, not having to discuss his odd living situation with anyone. By preference, he didn't have any friends, only his demon brothers, who had to put up with him and vice versa. Having a fireside chat about it all with Justin was not remotely on his agenda.

Particularly not the part about his involvement with Ember, which he was still trying to sort out himself.

"So who sits on the council these days?" he asked. He didn't care that the change of subject was obvious. Justin, to his credit, let it go.

"I'm curious, Raum, about your trust in someone who you haven't seen in a millennium. What makes you think I won't just hold you here and hand all three of you over? Mammon did offer the oh-so-appealing reward of not being utterly destroyed, plus a handful of *nefari* slaves thrown in for good measure. Because, you know, what we've all missed about your kind was the access to idiotic demons who can only occasionally speak in complete sentences."

Justin's smile was wry, and Raum remembered why he had always sort of liked the vampire king, as much as he generally liked anyone, that was. He was shrewd, dangerous, but not without a sense of humor. Still, Justin was right. There was no particular reason to trust him. Except…

Raum leaned slightly forward, wanting to make himself very clear. "You won't, because I'm going to kill Mammon. Problem solved for both of us."

Justin sipped at his drink and looked skeptically back at him. "Wow, why didn't I think of that? Just kill the bastard. Oh, yes, wait, he's protected by Lucifer himself, and he's a coward who never goes anywhere without a heavy guard." His voice hardened. "He wasn't kidding when he threatened to destroy Terra Noctem, Raum. And we've worked too hard for what we have to throw it away for some petty personal vendetta."

Raum opened his mouth, ready to launch an angry defense, but Justin put up his hand.

"Okay, maybe that's not quite fair. But it's hard for me to be sympathetic," Justin continued, "because your kind never had a problem using and discarding us at will. And now here you are, a thousand years later, with a half-Fallen Breaker and a request for me to please put my entire race on the line." He paused, a smile playing at the corners of his mouth. "By the way," he said smoothly, "does Ember know exactly how personal it is with you and her father?"

Raum glared from where he sat stiffly in the chair. "Not exactly," he admitted, still seething from the vitriol that had fallen so easily, so calmly, from Justin's tongue. It hadn't been his intention to act as a stand-in for his entire race so that Justin could take them collectively to task for being miserable creatures to deal with, which he knew they were, but it seemed as if he'd gotten the job anyway.

And the question about Ember had hit the mark quite effectively, which had always been Justin's unfortunate talent.

"Don't you think you might want to explain things to her?" asked Justin. "Far be it from me to interfere in your personal affairs, Raum…in fact, that's really the last place I want to go…but your Ember is no common *nefari*. You can see that just by looking at her, and the more comfortable she gets with it, the more her Fallen blood will show. She's handled this much, she can handle knowing the rest. In fact, I think she'd appreciate it." He paused. "I know something about being kept out of the loop, after all."

"She's got enough to deal with," Raum growled. "And she's not *my* anything. I'm acting as her Guardian until the angels get the Nexus problem sorted out. After that, she can do what she wants."

Justin relaxed into his seat and tilted his head, watching Raum curiously. "The Fallen have a nasty habit of underestimating people, I've noticed. You're making a mistake with her, Raum, whatever you decide to do about the connection you two have. Which, I have to say, anyone could feel a mile away. How did *that* happen?"

Raum flexed his hands, remembering the pain of the Light he had channeled, and looked away. That was something he had no intention of sharing. "Doesn't matter."

Justin sighed, and it surprised Raum to hear the sudden hint of bitterness in the vampire's voice when he spoke again.

"I hate to tell you this, Raum, but you're going to have to start trusting *someone*. Things are going to end badly if you withhold information just because you think everyone will screw it up but you. You're not in the Infernal City anymore."

"Believe me, I've noticed," Raum replied, giving Justin a dark look. This was, by far, the least enjoyable conversation he'd had in a long time, and considering who he'd been keeping company with, that was saying something. How he handled things with Ember was his own business.

She didn't need to know about him. He wanted her passion, not her damned heart. And if she tried to open the latter to him, it would do irreparable damage. That was what he had become, what he had been forever: a conduit to pain and suffering. That was his strength. He would need it, all of it, to destroy her father.

Even if she hated him for it. But as soon as he thought it, guilt stabbed deep into his chest. He had never cared what anyone else had thought of him. And yet somehow, the thought of hurting, of disappointing Ember, was almost impossible to bear. But how could he avoid doing it, if he didn't find a way to put some distance between them? Pain was all he knew.

"So," he said, turning the subject again. "Tell me about the Necromancium these days. Are all of the old races still intact?"

Justin offered a small half smile, but again he allowed the switch. "Most, though it was close with some for a while. The Enlightenment came just in time. There were a lot less pitchforks and stakings after that. We've changed, adapted. We have resources and influence that we never would have dreamed of the last time your kind were here. And I have to tell you," he continued, his eyes narrowing, "that harboring a demonic powder keg like the one you're so enamored of is inconvenient at best, necessary though it may be. If you're going to stay here, you're going to take the wishes and counsel of the Necromancium, me in particular, into account."

Raum shrugged. "Of course." He wasn't interested in the vampire's bluster.

"Oh, no," Justin said, and his eyes hardened. "This isn't like the old days, where you and your ilk wander in, use your scruffy relations for what they're worth and then pretend we don't exist when it's convenient. You will be magic-bound this time."

Raum glowered, feeling a quick rush of anger. "I will do no such—"

"You will," Justin replied, setting down his glass and leaning forward. "Or you will receive no help from us. Any of us. All the doors to the secret places on Earth will be shut to you. You rejoin the Necromancium, you do it as an equal, not as our superior. Governing the otherworld is a huge task even without the problems Hell likes to cause. You reenter magic-bound, as does every member of the council. The compact will be signed by your hand, in your blood, tying your fate to ours. We learned our lesson the last time."

Raum stood, shoving away from his chair and seething with indignation. It wasn't enough, apparently, to endure Mammon's treachery, the loss of his home and status, having to endure the "help" of the angels. Once again, he was going to have his lack of status rubbed in his face. His battered pride could take no more today.

"I'm tired," he ground out, "and I'd like to rest before the others arrive, and the council meets. I'm sure you're enjoying yourself, but any further humiliations you've got in store for me are going to have to wait."

He gave a stiff half bow and headed for the doors, gut churning. Never would any of the Lost Ones have dared demand that he bind himself to their rules with their blighted Earth magic back when he had come as a representative of Hell. He had been crafted before their existence was even dreamed of. He was untainted by human blood. Their rules shouldn't apply to him. He was…he was…

"Raum, I mean no disrespect to what you are. I can imagine what a shock to your system these past months have been."

His hand paused on the cool metal of the door. "Spare me your pity," he snarled. "You want me magic-bound, fine. I owe the seraphim. I owe the Necromancium. You all seem to want a pound of flesh, and I'm not in a position to deny you, so go for it, if it makes you feel good."

Justin's voice was wondering. "You honestly think this is about me getting off on some kind of old score-settling? God, you really are a self-centered bastard, Raum. That hasn't changed. For the record, I'd choose you over Mammon and his thugs any day, even if it means throwing that smug asshole Gadreel into the mix. But understand how much you're asking of me. Of us." Raum turned his head to glare at Justin, and the cool certainty in the vampire's eyes had been replaced by an intensity of emotion that stilled Raum's hand at the door.

"We've built an empire in the years since any of you bothered with us, a fully functioning world. Vampires, shifters, magic-wielders...we're not the ragged Lost Ones anymore, barely hanging on to the fringes. I don't want to see what we've built destroyed. Not for Heaven or Hell would I see this destroyed."

Raum could only nod, surprised by the depth of emotion in Justin's words. And despite his burning pride, he did understand, though he didn't particularly want to. Damn if he didn't even feel something unnervingly like sympathy. Whatever it was, it pulled at him, a sick and strange and sad feeling that stole over him in place of the anger and contempt that should have been there, should have had him storming out the door.

Something was wrong with him, Raum realized with dawning horror. Whether it was simply being on Earth too long, or, more likely, another side effect of taking on the responsibility of Ember Riddick, it was as though someone had found the place he'd buried all of his unwanted emotions and gotten out a shovel.

And he couldn't put them back. Somehow, he couldn't put them back.

He wondered what might be unearthed next, and it terrified him.

"I'll see you later tonight," Raum said. He needed air, to walk the silent streets and try to get his priorities back where they belonged. The desire to go to Ember was unnervingly strong, so he would ignore it, prove he could resist until he had his control back. Wanting her was understandable. The need to protect her, well, unwanted, but acceptable enough. But this compulsion he had to remain in her orbit, to discover all her secrets and worse, to reveal his own, had to stop. He would still be Raum when she was nothing but a whisper in the past. In the end, that was the only truth that mattered.

Pretending otherwise was for fools.

"Talk to your woman, Raum. You'll end up regretting it if you don't," Justin said.

"I have no regrets. And she's not my woman," Raum said, though his protest sounded half-hearted even to him.

Justin simply tilted his head and watched him with eyes that were far too shrewd for Raum's liking.

"Then you'll find regret soon enough. *Partner.*"

Chapter 11

"*Ember.*" The voice was low, musical and comfortingly familiar.

She gazed across the wastes, a light, hot breeze lifting her hair away from her face. Normally, there was nothing to see but sand and the deep and angry red sky. Today, however, was different. She stood on a wide path crafted of stone, worn and obviously well traveled. On either side of her, not far from where she stood, she could make out a river. The two rivers were like nothing she'd ever seen before, though. One was a dreamy blue-green that stood in marked contrast to the desert, a soothing color that made her want to head that way. A filmy mist hung over the surface of the water, and in the quiet, Ember could faintly make out the soothing rush of the water.

On the other side of her was a river that didn't seem to be made of water at all, but instead was a rapidly moving flow of white fire. It shifted and glowed as she watched, sparks shooting from it in spots where it roiled more violently. The noise of the fire was a snakelike hiss, punctuated by the occasional snap of a spark.

"Beautiful, isn't it, my daughter?"

Ember turned back, and there he was, watching her calmly. He was tall, powerfully built, with chin-length waves of hair the same shade of red as her own. He was dressed as he always was, fitted breeches and tall black boots, with no shirt to cover a muscular torso, and more importantly, the massive, beautiful wings that sprang from his back.

She reverted, as she always did in these dreams, to thinking like the child she had once been. Lonely, eager to please, needy…and torn between fear and awe at this creature's interest in her.

"Do you want me to summon the legions again?" she asked, anxious for the praise he always gave when she had accomplished one of his tasks. "Or open the chasm?"

"No, darling," he said, smiling again. And Ember found herself thinking that it was really more a baring of teeth than a true smile, because his eyes, golden mirrors of her own, stayed hard and flat.

"You and I need to talk. I'll be coming for you soon, to take you home with me. But the one who took you is making it…difficult." The smile stretched so that it was a grimace. "He's taken you someplace I can't see, and I don't know why." A muscle in his jaw jumped. "I need you to think, very hard, sweet. Think about where you are. Where the bastard has taken you."

Ember tried to concentrate, but she was coming up blank. She frowned, frustrated. Something surfaced, rising through the quagmire of her thoughts, and she grabbed a hold of it as hard as she could.

"He's not a bastard," she announced. "He saved my life."

She recoiled immediately at the mask of fury and rage her father's face morphed into. He was rarely annoyed with her. And he'd never been so angry.

"He doesn't give a damn about you, you stupid little bitch! All he cares about is using you to get to me! He's nothing, a second-rate demon who always thought he was better than he was. He never thought of the good of his kind...*our* kind. He only thought of himself, and that's exactly what he's doing right now!" He advanced on her, and Ember stumbled quickly backward to get away from him. Her ankle twisted beneath her, and she gave a yelp that was both pain and fear.

"Don't hurt me," she begged, "please, Daddy."

That stopped him. He paused, tipped back his head and hissed in what she hoped was a steadying breath. When he crouched down beside her, he wasn't smiling, but he didn't look as if he was going to hurt her, either. He looked...grim. And determined.

Her father reached out to tuck a stray curl behind her ear. "Close your eyes, daughter. Clear your mind. Then I'll be able to see where to find you. I'll be able to see..."

"Ember!"

She gasped as her eyes flew open, surfacing from sleep with a sharp jerk, hearing the echoes of an enraged scream in the recesses of her mind. Her heart pounded, and she was covered in a thin sheen of sweat, making her thin shirt stick to her skin despite the cool air in the room. She drank in the air, so sweet compared to where she had been, in greedy little sips. And slowly, as her breathing slowed, Ember realized that the desert had vanished, replaced by a comfortable bedroom that was bathed in the cheery warmth of the small lamp on an ornately carved nightstand.

And watching her with obvious concern was the kindest pair of red eyes she'd ever seen.

Then again, she hadn't seen very many eyes that shade yet, so her judgment probably wasn't all that trustworthy.

"Hey, are you all right? I wouldn't have woken you up, but you sounded like you were having one hell of a nightmare."

Ember blinked rapidly, trying to clear her muddled, sleep-fuzzed thoughts and focus. "Um. Yes? To both," she managed. Her mind began to work again, if sluggishly, and she knew she'd just been through a less than pleasant meeting with her father. Mammon. He was searching for her, a little desperately, from how he'd seemed. And he'd almost managed to get close enough to find out where they were. To get even further inside her head.

It was so frustrating, Ember thought helplessly. She was always confused, powerless to resist in those dreams. She wanted to hold her own against him, to ask her questions on her own terms. But it never worked out that way.

And God, he'd been so angry.

She knew she should tell Raum, and immediately. But as she thought it, the echoes of Mammon's furious words came back to her: *He doesn't give a damn about you...all he cares about is using you to get to me...*

That couldn't be true, though. Could it?

Unsettled because she really didn't know enough about him to know the answer, Ember turned her attention back to the woman who was perched on the side of the bed, looking expectantly at her. She had hair so blond it was nearly white, falling in loose waves over her shoulders, a marked contrast to her expressive, dark-lashed eyes. Her lips, a china-sdoll rosebud, were vibrantly red. There was an effortless grace even in the way she perched beside her, her long-limbed dancer's body coiled into an attitude of elegant repose.

Ember thought of what was now probably the unruly red mop on top of her own head and winced. The woman, to her credit, either didn't notice or was too polite to show it.

"I'm Drusilla. But please, call me Dru." Her grin widened, showing off a sharp little pair of fangs. "I'm not a stalker, by the way. You'd been out for so long that I was starting to worry, seeing as how Justin told me to get, as he put it, my sorry undead ass over here a few hours ago. I kind of overslept, though," she said apologetically. "Not much of an evening person."

Ember laughed, already liking the vampire. The ugliness of the dream was rapidly fading away, and her mood lightened along with its recession.

"No problem. What time is it anyway?" she asked.

"Ah, the evening is well underway in the city of eternal night," Dru said, waggling her eyebrows dramatically. "Bloodsuckers and shapeshifters abound, stalking the streets in shadowy— Okay, forget that, I'm starving. You want to go grab a bite? I can give you the grand tour after we eat."

Ember's stomach growled at the mention of food, and she realized that she was starving, as well. She hadn't eaten since last night, apart from a granola bar Raum had dug out of his duffel bag for her. At the thought of him, she felt the same flutter in her stomach that she always did. Was he still here, she wondered? What was he doing?

And could she be any more ridiculous?

"Yeah," she replied, "I'd love to. But, um…I'm not sure if there's anything for me to eat down here?"

"Oh, no worries," Dru said breezily, rising from the bed. "Like I said, it's not all vamps down here. We've got your witches, your shifters of various sorts and probably even a few trolls if you really wanted to look for them, which trust me, you don't. But anyway, we feed them all, so I'm sure we can find something for a she-demon to eat. There's an excellent burger joint down the street. At which I plan to enjoy a glass of O Negative spiked with Grey Goose. Breakfast of champions." She gave Ember's flannel pajama pants and college T-shirt a critical look.

"Do you want to borrow some clothes?"

Ember looked down at herself and pursed her lips. "I'd love to, except that you're about a foot taller than me. And annoyingly gorgeous, just for the record."

Dru laughed, her face lighting up with pleasure. "I knew I liked you. And I know I've got something. Come on, I'm right upstairs. I think we can smuggle you up there with a minimum of trouble."

"Thanks." Ember sighed, relieved as she swung her legs over the side of the bed and spotted the hairbrush and small collection of toiletries arranged neatly on the large, low dresser.

She had just opened her mouth to ask one of the million questions that immediately flooded her thoughts when the door to her room slammed open so hard that the heavy iron bounced against the wall. All thought dried up immediately at the sight of Raum, looking slightly disheveled and, though she was sure it must be a trick of her imagination, worried as he stormed into the middle of the small but luxuriantly appointed chamber.

He stopped short when he saw Dru, gave her a once-over that seemed to be all about threat assessment and then barked out a single, imperious command.

"Out!"

Dru's lovely face hardened considerably, but Ember had no doubts about who it was directed at. Still, she rose at the order of the man who seemed to fill the room completely.

"I guess we'll do a rain check on the food," Dru said to her, her smile steely. "If you need anything—"

"She won't," Raum said. "Now get the hell out of here."

Now it was Ember's turn to glare at him. "Nice."

"Don't worry about it," Dru said lightly, giving her a

quick pat on the shoulder before gliding regally to the door. "It isn't your fault that they found you before you found us. Though if you want him out of here, just call for me, and I'll bring reinforcements."

"You'll be taking them out of here in pieces," Raum replied flatly.

"I can see you haven't changed much," Dru sniffed, baring her fangs at Raum before stalking off. He slammed the door shut on her rapidly retreating back.

"Is there a particular reason you feel the need to be, I don't know, a *complete* asshole?" she asked, her anger on Dru's behalf burning brightly even as her mouth watered at the sight of him. And with the knowledge that they were, once again, alone.

Incredibly, she had missed him. Though considering his attitude right now, she was hard-pressed to figure out why.

Raum turned his eyes back on her, and what she saw on his face startled her. Yes, there was a fair amount of the simmering anger he always seemed to carry. But she hadn't imagined the worry. He strode quickly to her, grabbed her roughly by the shoulders and without a word began to poke and prod as he looked her over.

"What are you *doing?*" she asked as he tipped her chin up and gave her neck a thorough inspection.

"Making sure your new friend kept her fangs to herself," he growled, then apparently satisfied, let her chin drop. "I don't trust them."

"Yeah, well, the feeling seems to be mutual," Ember replied. "And shockingly, your friendly demeanor doesn't seem to have helped."

He didn't so much as crack a smile.

"Did Gadreel stay away from you?"

Ember stared at him in wonder and tried, very hard, not to lose her patience. Up until now, she hadn't been aware that it was possible for Raum to get worked up.

"I don't think he's even here, Raum," Ember replied, keeping her voice even. "He stuck around long enough to see where this place was, and then he took off."

Raum said nothing, though she couldn't miss the flash of relief across his sharp features. But he didn't look away, either, and his gaze, so intense, began to make her nervous. Maybe there was something wrong with the way she looked, and Dru had just been too nice to say so. Horns, maybe? She lifted a hand to her forehead immediately, and was immediately relieved not to feel anything strange poking out of it.

"What?" she finally demanded.

"You look…nice," he finally said, his deep voice guttural. Then he frowned. "Why did you ever bother wearing those ridiculous glasses?"

Ember raised her eyebrows. "I, ah…glasses?" She thought it was an odd topic to jump to, but whatever. She shrugged. "I thought it was easier to blend in that way, I guess."

The odd, intense expression had not left his face as he studied her. She fought the urge to squirm.

Finally, he said, "You're a beautiful woman. You shouldn't have tried to hide that."

She knew her mouth dropped open, but she couldn't help it. Flustered and pleased, Ember suddenly found herself at a loss for words. She'd give Raum credit: he could certainly take the wind out of her sails when he wanted to. And her irritation with him had completely vanished.

"Well, I, um…thanks," she stammered, suddenly feeling very unsure of herself. Thus far, she and Raum had either been arguing or pawing at one another. She wasn't quite sure what to do with this new facet of his personality.

"I'm a mess, though," she finished, self-consciously shoving her curls away from her face. "I just woke up. Where were you?"

"Signing a contract in blood," he grumbled. Ember was sure he was joking. Almost. They looked at one another a moment longer, and Ember thought she could actually feel the dynamic between them shifting ever so slightly. He had worried about her, more than she'd expected. And he had shown her a side of himself that was different. Warmer, Ember thought, than she had thought he was capable of being. The now-familiar heat kindled inside of her as Ember's gaze locked with his, but this time it was less a dangerous flash than a slow and steady increase in heat, a slow burn that was somehow even more compelling.

It couldn't last, though. And it was Raum who finally pulled away from that moment of connection, though Ember could still feel the gossamer threads of whatever they had just shared binding them.

"Why don't you get dressed? I'll take you to eat or something," he said, shifting his gaze away. Ember bit back a frustrated sigh as she watched his profile. She almost considered refusing, just because he never seemed inclined to *ask* her to do anything. But in the end, her rumbling stomach, and her curiosity, won out. She made a quick trip to the bathroom, pulled on the pair of jeans and T-shirt she'd salvaged from the bag of clothes that had been delivered to the apartment, and set out. It was almost a date, Ember thought, sneaking a curious glance at the black-clad demon who squired her out onto the street and gave a death glare to anyone who looked at her twice.

Almost. Not quite. But it was an interesting start.

They wound up at a small, casual Italian place around the corner, tucked into a private booth that shielded them from the curious looks of everyone they came across.

Ember watched Raum settle himself into the seat and thought, with a smile, that he probably didn't mind the excuse to hide. A people person he was not. Strange that it didn't bother her too much.

"You're going to be a celebrity around here, I think," she said. "Everyone stares. And they don't look like they want to kill you yet, so that's good, right?"

"That's a matter of opinion." He deadpanned it, but Raum's smile was evident in his voice.

This was, Ember realized, the first time they'd spent time together where they weren't on edge waiting for another demon to come around the corner. He kept sneaking looks at her, as though he wasn't quite sure what he was supposed to be saying or doing in this situation. It occurred to Ember, rather suddenly, that this might be the first time Raum had ever taken a woman to dinner. Ever. She watched him concentrate on his menu and tried not to smile as she looked down at her own.

Who would have thought that big, scary, dangerously sexy Raum could come off as a little awkward? It was kind of…cute.

"Wow," she said blandly. Raum raised his gaze, looking puzzled.

"What?"

"I'm just thinking it's good I'm not squeamish, or this menu would make me pass out.

"I'm kind of torn between a burger and fries or a leg of…well, actually, it looks like they have a variety of legs. And they all look to be on the hoof. Or only recently off it."

Raum lifted one black brow, but his eyes were glittering. "You have a problem with fresh food?"

She snorted. "No. Except I have this sudden urge to become a vegetarian."

The conversation flowed more easily than she'd expected, even though Ember felt as if she did most of the talking. She and Raum wound up sharing a large platter of cheddar bacon fries, and as the relaxed chatter of the other diners ebbed and flowed around them, Ember found herself drawn into chatting easily about her business, the charming old house she was locked in constant battle with, even, a little, the psycho mother who somehow found it appropriate to send her everything from communion wafers to vials of holy water for birthdays and Christmas, probably in hopes of annihilating her.

It was a little funny, even as it was sad. But she was a

big girl now. And Raum was such an attentive listener, it didn't feel strange to spill it to him. There were things she skirted, of course: how unhappy her childhood had been, the unfortunate events that had led to her move to Johnstown. But he seemed surprisingly, genuinely interested in what she had to say.

Eventually, though, between the eating and the talking, Ember had to come up for air.

"Wow," she said looking down at the nearly clean platter. "What hurts more right now, your stomach or your ears?"

His smile was slow, warm in a way that heated her to her core.

"You do talk a lot."

She stuck her tongue out at him, and they both chuckled together. It was amazing how much he had relaxed over the course of the meal. Of course, that also let Ember know exactly how uptight Raum had been since they'd met. But the surprise of the night was that she didn't just *want* this surly fallen angel. It seemed she might actually even *like* him.

"I might, repeat *might,* resemble that remark. My jaw has limits, though. Why don't you tell me about you?" Ember asked, propping her chin on her hands and leaning forward.

Only to feel her stomach sink as she watched Raum's look go instantly from open to shuttered. He shrugged, but she could see the tension return to his shoulders.

Damn, she thought.

"There isn't much to tell."

She gave him a beleaguered look, determined to get

something out of him. "Be serious, Raum. I think you now know everything about me up to and including the name of my third-grade teacher. I may be a half demon, but I'm boring. You're something I didn't even think existed. How can there not be much to tell?"

"Eternity isn't all that interesting," he said, and she did hear a faint ring of truth in that. Still, dissatisfied, she pressed again.

"So is your past littered with ex-wives and scandal or what?" she asked, trying for an easy smile even though this felt like pulling teeth all of a sudden.

That did, at least, elicit a small laugh. "No. The Fallen don't marry. Who would we marry?"

"You mean, who would put up with you forever. But I'm living proof that your kind does sleep around," Ember remarked. Raum smirked.

"Breaking that particular rule is one of the reasons we Fell."

She tilted her head to the side and looked at him closely, intensely curious now. "Is that why *you* Fell?"

His discomfort was immediate, and very obvious. "No. I just don't like rules—period."

"Or humans, I'm sure," Ember added. She had, after all, been to Sunday school a few times. Before Dina had decided it wasn't doing any good, at least.

"I like *you* well enough," Raum hedged, and that surprised a laugh out of her.

"Be still, my beating heart," she deadpanned, patting her chest. "So I guess you don't want to tell me what Hell was like?"

"Hot."

"Or Heaven?"

"Boring."

Ember sighed, and then she caught the wicked twinkle in Raum's sea-green eyes. "You're messing with me," she accused him, and his lazy grin was a definite affirmative, apart from also taking her breath away. He hadn't clammed all the way back up after all. But considering what his smile did to her, she couldn't decide if that was a good or a bad thing. It definitely wasn't in her own best interest. But then, very little she wanted ever was.

"Okay, fine," Ember said. "I give up." She poked at the remains of the eggplant with her fork, not really interested in eating it but suddenly unsure where to go from there. To her surprise, for once, he was the one who picked a subject.

"I won't be able to be with you all the time down here," he said. "Justin's promised you'll be safe, and he's adamant that Drusilla is about as mean as they come when she needs to be, but you need to be careful, and stay close to the apartment. I have—" he curled his lip "—*obligations* now that I'm expected to honor. But I want you to come and find me immediately if anything seems off and I'm not right there."

She wasn't sure whether to be touched by his concern or irritated in his lack of faith in her ability. She guessed it was a little of both.

"Of course," she said, herself not liking the thought of being without him more often despite her resentment of his high-handedness. "But I've got some obligations, too. When do you think I'll be able to go home?"

The careful blankness in his gaze told her all she needed to know.

"Raum," Ember said, trying to keep the urgency out of her voice. "I appreciate the hideout and everything, really. But I have a life. And once this is all over with, I have to go back to making a living. I can't just stay down here forever!"

At least, she didn't think she could. But the thought brought her up short: might she be able to stay? And if she could, would she want to?

"Levi is bringing the others," Raum said carefully. "And we'll do all we can. But you can't go back until this is sorted out, Ember. It would be too dangerous..."

"I know, I know," Ember interjected, trying not to sound as frustrated as she felt. And he was right—she couldn't run the risk of hurting all of those people. She tried to sound flip when she continued. "But hey, now that I know how to defeat a cave demon, I'm all good, right?"

A ghost of a smile played at the corners of his mouth, though Ember could see his concern hadn't evaporated.

"It's a start."

That tension was back, in the lines at the corners of his eyes, his mouth, the line of his shoulders. Before she could think better of it, she reached across the table and put her hand on his, feeling how tightly he was holding himself. It touched her, unexpectedly. Raum was the most self-contained creature she'd ever encountered. She wanted, though it was likely futile, to know what he kept inside.

"What's wrong?" she asked softly, sensing that the tension was different than before, that it contained far less anger than usual.

He looked down at their hands, and she felt his relax ever so slightly before he raised his eyes to hers again. So *beautiful*, she thought, and something throbbed painfully in the vicinity of her heart.

"I...worry," he said, his voice halting, a frown creasing his forehead. "About all of this. About...you."

She tipped her chin down to regard him. "Since you're supposed to be my Guardian, I can't say I'm sorry about that." But his frown stayed.

"I am. I don't like it."

She sighed, torn between exasperation and amusement.

"Tough, Raum," she said. "To know me is to like me. And to guard me is to worry that I will inadvertently wreck the world as we know it."

"I'm beginning to understand that," he said, but his tone was back to being friendly, if weary. "Come on, I've got to get back and open another vein for the Necromancium. But I'll take you home."

Home. She wished. But beneath that wistful longing for things she couldn't have, Ember quietly thrilled at his words. He might be about as wrong for her as it got, but it was nice to know that someone gave a damn. That *he* gave a damn.

Even if it ticked him off.

Chapter 12

By the time Ember awakened to her third night in Terra Noctem, she wasn't worried about what Raum was doing anymore.

She was ready to kick his ass.

"Some protection," Ember muttered, slamming drawers as she hunted for the perfect outfit in which to inflict pain and destruction on her missing Guardian. As far as she knew, between yesterday and today, neither Raum nor Gadreel had set foot in the apartment the three of them were supposed to share. While part of her calmly asserted that going into withdrawal over him was ridiculous, since he wasn't exactly obligated to hang out with her all the time and he'd *said* he would be busy, the rest of her was happily ruled by her temper. Especially since, in her world, you didn't tell a girl you *worried* about her—especially in that dark, sexy, oh-so-intimate voice he'd used—and then go out of your way to ignore her.

Which he seemed to be doing, since Raum's and Gadreel's presence was the freaking talk of the city.

At least Dru had indulged her in some much-needed retail therapy, complete with the sort of easy female banter that Ember had been missing most of her life. She'd fallen into bed this morning feeling as if she had a new friend, and they'd made plans to meet up tonight.

After the ass-kicking.

At least there hadn't been any more semiconscious heart-to-hearts with dear old dad, Ember thought, pulling on a pair of dark, low-slung jeans. It was, at least, a reprieve from having to decide what to do about that, if anything. She was glad for it, even as she pushed away the nagging feeling that she was ignoring the reality of the visits at her peril. But Raum had insisted she was safe here. She decided to take him at his word, even though Raum's sudden switch from concerned hero to aloof jerk left her with some serious doubts about his commitment to her well-being. Her mental well-being, anyway.

Ember zipped into the funky black-and-purple bustier Dru had talked her into and turned from side to side in the mirror, considering. It wasn't normally something she would have picked up, but there was a definite Goth-y vibe going on with a lot of the residents of the city, and it was fun to try something new. Plus, it made her boobs look really good, Ember decided. Always a bonus.

She let her hair fall in wild curls around her shoulders,

shoved her feet into a pair of dangerously high heels and painted a thin coat of murderous red onto her lips before striding out the door.

When she hit the street, already bustling with activity, she found herself returning the waves of a few of the people Dru had introduced her to last night. It was nothing short of amazing, Ember thought as a small group of pale-skinned men craned their necks around to stare at her as she passed, but she already felt more comfortable here than she'd ever felt anywhere. Vampires, she'd realized, were plenty sexually magnetic in their own right, and no one here seemed to think she was much different than the norm. And if she was so inclined, she was pretty sure that either a shifter or a vampire would make an acceptable, and resilient enough, partner.

Unfortunately, for the first time in her life, she was so hung up on one man that she couldn't find a single other one who appealed to her that way.

There was a huge crowd outside the place she and Dru had eaten and had—quite a few—drinks the night before. Blackheart's, it was called, and Ember had loved the decadence of the inside, with all the plush crimson velvet and deep mahogany wood. Dru had opined that it always reminded her of a cross between a coffin and a bordello, and Ember agreed that the unusual combination alone was reason enough to love it. The food, however, had been fantastic in it own right.

It seemed as if plenty of other people thought so, too, Ember thought, slowing to take in the crowd. There were a number of tall, imposing-looking men with shaggy hair keeping everyone back, and the growls told her they weren't vampires, but werewolves. There were a few packs that had made the city their home, according to Dru, and still others up above. These looked like law enforcement.

"Oh, come on, let us see, Jenner!" snapped a dark-haired girl who couldn't have been any more than eighteen. She was up in one of the wolves' faces, gesticulating angrily.

"Sorry, Gina, but they're having some kind of meeting, and most of them just got into town. Justin says it's private. You can see them when they come out."

A pretty blonde bumped Ember's elbow in the crush, then turned to apologize. "Sorry! I wasn't going to come, but I've never seen a fallen angel before, have you?" she asked. Ember shook her head as understanding sank in. It sounded as if the rest of the Fallen had blown into town. And of course, no one had bothered to let her know. She gritted her teeth.

"I heard they're pretty incredible to look at," the woman continued, oblivious to Ember's rising temper. "But then, I guess that makes sense. Have a great night!"

Ember watched the woman bounce off to join the throng, a red haze descending over her vision. She'd been left to her own devices, and Raum was playing rock star. Well, they'd just see about that.

She headed straight for the door to Blackheart's, unsurprised when one of the wolves moved to block her way.

"Sorry, miss, you can't go in."

In response, Ember planted her hands on her hips and bared her teeth at the guard, willing the demon in her to the surface. Heat flashed over her skin as she allowed it out, inwardly pleased that when she was just pissed off, as opposed to in mortal danger or aroused, she seemed to have pretty good control.

"I came in with the demons," Ember said flatly, "because I am one. Or did no one bother to mention there was a woman with them?"

The wolf's gold eyes widened with understanding, and Ember decided he was one lucky dog.

"Of course, Miss Riddick. Justin didn't mention you were coming. Go on in."

She knew that necks were craning in the crowd to see who had been allowed in, but Ember barely spared them a glance, intent on her mission of destruction. She'd been angry when she woke up. The anger was now borderline nuclear.

They're users...he doesn't give a damn about you... using you to get to me...

Dru's words, and Mammon's, played on a loop in her head as she pushed through the smoky glass doors of the restaurant. She stopped short only a few paces in, however, when she got a look at the men hanging out at the large circular bar that dominated the main room of the place.

They were stunning. That was all Ember could think as her brain tried to assimilate the fact that so much raw male sex appeal was crammed into one place. They were as different from the other as night was from day, each exhibiting a singular beauty that no human could possibly match. She saw Gadreel's blond head, tipped forward in deep discussion with another man whose hair was as white-blond as Dru's. Two brunettes, one with short, spiky hair and a fascinating tribal tattoo that curled down the length of one arm, the other with the steely look of a battle-hardened warrior. A redhead with a grin that could have set ice on fire.

She knew the second her presence had been noticed as conversation slowly ground to a halt and several pairs of unusually colored eyes fixed on her with laserlike intensity.

"Damn," someone muttered as she headed for Gadreel's broad back. He was so deeply engrossed in his conversation that he didn't turn until she was almost on top of him, but his reaction was worth it.

Apparently, Dru had been right about the shirt.

Gadreel's jade-green eyes flashed with light as they slowly slid down the length of her, and then back up again before meeting her defiant gaze with a look that held nothing but heat and intense sexual promise.

"Ember," he purred, drawing out the final *r* so that it scraped deliciously across her nerves. "I think you're going to have to come sit with me."

She arched an eyebrow. "I don't see an empty stool beside you."

His smile was lazy and utterly wicked. "I have an empty lap, don't I?"

"And big dreams," Ember replied, flagging down the bartender to order a drink.

"My dreams are not nearly as big as other parts of me."

Ember couldn't help but laugh at the cocky grin on his handsome face, though it made it a little harder to hang on to her mad like she needed to. Meanwhile, Gadreel's companion smacked him in the shoulder.

"Yeah, your head's way bigger. And I don't mean the little one," said the other blonde. "Are you going to introduce me or what?"

Gadreel rolled his eyes and swiped Ember's drink as soon as it arrived to take a swig. "Ember, Murmur. Murmur, Ember. Hellfire, woman, what is this you're drinking? It tastes like lighter fluid and Tabasco sauce."

She gave him a look and plucked it out of his hand. "It's a Prairie Fire. And it pretty much *is* lighter fluid and Tabasco. I like spicy things."

"Hmm, we have that in common," Gadreel replied, and Ember was suddenly very certain that Gadreel would be perfectly willing to abscond with her to the nearest hotel, bathroom or dark corner if she so much as winked at him. Part of her wished she could muster the desire, but it just wasn't there. And she didn't know why.

Well, yeah, she did. But she didn't like it. Not right now, anyway.

"You're a lot prettier than Mammon," Murmur offered, leaning casually against the bar. Ember took in his tousled hair, a shade that was nearly platinum, and eyes that were the bright blue of a winter sky. There was nothing dark about his looks, but Ember was sure his wings were as black as the rest.

"Shorter, too."

"Thanks," Ember replied with a smirk, and Murmur chuckled.

"Maybe you should come sit with me instead. I'll protect you from Gadreel. He's a lush."

"She's not sitting with either of you."

His voice, directly behind her, sent a shiver of pleasure directly up her spine, and her breath caught in her throat. It had only been days, but Ember was stunned to discover that she was as hungry for him as if he'd been away for years. Her toes curled inside her shoes, and she fought the urge to arch back against him and stretch like a cat.

Gadreel looked at her, then at the dark angel behind her, and pressed his lips together with obvious annoyance. "Oh, goody. Captain Fun has arrived."

Ember turned slowly around, trying to brace herself to deal with her own reaction to his nearness. Still, simmering heat coiled through her system the instant she looked at him, tipping her head back to meet his disapproving gaze with a defiant one of her own. It was hard to maintain, though, when his gaze dropped to take in her clothes. Everywhere his eyes lingered, it felt like a warm caress, and her knees threatened to go liquid.

"Nice to see you," she said, hoping she sounded cooler than she felt. "I was starting to think you were hiding."

His eyes were hot, glowing when they met hers again. "Actually, I'm late because I went by to get you. Of course, all I found was an empty bed and your clothes all over the floor. If you weren't here, I was going to go looking for you."

"Oh, that's convenient. What was I supposed to do, wait around for you to remember I was here?" she asked, extending one long claw and poking him in the chest with it. He frowned down at it. "Would have been nice if you'd stopped by yesterday. Checked to see I'd settled in. Bothered to return *even once* to the apartment I was given to understand was going to be occupied by *all three* of us. You know, stuff you might expect from even a *replacement* Guardian Angel."

"Ouch," Murmur said behind her, and Ember realized that the entire place had gone silent again in order to listen to the budding argument.

"Just because I'm not right there doesn't mean I'm not paying attention," Raum growled. "I knew you were fine."

"One minute you're telling me I'm not going to be able to get rid of you, and the next, I can't even *find* you," Ember snapped, glaring at him now. "What if I hadn't been fine? I was alone in that apartment! I could have walked right out of this place, actually, but what good would that have done? You wouldn't have noticed! And you know why? Because you were too busy with your new vampire buddy turning the magic of testosterone into some more grand plans for my existence." She slammed her hands onto her hips and stood up on her tiptoes to get as close to in his face as she could. "My mother's geriatric poodle is a better bodyguard than you, Mr. Be-Careful-I-Worry." She saw the anger flash in his eyes, as deadly as lightning in a midnight sky, and wondered too late if she might have wanted to think about picking a fight with an ancient fallen angel before she actually went off and did it.

Raum leaned down close to her, close enough that she was only a breath away from being able to take his full bottom lip in her mouth and give it a nip. The anger seemed only to have made her attraction to him more intense, Ember realized, dismayed. She drew in a ragged breath that betrayed it completely, but she was powerless to hide her need when he was so achingly close.

"This is not the place, Ember." His voice was calm, deadly. But the lack of emotion in his expression told her what she'd needed to know. She really was just a job to him, pleasant dinner and raging lust notwithstanding. And now that she had other people to protect her, he was more than ready to walk away.

Rejection. She should be used to it by now. But God, this hurt.

With a furious snarl, Ember backed away from him, tearing herself free of the magnetic pull he exerted on her as well as she could. Channeling the pain into anger was the only way she was going to make it out of here without screaming.

"You know what? You're right. It's not the place," she gritted out. "Enjoy your little VIP party, Raum. I'll see you around."

She whirled and stormed out in a blind rage, ignoring the entertained hoots and hollers of the other Fallen. She was thrilled she'd given them such a great show. Ember slammed out of the front doors, ignoring the guard's request for her to have a good night, and stomped down the street to her building. Her fury and her helpless, unrequited attraction had created a toxic storm inside of her that needed to find a way out, and soon. Because she wanted to rip, to tear, to bite. If it got any worse, she was going to need someone to chain her to a post until she calmed down.

There were few people she'd ever allowed to make her this angry. One had tried to take something precious from her late one night, alone on a beach. For this, and for what he had stolen from a number of other young women, she'd ensured that he'd ended up hospitalized for months before the trial, supposedly wounded with his own knife when she'd wrested it from him and attacked in self-defense.

No one would ever know that she hadn't needed a knife. And until that night, Ember hadn't really known what she was capable of. She hadn't thought she could be a killer. But she had wanted that man's blood, and the only thing that had stopped her from getting all of it had been the sirens. The fear of becoming that thing she had transformed into again, but permanently, was one of the main things keeping her here, even though she chafed at the confinement.

Even though now she had nothing. Nothing but her rage and her nonsensical need for a man who wasn't even human, and who couldn't belong to her…who didn't even want to belong to her. The one man she had ever wanted whom she couldn't have. And the only one she seemed able to feel any desire for since the moment she'd laid eyes on him.

Of all the injustices she'd had to endure for being as she was, this, in some ways, hurt the worst.

Ember slammed into the apartment so hard that the walls shook and headed into the bedroom. She stopped in front of the mirror and glared at the golden-eyed demoness who stared angrily back. Even through her fury, she could see that in some ways, she'd never looked as alive, as vital and as much *herself* as she did here. But what the hell good was it?

She bared her fangs at her reflection and whirled away. All of her anger needed an outlet, and the pressure was building...

Then the door slammed again, and Raum was stalking toward her, eyes burning, wholly a creature of the night. All the air seemed to go out of the room at once, and Ember could hear the rapid thudding of her own traitorous heart.

It soared when she saw what was now so plainly written across his face.

"We're going to take care of this right now," he snarled.

"Fine with me," Ember shot back.

With the grace and agility of a sleek jungle cat, she was on him in a single powerful leap, clearing the distance between them as though it were only inches rather than the length of the room. He caught her and crushed her to him as they came together in a mad frenzy of need, licking, biting, devouring one another with a hunger that seemed so fathomless it would never be assuaged.

With a ragged groan, Raum took her to the floor, pinning her beneath him as he continued his brutal assault on her senses. The feel of him, the weight of him against her flooded Ember's system with intense heat. Then Raum thrust his hips against her, letting her feel how hard she made him, and the crush of pleasure was intense, immediate. Ember arched beneath him with a hoarse cry, giving over completely to some primal, inhuman instinct to sink her teeth into the tender flesh between Raum's shoulder and the base of his neck. Marking him.

His blood was wicked ambrosia, dark wine that intoxicated her immediately.

Mine.

She felt his body jerk against hers, his fingers dig into her skin. He made a guttural sound of raw pleasure that was nearly her undoing. Ember thrashed beneath him wildly, caught in a haze of longing so intense that she could do nothing to fight it. She had tasted him, marked him. And her body demanded release from the passion that now imprisoned her.

"Please," she moaned, grinding her hips against his.

He rose above her long enough to fist his hand in the neckline of her bustier and tear it from her as though it were nothing but gossamer, baring her breasts as her nipples tightened into hard pebbles in the face of his burning gaze.

"I've tried to stop myself, Ember," he said hoarsely. "But I just can't."

His words, in that dark magic voice, twisted inside her where she was already tight and throbbing. With one more scorching look at her, Raum lowered his head and began to feast, taking one nipple in his mouth and giving it long, hard pull.

Ember closed her eyes in pure bliss, only a soft, choked sound escaping her throat as she tried to remember to breathe. She dug her fingers into the coils of Raum's hair, arching into him as he swirled his tongue around the tight bud, alternately licking and sucking. He wedged his thigh between her legs and pressed into her, urging her to ride it while he pleasured her, lavishing attention on first one breast, then the other. Ember moved restlessly against him, sensing some blinding peak not far off, almost close enough to touch...almost.

She raked her claws down the thin fabric of his shirt, heard it give way beneath her fingers as she dragged it off him. Then they were as she had imagined so many times: skin to skin.

"Like this." Ember sighed, her head falling back in pure pleasure. "Just like this." Then, with a feral growl, Raum claimed her mouth again as hard, smooth muscle pressed against the bare skin of her breasts. His kiss was anything but gentle. And yet in it, there was a raw need that rocked Ember to her core. She had never wanted romance: she wanted possession.

Her first climax blindsided her, slamming into her body without warning as Raum rocked his hips into her again. Ember gave a hoarse cry as the world faded out for a shattering instant and she gripped him hard with her thighs, riding a cresting wave of pleasure that reverberated through her even as Raum's rhythm never faltered.

Still, she wanted more. In a blur of motion that caught

him off guard, she had him flat on his back beneath her. His expression was all hungry, violent need, and he growled again at her, low, deep. Still, he made no move to regain the control, seeming to sense that she, too, needed to take control. Enjoying the view of him, spread out beneath her like some ancient and decadent god, Ember slid her hands up the bare expanse of Raum's torso, savoring the way the muscles contracted and jumped beneath her touch. She slid up the length of him, lowering herself to claim his mouth in a hot, demanding kiss that left her dizzy before running her tongue down over the hard line of his jaw, down his neck, over the twin pinpricks where she'd marked him and down his chest where she could graze her teeth over each tight nipple. He tasted of spice and darkness, Ember thought, moving lower. She wanted to know if he tasted that way everywhere….

But Raum had apparently had enough of submission. In one quick movement she was back beneath him, and he was dragging her jeans off, as well as the lacy black scrap of material she wore under them. Ember helped him, and they fumbled his jeans off together. Then there were no barriers left between them, skin on silken skin as Raum dragged her back to the floor. His hands everywhere then, stroking her, slipping between them to stroke the swollen nub at the apex of her thighs where her body now wept for him. And inside, sensation rose once again, but more intense than before.

Ember registered it only dimly as she indulged her own insatiable need, cruising her hands over all of his gloriously bare skin, wrapping her hand around his shaft and purring with delight when his head rocked back, letting her see how her stroke affected him. For Ember, the universe had contracted until there was only the two of them. There was nothing but Raum, and those blazing eyes that seemed to her to be, in that moment, windows into eternity. And still he stroked her, circling her sex with expert fingers now slick with moisture. Her breath came in sharp pants now, matching those of the man whom she was now giving herself to, body and soul. Power shimmered in the air around them, a silvery mist that rose from their skin and glittered like suspended rain. But the wonder of it was nothing compared to what Ember felt her body racing toward.

"Come to me," she rasped as she writhed beneath him, lifting her hips into his wicked touch. *"Now."*

For once, he was in the mood to do as he was told. With a single, guttural cry, he gripped her hips and drove into her, burying himself to the hilt.

She gasped his name as he tore through the final barrier, pain and pleasure mingling into one as the thing she'd never been able to give to another was breached in one hard stroke. All around the apartment, the lights began to flicker wildly. Somewhere in the bathroom, a glass bottle shattered. Then another. And another.

He stilled above her, and Ember knew he realized what he had just done. She turned her head away, suddenly afraid that if she looked, she would see nothing but his anger. She didn't want anything to mar the perfection of this, the two of them joined in a way she had given up dreaming she would ever experience. And this was so much better than any fantasy.

He said her name. Once, and then again, his dark voice gliding over her skin like a caress. Finally, she gave in, and what she saw in his eyes took her breath away all over again. There was no anger, only a naked wonder that transformed his face into something so beautiful it was almost heartbreaking.

For just an instant, she could see the angel he had once been.

Then he lowered his forehead to hers, reverently, and he was only Raum again.

The man she was falling in love with.

Ember wound her fingers in his hair and savored the way he looked at her, as though she were the most beautiful woman on Earth or anywhere else. She knew it was wrong, that it was hopeless. But she also knew that she was in the process of taking that final inner leap into an emotion that she knew, somehow, she could only ever feel for him. He was to be her only.

"Only you," she whispered breathlessly, managing a small smile as she felt herself tightening around him. It was all she could allow herself to say, knowing it would be foolish to bare her heart. But she tried to imbue those simple words with as much emotion as they would hold, and hoped that somewhere in whatever he might have for a heart, he would know.

"But did I hurt—?"

"No," she murmured, drunk with the pleasure of having him inside of her. She pressed her fingers against his lips, looked into his beautiful, worried eyes. "No. I want this. I want you."

Raum shuddered against her, and his kisses turned

soft, tender as he pressed them to her lips, her cheeks, her eyelids. Ember pushed up against him, tentatively at first, but then more forcefully as the two of them fell into the ancient rhythm that joined man and woman. Raum's thrusts became more urgent, winding Ember ever tighter as she was swept toward an oncoming wave of sensation that dwarfed anything she had felt before.

Then, on a burst of blinding light, the world came apart.

She cried out. His name.

Ember jerked upward against him as it tore through her, the waves of it carrying her on a current of power too long denied. Pictures flew from the walls, vases and plates flew from their shelves to shatter in midair and the entire building was rocked on its foundations as the floor beneath them trembled. Still, Ember could do nothing but cling to Raum, riding it out, shaking with the force of sheer, unbridled pleasure. It was only then that he allowed himself to let go, emptying himself into her with a harsh cry and a final hard thrust of his hips.

Some time later, the two of them lay in a tangle of limbs on the floor, Ember curled contentedly into his heat and absently stroking his chest while Raum rubbed a lazy circle over and over on her back. She knew she should at least get him to move to the bed, but that would require walking, which was not on the agenda for the time being. Besides, she was pretty sure the entire apartment was littered with shards of broken glass.

Who knew that demon virginity was such a force to be reckoned with?

She snuggled closer with a contented sigh, savoring the feel of Raum's arms around her, the musky scent of their lovemaking that still hung in the air. There was, she knew, no falling about it anymore. The demon had her heart. But knowing that he wouldn't want it, a thing that Ember pushed from her thoughts along with the sadness it came with, Ember knew she would never tell him. She would just enjoy what they had, whatever that turned out to be. And however long it lasted.

His voice rumbled against her ear, which was pressed against his chest.

"I meant to ask…what were you mad at me about again?"

She smiled at the warm humor in his tone, and decided that she could admit to a little of what she felt. Only a little.

"I missed you," she said simply.

"Oh," he said, and she could hear the surprise in his voice. More telling, though, was that he pulled her closer, a small action that felt, to her, bigger than the earthquake they'd caused.

And hope, fragile and tentative, bloomed deep in her chest as she listened to the steady beat of Raum's eternal heart.

Chapter 13

Magic-bound: that was how the Necromancium had wanted him.

Well, Raum sure as hell was, and in more ways than he'd counted on. Especially if you factored in one irresistible she-demon who seemed to have a predilection for hopeless and unpleasant fallen angels.

Not that he was complaining.

Raum turned the doorknob and stepped inside the apartment he supposed he was now sharing with Ember. After all, he'd stayed there, even slept a little, and certainly shared Ember's bed for the past few nights. He was only just beginning to sort out what exactly that meant, but he was beyond grateful that Gadreel had opted to spend his nights with whatever willing female would have him.

She had given him her virginity. It still stunned him,

that she would honor him with such a gift when he had done nothing to deserve it. He was still terrified that somehow, he would hurt her, or that his touch would end up scarring her in ways that would not heal. But that night had convinced him of one thing: he could no more stay away from Ember Riddick than the planet could stop orbiting the sun. Come what may, he was done trying to deny himself what he wanted. And, it seemed, what she wanted.

The only problem was that Justin's words to him from that first meeting had returned to haunt him with a vengeance, insisting that he should tell Ember everything. That he would regret it if he did not.

But if he told her now, told her that he and Mammon were bitterest enemies, that her father was the reason he'd had to flee Hell...would she believe that his feelings for her were anything but a lie? He planned to kill one of her parents. That was the truth, and it would not change. Not for her, not for anything. Neither of them would be free until Mammon was dust.

But there was a strong possibility she wouldn't see it that way. And in his selfishness, which Raum readily acknowledged to himself, he would not risk this strange new connection that had bloomed between them. Ember was his. At least for now.

The truth could wait.

Raum stopped in the doorway to look at her, curled sleeping on the bed with a book clasped loosely in her hand. Her face, in sleep, held an innocence that took hold somewhere inside of him, in one of the places he had locked up long ago, and began to tug painfully.

His breath stilled as he watched her, unable to look away. Ember breathed deeply, evenly, her rosebud lips parted slightly in sleep, her long dark lashes twined together. And still, looking closer, he could see the faint smudges under her eyes were very much in evidence, that her skin, always fair, was a little too pale.

And as he watched, she stirred slightly, frowned.

"No," she murmured thickly. "No, it's not…not true…"

The dreams again. Raum felt that pull inside increase, dragging him toward her, dredging up emotions that he had no business entertaining. And yet there they were. He shoved them aside as well as he could and strode to the bed, settling himself beside her and pulling Ember into his lap, cradling her like a child.

Her eyelids fluttered open at the movement, luminous gold, and though he could see the weariness in them, there was something else there. It terrified him, even as he moved inexorably toward the edge of a precipice he had never seen looming.

"Hey," she said softly, her voice rough with sleep. "Thought I was waiting up for you."

He smiled. "Meeting went late. Never underestimate the long-windedness of a bunch of immortals."

Her lips curved upward. "So how did it go? Are you all welcomed back with open arms yet or what?"

Raum's smile faded when he thought of what had transpired, the demands that had been made of him, of all of them. Somehow, after ages of doing as he pleased, he had wandered into a position that entailed heavy responsibility. If he'd been worried that the races of the

Necromancium wouldn't respect his kind's power any longer, he'd been wrong. But they wanted to use it. And if he'd thought to make a break from the angels, he'd been very, very wrong.

"Not exactly," he finally allowed. "But there was… progress. What about you? Bad dreams again?" he asked, shifting the topic to something less immediately irritating. It still rankled, Justin's insistence that the Fallen rebels maintain their obligation to Heaven. He, and the others, wanted to forge some kind of truce between the Necromancium and the white wings, who traditionally either ignored the dark races or used them for target practice. In a way, he understood their desire to be in on the war against Hell, to prove themselves as a power to be reckoned with. But it was a spider's web, intricate and deadly, and he was caught squarely in the middle of it.

Ember looked as though she wanted to push him for more information, but thankfully, she seemed to sense that he was too raw yet to discuss it. He didn't expect her to answer the question, though. Every time he asked about her nocturnal mutterings, Ember shut down on him. It worried him, but he wasn't quite ready to demand an answer. Not yet.

But soon, Raum thought, absently tracing a finger down one pale cheek.

His hand stilled as Ember, not for the first time, proved his instincts utterly wrong.

"Okay. I'll tell you about my dreams," she said solemnly. "I think it's time. But I want something from you first."

Raum's eyes narrowed as every dark suspicion he'd had about Ember's nightmares crowded into his mind at once. His first instinct was to shout at her until she gave him what he wanted. But he had learned already that no such thing would ever work with Ember, no matter how desperately he needed the information. She was in danger. Knowing it, knowing she had been keeping something from him, had Raum's temper, edged with worry, snapping at the end of its leash.

And yet faintly, he heard himself saying, "What do you want of me?"

He hated bargains that were not stacked in his favor, never entered into ones he had not concocted himself as a general rule. But in this, looking into Ember's wan face, he had no choice.

"You know everything about me," Ember said softly, and he couldn't miss the sadness in her voice. "But you never tell me anything about yourself."

He felt his back going up, despite his best efforts. His past had always been off-limits. Or it would have been, if he'd ever chosen to have a friend.

"But I told you," he said, trying to sound nonchalant. "There's very little to tell."

Ember sighed heavily and shook her head, a stray curl falling over one eye. Raum reached out to tuck it back behind her ear, a tender gesture he hadn't even realized he was making until he was halfway through it. He didn't want to cause her pain. It was ridiculous, but while Raum had once been known for his skills at lying, he made it a point not to lie to himself.

"I'm not giving you any more, Raum," Ember said.

"Not even this. Not until you give a little yourself. It's tiring, being the only one talking all the time. Not that you would understand that."

Her gentle reproach stung. He didn't let her do all the talking…did he? Raum mulled over the things they had done, the places they had been, and tried to recall times when he had raised a subject himself in conversation.

"No, you really don't talk much, Raum," Ember said, as though she knew exactly what he was thinking. "Or when you do, it's always surface stuff. That's fine, most of the time. But you know me now." Her soft golden eyes were pleading. "I want to know you."

Raum stiffened and drew back a little. Amidst all the uncertainty in his life right now, one thing he was absolutely sure of was that if he opened himself up to Ember that way, shared more of himself with her, that he would be over whatever terrifying edge he was creeping closer to all the time. He wasn't used to depending on anyone, and wasn't inclined to begin.

Even though he, too, was weary in his own ways. And the thought of sharing a little of his burden with Ember was dangerously appealing.

"Is what you have to tell me about these dreams important?" he asked. Then he could barely keep from snarling out the next words. "Is it Mammon?"

Ember shook her head slowly. "No. I'm not saying another word. You first."

Raum stared at her, his temper prickling. No one demanded anything from him, not if they wanted to live. And yet here was this slip of a woman, holding needed information over his head simply to get her own way. It was infuriating. It was unthinkable. It was…

It was exactly like something he would do, and had done, many times.

"You would endanger yourself, endanger all of us, for this? For some useless story?" he asked, his voice tight. He saw her shoulders stiffen, but Ember nodded.

"What I want is a small price to pay, Raum. But if this is the only way I can get you to talk, really talk, to me, then yes."

Raum could see that she was deadly serious, and knew he had already lost. There was no way he would leave her without knowing what was the matter with Ember's dreams, and she knew it. His anger mixed with some small amount of grudging admiration for her underhanded tactics.

"Clever little demon," he said, echoing the words he had said to her at their first meeting. This time, however, they weren't intended as a compliment. And he could see that Ember knew it. But she wouldn't back down, either. So he braced himself.

"All right, then, Ember. What is it you would have me tell you? The names of all those I've killed? That would take a long time."

"I want to know about your Fall," she said. A simple request. And one that punched through him like nothing else would have. It was not spoken of in Hell. Such topics were outlawed, even if anyone had wished to discuss it, which no one did.

"Why?" he asked, willing her to take back the request. "Why isn't it enough to be with me as I am, as we are, instead of dwelling on the past? That was ages ago. It doesn't matter how or why I Fell."

"It matters to me," Ember said, and beneath the soft tones of her voice he could hear steel. She wasn't backing down from this.

"But…why?"

"Because I want to know you, Raum."

He exhaled through his nose, frustrated. Tried desperately to think of a way to circumvent the topic. And realized, finally, that he was going to have to tell Ember what he had never discussed with another living creature.

Incredibly, he felt her take his hand. "Please," she said softly. He still didn't understand why it was so important to her, to know the singularly most painful part of his past. But beneath his resentment, that feel of her hand on his made him feel something wholly unexpected: that he would no longer have to carry his burden alone. And with that thought came an almost dizzying relief.

So he looked away from her, and began.

"I was young then, beautiful and proud of what I had been made to do. I was a Throne, one of the higher ranks of archangels, and I was determined to do great things. To outshine all others." And he remembered it, as the words fell from his lips. The golden sunlight and endless meadows of his own little corner of Paradise, the feel of the air on his wings as he soared with the others of his rank.

"I bet you shone pretty brightly," Ember said, and he supposed she was imagining him as he had once been. But she couldn't know, couldn't possibly know how beautiful he had really been. He had been so young, so utterly unsullied by any world other than his own. And the memory, he found with little surprise, still hurt. Innocence never lasted. Not for any of them.

"I did all right," Raum allowed. "But I had a mentor who was less impressed with me than I was with myself. He was always pushing, always trying to cram more knowledge into my head when I could see little use for it." He smiled a little then, at his own youthful ignorance. "After all, I was already an angel. I had been born perfect, and knew everything."

"I guess that your mentor didn't agree?"

"No, Uriel was decidedly unimpressed," Raum replied, and a glance at Ember told him she was as surprised by the revelation as he'd expected her to be.

"This is the same Uriel that—" she started.

"The same. My rotten luck. And he's still not impressed," said Raum. "But things went along well enough. I was…happy," he allowed. And though the exact memory of that emotion eluded him, a ghost of it lingered in him still—a whisper of hope and promise and laughter that haunted him—no matter how hard he'd tried to expel it. It had been a lie, he thought.

At least, that was always what he had known to be true. But that old ghost, he could now admit, had been whispering more loudly in the weeks and months leading to his escape. Willing him to chase it once again. Promising impossible things should he dare to try.

"So what happened?" Ember prompted gently, and Raum realized he'd lapsed into silence.

"Humans happened," he said, tipping his head a little

to look at her. She nodded, and somehow the sadness he saw written on her face helped lessen his own, just a little.

"I can't imagine how that must have felt," she said, "to lose your place like that."

"I don't pretend to understand now, any more than I did then, what He was thinking," Raum said with a shrug, finding the telling easier as he went along. "But I was tired of Uriel, tired of not being recognized for my own brilliance, and being told that my new job was to try and herd a bunch of willful primates into the sort of afterlife that had been denied my kind was the last straw. I had known a few already who had fallen, who'd left to start their own version of Paradise, where humans would only ever be allowed in at the mercy of their superiors—us."

"So you just…woke up one day and left?" Ember asked.

Raum looked at her and shook his head no, trying to form the words. But there was no real way to describe the agony he had gone through in the days and hours leading up to his decision. The punishment, by then, was already clear. There would be no forgiveness, and no coming back. And it had tormented him, more than he'd thought it would. But in the end, his youthful and wounded pride had decided him.

"I Fell in the early morning," he said, "on a beautiful summer's day. I remember looking around one last time, standing in the meadow near my home, smelling the flowers and hearing the birds sing. And then I closed my eyes. When I opened them again, it was all gone."

Ember's brown creased slightly, and he knew she didn't understand. How could she? But he wouldn't tell her what had passed through his mind as he'd closed his eyes, the things he had said in his turning away.

"Did it...hurt?" she asked.

"It was," he said, looking directly at her now, "the singularly most painful event in all of my existence. At that point I had to embrace the darkness or die. It was the thing I hadn't understood, that I wouldn't be able to so much as tolerate the Light. But in time, I found... other things...to sustain me. And there's your story, Ember. Here I am." He watched her closely, looking for any sign of revulsion, or worse, pity.

Instead, all he saw was his Ember, full of empathy for the foolish angel he had once been.

"Did you...do you still think you did the right thing?"

It was the question he had hoped she wouldn't ask him. And the one he couldn't answer. Because every fallen angel carried a little piece of what Hell was inside of him. And his piece was just that: the Hell of not knowing whether he had been right...and having to live with the suspicion that when all was said and done, he had made a terrible mistake.

"It doesn't matter," he said, his anger at Ember gone. And though he was loath to admit it, his burden was indeed a little lighter for the sharing. He still didn't intend to make a habit of it. But what could he tell her, Raum realized, that was more intimate than this? It was the core of who he was.

Shaken, Raum buried all of the roiling emotions

his tale had dredged back up. His hand tightened on Ember's, less affectionate than a warning. Her eyes widened, and he could see her confusion. But he could not let her know how close he had let her get. And how close he was to tumbling, out of control, into the thing he had feared since his happiness had died so long ago.

"Now tell me," he said, "about your dreams."

It was only much later, as Ember lay sleeping in his arms, that Raum could think clearly again.

The telling of it had exhausted her, of course. And he'd been happy to put what strength they'd each had left at that point to better, more pleasurable uses. But in the end, Raum had to admit that Ember's confession had been worth the price of his sorry tale.

He stroked her hair absently, lost in thought. Ember needed him more than he'd realized…and more than she had wanted to admit. It was interesting, that not wanting help was something the two of them shared in common. They were also both incredibly stubborn. And, he supposed they'd each given the other enough things to worry over tonight.

Raum thought it was a fair enough trade: he wasn't feeling as steady as he should, either, with all his unpleasant memories dredged up. At least now he knew how Mammon had tracked them, and how he intended to find his daughter once again. Security would be tightened, he was sure, once he spoke to Justin when the sun went down. But the bulk of Ember's added protection, Raum knew, fell to him.

There might be others who could do what needed to

be done. But he would never let them near her. And it was time he accepted that. No man would guard Ember Riddick's dreams but him. It was ironic, Raum thought with a faint and rueful smile, that he, of all creatures, should be responsible for giving a human peace. But Ember needed to rest. And at that point, he knew he had no choice.

He had resisted dipping into her dreams, fearing that it would only intensify their connection. It was an ability he'd rarely used, and then only to work against whatever foolish human he was toying with. But he'd sworn to protect her. And though his word, in the past, was made to be broken, in this he refused to back away.

So thinking, Raum curled more tightly around Ember and closed his eyes, sliding into her mind as easily as he might have slid into a deep, warm pool. Even as she welcomed him with undisguised delight into the lush forest of her dream, he felt the distant anger of another mind, locked out as he wound his protection around her sanctuary of pure thought.

That was soon forgotten, though, as Ember, clad in a flowing gown fit for a goddess, caught his hand in hers and looked at him with a barely remembered emotion that was no longer remotely disguised. And seeing it so clearly, after so many millennia without it, took his breath away.

"Come with me," she said, pulling him into the magic of her thoughts, despite the fact that he had come to her dressed as the warrior he had always been. His wings rose behind him, black as sin, and he wore only the leather pants and tall boots that afforded him freedom

of movement in battle. In his hand, he clutched the double-headed ax that had drawn the blood of countless wretched souls.

And still, Ember took his hand.

"Why?" he asked, truly bewildered that such a creature should look at him so, even seeing him as he truly was.

Ember's smile was as warm as the sun, as inviting as the moonlight he so often flew beneath.

"Because I love you," she said, as though it were the simplest, most obvious thing in the world. He knew he should resist, even as something he'd thought he'd killed long ago stirred in his breast in return. But as she led, he followed. And in sleep, he was unafraid.

In the darkness beyond both of them, where it could not touch them, something terrible howled its fury, and vowed vengeance.

Chapter 14

"Please take me to Amphora."

"No."

"But I want—"

"No."

Ember scowled at Raum's back and tried not to notice the way the muscles rippled as he pulled on a shirt. It was exactly as she'd feared: telling Raum about her dreams of Mammon had sharply curtailed her freedom. Terra Noctem, though cool, was making her a little stir-crazy right now. She exhaled loudly through her nose and tried again.

"Raum, I've done everything that's been asked of me. But seriously? I was not made to stay underground on a permanent basis. Everyone else goes above pretty regularly. So I don't get why you can't at least take me to the vamp club so I can breathe a little. I think we've established I'm not going to take off, and they're just *dreams*. It's not like he was actually showing up in my room every night!"

He turned to regard her, and because of his pause Ember had a quick second of hope that he might bend a little.

"No."

Ember gritted her teeth. She should have realized by now that *Raum* and *bend* should never be used in the same sentence. Still, it was beyond frustrating. Alpha males, she was coming to understand, were great in theory but kind of a pain in the ass in reality.

Even if the sex was indescribably amazing.

Ember sat up in bed and pulled her knees to her chest, glaring at him while he pointedly ignored her. She shoved a hand through her hair and sighed again. At least she was feeling good enough to argue with him, she supposed. Her nightmares had vanished the past few nights, replaced by the most amazing dreams about the man who was sullenly dressing in front of her.

She knew that somehow, Ram had figured out how to give her the rest she so desperately needed. She would have thanked him, if she hadn't known that he'd probably just give her a surly grunt as a reply. The man wasn't big on being recognized for his contributions. Which was fascinating, considering that lack of recognition had apparently been one of the things that had driven him to his Fall.

His story haunted her, as did the memory of the ancient, fathomless pain in his eyes when he told it. He'd seemed to think it would drive her away from him.

All it had done, Ember thought, was to make her love him more. It had been so easy, to listen and hear what he was really saying: he knew he had made a mistake. And he had spent lifetimes deadening his own pain by causing it for others.

She ached for him. And more than ever, she was certain that beneath the gruff and difficult exterior lurked the heart of a good man. But she would never tell him that, Ember thought with a smirk, lest he freak out and try to stab it to death.

Since he was leaving anyway, Ember tucked up her knees and finally asked Raum a question that had been plaguing her ever since she'd told him what was really going on in her head at night. He might go off in a huff, but he wouldn't be making an extra trip, she figured.

"So you never told me what he's like," Ember said. As she'd expected, it got Raum's attention. He turned to look at her warily.

"Who?"

"Mammon," she said. "You know, my father? Nobody seems to want to talk about him, but I think I'm allowed to be curious."

Raum didn't bolt, fortunately. But his lip curled, which wasn't a much better sign of forthcoming information.

"He's a highly placed demon in Hell, Ember. That should tell you everything you need to know."

Ember rolled her eyes back into her head, sick of that answer. "Bull, Raum. It's pertinent even if you don't want it to be. I mean, does being his daughter make me completely evil? Because I don't feel evil. I'm actually pretty nice most of the time. And all these vampires and whatever else, they seem pretty normal as far as personalities go. Some I like. Some I don't. But none of them seem like they're all about turning the world into a river of blood or anything."

He looked at her for a long moment before responding, and Ember was suddenly sure he knew exactly where she was headed with all of this. His response, though, was fairly neutral.

"You're half human, though" he said. "It makes a big difference. You're more," he paused, searching for the right word, "nuanced."

"And you're not?" she asked, her voice rife with skepticism.

"No," he said automatically. She'd known he would. But she could also see he didn't really believe it.

"So you're telling me that I was rescued by, and am sleeping with, the embodiment of pure evil." Ember said it drily, interested to see what he'd say with some prodding. Raum, however, was having none of it. She saw him look longingly at the door, but knew he wouldn't just go running. Yet.

He did, however, seem to know right where to hit her to end the conversation.

So much for being sneaky.

"Ember," Raum said gently, "think what you like about me, about the seven of us, misguided though it is. Whatever we are, we won't hurt you. But looking at Mammon that way is a mistake. He is not remotely human. And he has the ear of the king of Hell, a position he's worked very hard to get. He only wants you for what you can give him. There is no love there, sweetheart. He isn't capable of love."

It hurt her. And though Raum had her heart, she still found she couldn't quite accept it.

"How can he be all bad, Raum? I'm not, despite the things I've done."

Now he came to sit by her on the bed, his eyes bright with concern. "You've done nothing. And if you're referring to the man who tried to rape you, he got what he deserved."

So he knew. Ember wished she were surprised. But then, that night in Florida was something that had haunted her for a year now. Why shouldn't it follow her here, as well?

There had never been any question that it had been self-defense. The fact that she'd defended herself was not, in Ember's mind, the problem. Charlie Davies was scum, a serial rapist who should be locked up permanently, and would be if she had anything to do with it.

No, it was more how she'd defended herself that was the problem. The way she'd managed to put her attacker in the ICU for weeks, minus a hand, and probably even now muttering incoherently about glowing eyes and claws.

"I know he deserved it," Ember said softly. "But when it happened…it's like this switch flipped inside of me. There was no way I was going to let him hurt me. I wanted to teach him a lesson." Her eyes dropped, and her cheeks heated with the memory of what she had become: nothing less than a monster.

"He deserved it," Raum said, his tone brooking no argument. "And more."

"Maybe." Ember sighed. "Jail, he certainly deserved. But I'm not interested in being some kind of purveyor of vigilante justice. I'm no Batman."

Raum frowned. "Bat-who?"

Ember shook her head, and this time her smile was genuine. For all that he talked like a normal human, he was totally ignorant of pop culture. "I'll show you the movie sometime."

"You let the demon out," Raum said approvingly. "As you should have. It saved you, Ember. What do you think would have happened had you been just a human?"

She shook her head, disgusted with the memories and wishing she hadn't brought it up. "While it was happening, I...*enjoyed* it, Raum, hurting him. It was like I quit being me and started being something terrible. Something dark. I don't know why I stopped hurting him. He was screaming. Somehow that got through, just before the cops showed up, and I grabbed his knife so that it wouldn't look like...God, I don't know *what* it would have looked like. And then I was being painted as poor Ember, the helpless victim, when I'd sliced this guy's hand off. I couldn't take it. That was when I decided I had to go, start over someplace else. I'd drawn him just by being what I am, and then I found myself taking pleasure in destroying him." She shuddered. "It scared the hell out of me. And I swore it was never going to happen again." She looked at him beseechingly. "It isn't, is it?"

"That's why we're doing our best to keep Mammon

away from you," Raum said. "And why you're going to have to deal with being stuck underground for a while longer." He gave her a soft kiss before rising, and Ember knew that for him, the subject was now closed. But he surprised her when he added one more thing.

"You're not at all like Mammon, Ember. He enjoys killing. Remember that."

Something in his voice struck her as odd. Ember frowned up at him. "Were you and he friends?" she asked.

His eyes shuttered immediately, and Ember wanted to growl in frustration. Why did he insist on being so closed off from her? He'd shared the story of his Fall, yes, but not without heavy coercion. And this time, she had nothing to bargain with to get the truth.

"Demons don't have friends," Raum said. "But we all know one another well."

"You've got friends," Ember said, fighting back her irritation with him. Just when she'd think he was changing for the better, he put on the brakes and re-trenched. She'd seen it over and over again since they'd met. And sure enough, his next words were just what she expected.

"They're not my friends," Raum growled. "Being stuck with them doesn't make them friends."

"Okay, whatever." Ember sighed, and tucked a stray curl behind her ear. "But after meeting you and your *associates,* I think that even fallen angels have a lot more *nuance* than you want to think. You're all different. And I don't think you're all bad, either."

She saw with dismay that Raum's eyes had gone dead

cold. She felt herself starting to clench her jaw, a fairly constant problem where conversations with Raum were concerned, and forced herself to relax it.

"Damn it, Raum, why do you always get angry when I make the tiniest little suggestion that you're not such a bad guy?" she asked, letting her exasperation out. "Is it that awful that I l—that I *like* you?"

Oh God, she'd almost said it. Right out loud. And from the sudden look of terror on Raum's face, he knew it. *Oh God oh God oh God...*

"I have never pretended to be other than what I am," Raum said flatly, and there was something in his voice she had never heard before. Something ugly and dark.

"And what is that, Raum?" Ember asked, anger and growing desperation warring for supremacy within her. She didn't want to have this conversation. Not now, not ever. But it seemed she wasn't going to have a choice. And maybe it was better that she knew exactly where they stood, after all.

"What exactly are you, huh? I wish you'd enlighten me, because I'm confused. Are you the badass without a conscience, or are you the man who holds me while I sleep and worries about me enough to drive me crazy? Which is it?"

He stiffened, glaring at her as though he didn't even know her. And Ember knew, without him even saying, what the answer would be. She didn't think it was true... but what mattered was what Raum thought to be true. And she couldn't, she was realizing, do anything to change that.

Silently, she cursed herself for starting this. Every

time they had skirted the question of feelings, Raum had gotten his back up. The problem was, she couldn't keep herself from wanting more from him than she was getting. And her suspicion that he was still keeping things, important things, from her had only increased. She'd hoped that by being honest about her dreams of Mammon, Raum would begin to open up to her in turn…sort of a good-faith gesture on his part that their relationship, whatever it was, was deepening.

But it hadn't happened. And right now, Raum looked farther away than ever. She was a fool for loving a fallen angel. She knew it. The problem was, she couldn't seem to help it.

"I am Raum, Destroyer of Dignities and Robber of Kings," he said, his voice filling the room as though he had shouted, though his voice remained deep and even. "I have met the souls of the damned at the gate of Hell and dragged them into the Pits while they screamed for mercy. I have set villages aflame and cut down the righteous in Lucifer's name. And I did it with no regret, because I have no heart. I am a demon, Ember. I will still be here when you and all of Terra Noctem are dust. I'm not a human, and I'm not going to act like one. And if you believed otherwise, then I'm sorry." His voice softened only slightly, but that didn't make the words any less of a blow. "You were wrong."

His words, so unfeeling, crashed over her in a wave that would have taken her to her knees if she'd been standing. Because he'd meant it. Every word. And no amount of searching for hidden meaning or dancing around the subject any more was going to fix that.

Ember felt hot and hopeless tears rising in her throat, and only barely managed to hold them back.

She had given him what she had. And he had, in her eyes, just taken what small amount he'd seemed to give her in return back. It was time, Ember realized with a dull sort of horror, to call this thing with him what it was. A fling on his part. And a fantasy on hers.

"If all that's true," she asked, her voice little more than a hoarse whisper, "what are we doing here?"

She silently willed him to say something, anything that would restore the hope he had just ground to dust beneath his boot heel, to prove her instincts wrong. And there was, she saw, at least some emotion in his glowing eyes now, something powerful and indefinable. But he turned away from her and started for the door. There were no words. But it was an answer.

"Raum?" she asked, hoping she didn't sound as utterly devastated as she felt. He stopped, his hand suspended in midair as he reached for the knob. "Answer me. If you really have no heart, if you really are all that you say, then what are you doing…with me?"

He didn't even look at her, but paused, seeming lost in thought for long moments.

"I don't know," he finally said, so softly she could barely hear him.

Then he was gone. And, Ember thought as she let herself dissolve into tears, he'd made sure to leave the one heart between them broken.

Amphora, the crown jewel of the Necromancium empire, sat nestled between impersonal high-rises in the heart of D.C. Once an old government building done in the neoclassic style, it had been outgrown, crumbling and slated for destruction before Justin—Dru, in fact— had seen its potential. Now it was a dark, lush meeting ground for the underworld and often unsuspecting humans, a bastion of justice tuned rather more Dionysian. Opening only at sunset, part of the mysterious appeal that made it an attraction for residents and visitors alike, the sprawling marble temple now housed an acclaimed restaurant, a popular cocktail lounge featuring live music, a multitude of private rooms for more exclusive gatherings and one of the most fascinating draws—a sunken garden above which the buildings of the city soared.

It was to the garden that Raum headed, once he emerged from the well-worn path upward from the city far beneath. Terra Noctem had been many places over the course of its existence, shifting about beneath the Earth thanks to the magic will of witch and warlock alike. But it seemed fitting to Raum that they had for so long now left it situated beneath the American capitol. Perhaps it gave the council a sense of power, to play with the men and women who fancied they ruled the world.

Maybe the blood of the powerful tasted better. He had no idea.

It was early evening yet, and moody, sexy jazz had just begun to drift from the cocktail lounge. A harvest moon rode the sky, low and orange, visible between the surrounding buildings as it rose over the garden, a place of shadow and whimsy that had seen more than one human willingly taste eternity.

He was normally fascinated by all that the Necromancium had done. Tonight, however, the ambiance was lost on him. Because he was fairly sure that he had just managed to lose Ember, and all for the crime of being the only human to ever see any good in him. The only one to ever love him.

Raum closed his eyes as he paused at the top of the stone steps that led down into the sunken garden, and breathed in deeply. He needed to steady himself. To put the turmoil with Ember, who was foolishly hopeful that her father would be capable of being a true parent to her, aside.

She might be Mammon's daughter, but Ember was just like every other creature of the Light he had ever reviled. She saw goodness where there was none, possibility where there were only locked doors. And she scared the hell out of him…because she'd begun to make him wonder if some of the things she dreamed possible could be true.

The table was small, of wrought iron, and tucked in a partially secluded spot between a small fountain and a hedge clipped into the shape of a faun. Raum slid into the one available seat, looked into a pair of puzzled eyes that were the blue of Heaven at daybreak. He needed to concentrate on the matter at hand, Raum told himself.

"I wasn't sure you'd come," he confessed, bracing his elbows on the table and folding his hands in front of him.

Uriel looked surprised. "Did you not get my reply?"

"No, I did," Raum said, and shifted uncomfortably. "I just...well, this isn't really your kind of place."

Uriel smirked and looked around. "No. It isn't. But I couldn't refuse. I was too shocked to receive a message from anyone other than Leviathan. So what's so important that you've invited me out for a drink?"

"I wanted to talk to you about the situation with the Nexus."

"Interesting," Uriel said. "In fact, I wanted to speak to you about the same thing. It's been found."

Raum stared, incredulous. It was the last bit of news he'd been expecting. "How? When?"

"Only just. Gadreel arrived back in Johnstown three days ago, against his better judgment. Still he and Murmur managed to work together long enough to find it for us. Though I'm not sure they'll be speaking to one another for a while, from the sound of things."

"Where is it?" Raum pressed, his mind reeling with the implications. If the Nexus had been found, it was only a matter of time before it was closed, likely spilling angel blood in the process. But it would only solve a part of the problem.

Uriel's expression was as stoic as ever, unreadable. If he was excited or interested, he didn't show it. "Ember was drawn more strongly to the Nexus point than we knew. And considering she was there for a year, we are very, very lucky that nothing had happened when we found her."

"You mean, when I found her," Raum snapped, more

sharply than he'd intended. When Uriel's eyebrows rose, he simply continued, "It's her house, isn't it?"

"Very near it," Uriel said. "Are you sure there's nothing wrong?"

"Spare me the angelic-counselor routine," Raum grumbled. "No. But I don't think we want to seal the Nexus just yet. That's why I asked you here."

Uriel nodded, surprising Raum. "No. He'll never let her go that easily. And her ability can be used elsewhere, if he finds her. We've been considering…whether Ember might be willing to try to draw Mammon out. But I don't know how she would feel about that. Her only other option is to stay below permanently. And there is no guarantee Mammon won't eventually figure it out and destroy the city."

"Exactly," Raum said, pleased, if a little chagrined, to find that he and his old mentor were so much on the same page. "We use her to draw him out, and then we destroy him. It's dangerous, but it's the only way. Otherwise it won't end."

Uriel looked thoughtfully at him. "But Ember needs to agree. Her choice. Her father."

"Hell with that!" Raum snarled, drawing surprised looks from the customers around them with the force of his voice. He lowered it when he realized he'd drawn attention to them, but only a little. "Her father is scum. I know that better than anyone. And Ember makes bad choices. Her opinion in this doesn't count. It's for her own good."

"Raum," Uriel said, censure in his sonorous voice.

"Oh, don't," Raum said, shoving himself back in his

chair and crossing his arms over his chest defiantly. "I don't need a lecture on free will. Ember needs to do this, and she will."

"It's not your decision, Raum. It's hers."

Raum widened his eyes, exasperated. "The woman has this crazy idea her father loves her, Uriel! You and I both know that's not possible!"

Uriel's expression was guarded. "I've seen things just as strange. Just as improbable."

"Damn it!" Raum cried, slamming his fist down on the table hard enough to make the glasses jump. Uriel barely saved his from toppling.

"You're insane, both of you!" he ranted, not caring now about the looks he was drawing. "Things don't change. Not that much. Pretending it can be different doesn't make it possible. You're talking about sacrificing thousands of lives because one woman refuses to believe in reality. And you wonder why I left?"

Uriel simply watched him go off, looking unperturbed as Raum finished and waited, furious, for some sort of denial, some stupid argument he could use as an excuse to fight. Because he was itching for one now, feeling as if he had become the sole voice of sanity in all of this. At length, Uriel finally spoke. But they weren't the words Raum was hoping to hear.

"Tell me what's troubling you, Raum. Maybe I can help."

He hadn't intended to say it. Not now, not ever. But Raum heard it falling from his lips anyway. If nothing else, Uriel was the one being who would not ridicule him for it, who might try to understand.

"Ember Riddick is in love with me."

Uriel's hand paused in midair on its way to pick up his glass again. Raum watched him blink once, twice, as though ascertaining he hadn't misheard somehow, and then his motion resumed, though slowly. He took a thoughtful sip before replying, in a measured tone.

"Are you certain of this?"

Raum frowned down at his hands, folded on the table. "Yes," he said, his voice low. "I knew things were... changing...but it wasn't until I had to start protecting her dreams that I understood exactly what that change was."

"So she's told you she loves you in her dreams," Uriel said, as though he was digesting the words himself. "And this bothers you."

"Of course it bothers me," Raum growled, digging his hands into his hair. "I didn't sign on for this emotional stuff, Uriel. I said I would protect her, and I have. I said I would help you and the others hold back Hell, and I have. You didn't bother to mention that she was Mammon's daughter, and I didn't bolt. Or kill her just to be spiteful."

"We didn't know, either, at first," Uriel pointed out. "We only knew something was off. Again, the Infernal Council took us by surprise with this. I'm afraid they've been ahead of the curve for a while without our knowledge."

"Whatever," Raum said, letting it go. "Doesn't matter. She's not him. Nothing like him, in fact, which is amazing. Just the looks, and even that...well, she's better looking by a long shot."

Uriel tilted his head, a faint crease appearing between his brows. "I see," he said, and in that breath was a wealth of meaning.

"I don't think you really do," Raum said, frustrated. "I've been...we've been...well, that doesn't really matter, either, but things have gotten—"

"You have feelings for Ember, as well," Uriel said, and when Raum returned his full attention to him, the angel looked nothing short of amazed. It wasn't an expression he'd ever seen on Uriel, and he couldn't decide whether to be pleased that he'd put it there or just horrified.

Raum exhaled loudly, dropped his head onto the table, and finally, finally admitted the truth. "I don't know. Maybe," he muttered. When Uriel offered nothing, not a single word, not a whiff of support or sympathy, he added, "You're not helping. You're supposed to be helping. Giving a shit when it's completely nonsensical is your area, isn't it?"

"I thought Ember was nonsensical," Uriel said. When Raum didn't even bother with a response, he tried again. "First, tell me why you care for her. Then I'll see what I can do in the advice department," Uriel finally said. Raum lifted his head and saw that Uriel seemed, at least outwardly, to be serious, so he gave it a try.

"Okay. Ember...is different."

Uriel gave him an arch look. "I think you might want to elaborate."

Raum gritted his teeth. It was hard, harder than he'd expected, getting this out. "She makes me laugh. She *tries* to make me laugh, as well. She pisses me off, but I don't want to hurt her. In fact, I usually wind up more worried about *her* being pissed off. She's too sexy for her own good, but she has no idea. I like her smile. I like her smell, and her voice. And when I think of anyone hurting her I feel...I *feel*..."

He stalled out there, unable to quite articulate how that made him feel. But there was a rage that rivaled what he'd had in his darkest moments, mixed with fear and sorrow that threatened to take him to his knees.

"Don't tell me that after all this time, you've finally learned what it is to love," Uriel said quietly.

"No! Yes... I don't know!" Raum snarled, slamming his fist down on the table again. This time, he toppled his beer, though he couldn't bring himself to care. "I can't love her. I told her I had no heart, and I may have broken hers." He looked helplessly at Uriel, shaking his head. The angel had just articulated his greatest fear, and yet the moment it had been spoken, Raum knew it was true.

He loved her.

Raum sat, stunned by the truth of it, as all around him, people went about their lives. And yet inside, everything went still. He thought, fleetingly, of life without his fascinating little she-demon, and realized he wanted no part of it. He had fallen again. But this time, there was no shame. Only a rush of warmth, and a fleeting memory, like unexpectedly catching the refrain of a forgotten and much-loved song drifting on the breeze, of what it had once been to be full of grace.

"You remember," Uriel murmured. "You really do love her. I can see it."

Raum shuddered in a breath, his first in this strange

new world he had entered. A world where even one as fallen as he could find his heart.

"It's impossible," he said hoarsely. "I'm immortal, Uriel. She has a soul, something neither you nor I will ever have. How can I love her?"

"Raum, if you've remembered love, then you can remember one more thing, one more universal truth. Love never fails." Uriel's eyes were incredibly kind, and for once, Raum felt no need to shun it and turn away.

"I'm only an angel, Raum. I don't understand everything, or even most of everything. So much is above me, beyond me. The seraphim were made to be warriors, not philosophers or counselors. But that is one thing I have found to be true. Love never fails. Even death can't defeat it. Focus on that, instead of the fear, and the rest will work itself out in time."

Raum shook his head. "I don't know that it will. But I don't seem to have any control over it."

Uriel smiled, in the old way that Raum had nearly forgotten. Like a friend. There was a strange tightening sensation in his chest, and it was a few moments before Raum recognized another lost emotion: regret. They had fought, the two of them, since nearly the beginning of human time. It all suddenly seemed very pointless.

"I have only one thing to say that may be of use, then," Uriel said. "And that is that you probably ought to share the rest of whatever you need to say with Ember, instead of me."

"But I hurt her. Purposely," he admitted, appalled at himself now for what he had done. He had tried to push her away, and this time, he feared he might actually have succeeded. Justin had been right, after all. He had so many regrets he thought he might drown in them.

"You can heal it. I have faith in you." Uriel got to his feet, but not before Raum had seen the love and compassion on the angel's face that was a startling echo of long ago. It shocked him to his core...more, it humbled him in a way he had not thought possible any longer.

But this seemed a night for impossible things.

"Thank you for coming to me with this," Uriel said. "Believe it or not, I needed some good news."

Raum stood and inclined his head. "What about the rest of what we discussed? The Nexus?"

"Talk to Ember," Uriel said. "If you love her, trust her. It's her choice." Then he smiled. "Now go, before I chase *you* down there with a fire sword."

The night was young and, for the first time in a long time, ripe with possibilities heretofore not even imagined. With a final grin at Uriel, Raum rushed through the garden and back into Amphora, which was now crowded with more people than he ever cared to be around. Heedless of whether there was a clear path or not, he jostled, shoved and, finally, plowed his way through the crowd to get back to the lower level and the gates that opened back into the passage to the underground city.

Now that he had accepted what was in his heart, he was almost desperate to share it with Ember. Maybe Uriel was right, he thought, an almost violent hope springing to life within him. Maybe they would find a way. Maybe it was possible for one such as him to have a future that included someone like Ember.

His preoccupation made him blind until it was too late. The gates to the tunnels stood open, but unmanned, and his steps echoed off the cold marble floor in the unnatural stillness as he approached them, caught up in dreams.

"Hello, brother. It's lovely to see you, but you really do need to stop getting in my way."

He felt the claws at his neck, and then his hope, and the world, went pitch-black.

Chapter 15

Ember eyed the surly, uncommunicative fallen angel lurking at the edge of the building, glaring at the world with the violet eyes that would, on another man, have been irresistible. Her temporary babysitter seemed to be taking his duty very seriously. She'd tried to explain to him, once she'd gotten the nerve up, that she was pretty much fine as long as he checked in occasionally. What she'd gotten was a surly grunt and a dirty look, and more stalking.

Of all the Fallen, leave it to Raum to pick the only one she actually found scary to guard her in his absence.

Ember propped her hand on her fist while Dru chattered on about some fight between a shifter and a vamp at a club up in D.C. The two of them were cozily ensconced at a table at a little café called the Half Light. Terra Noctem was full of fascinating little nooks like this, and Ember still hadn't quite shaken the feeling that she'd wandered into the real-life version of Harry Potter's Diagon Alley. This version, however, was a lot sexier, and at least as dangerous.

"Okay, what's up? I started making things up about five minutes ago and you haven't said a word."

Ember blinked, startled, and then grinned sheepishly as Dru's words sank in. "Sorry. What did I miss?"

"The Huns had just invaded the Capitol Building."

She burst out laughing despite her miserable mood. "Now I'm really sorry I wasn't paying attention."

Dru's ruby lips curved into a self-satisfied smile. "You should be. You missed the orgy at the foot of the Washington Monument altogether. So, seriously, Ember, what's wrong? You haven't been with it all evening. Does it have something to do with Mr. Happy over there?" she asked, jerking her head in Meresin's direction.

Dru had become a closer girlfriend than Ember had ever dreamed she'd have, and in a very short period of time. But her position on the Fallen had never been anything but crystal clear. She didn't particularly like them, and she certainly didn't trust them. Unfortunately, that had put an important chunk of Ember's life off-limits for conversation in all but the vaguest sense.

What the hell, Ember thought. Dru was sympathetic, even if she didn't agree. And she needed to talk about it. Because ever since Raum had stormed out, she'd felt as if she was dying inside. The tears had stopped, eventually. And she hadn't had the heart to tell Dru no when the vampire had arrived with a dinner invitation.

Or maybe she just hadn't wanted to talk about it yet. But she did now.

"I don't know what I'm doing," she admitted, the words tumbling out in a rush. "He doesn't love me. I don't think he can. But I can't help it, because I'm an idiot, and now he's gone…."

And, oh God, the tears were back.

"Oh, sweetie, no, don't…oh, man, I'm sorry, Ember, I had no idea what was going on," Dru cried, distressed. She immediately came around the table and wrapped her arms around Ember's shaking shoulders.

Ember was mortified, but she couldn't seem to stop once she started. She rarely cried; it was a lesson well-learned as a child, when tears would only get her berated. Now, though, it seemed as if she'd opened the floodgates for something that had been building since this whole insane adventure had started. So she cried, and felt stupid and continued to cry.

The worst of it was, she knew she was right about him. Raum could be a mighty pain in the ass, and he was as prickly as they came, but he had saved her life when it probably would have made more sense to just let her go. He had hovered protectively to the point of annoyance. And when they were in bed, he made her feel not only wanted, but worshipped.

No, he was capable of a lot more than he gave himself any credit for. But the question was whether he would ever give himself the chance to *be* more than just an exiled demon. He was still determined to hold back. For as much as he would tell her, about himself or anything else, he might as well have been from Mars. And right now, he felt twice as far away.

Finally, the storm ebbed enough for her to regain her powers of speech.

"I j-just want to stop feeling th-this way about him if he can't return it," she sniffled against Dru's cool skin, which smelled faintly of incense.

Dru pulled away and brushed a gentle hand down Ember's cheek. Her red eyes were full of compassion. "I warned you, babe. They're not human, and they're takers. This actually isn't a bad bunch, but they're always takers. I'm just sorry you had to find out this way."

Ember huffed out a shaky breath, then grabbed her napkin and wiped her eyes with it. She could see the curious looks from the other customers out of the corner of her eye, but she was glad that no one seemed inclined to say anything.

"You really hate them, don't you?" she asked, amazed that their opinions of the Fallen could be so different.

Dru shrugged. "*Hate's* too strong a word. This group is better than before. I remember the ones who used to show up here, and the attitude is different." She smirked, then added, "Still bad, but different. But I want something concrete before I quit worrying. I want proof that *these* Fallen will help us, that they mean it. Because they always, and I mean *always*, have their own agenda."

"He told me to trust him," Ember said softly. "I start to think there's more, that I'm getting through. He sure doesn't like it when I'm out of his sight." She frowned. "That is, he didn't. But then tonight, I almost told him how I felt about him. And I think he knew. Because he freaked out."

"Freaked out?" Dru asked frowning, and Ember knew she was thinking of something violent.

"Nothing like that," Ember said, shaking her head. "He told me he had no heart, that he'd only ever be a demon and that I was wrong about him. And then he just…left. He had a meeting at Amphora, and he just walked away from me. Like I didn't mean anything."

Mammon's words, the ones that had gotten inside her head and refused to leave her, whispered insidiously in her memory: *I'm the only one who has ever cared for you. He'll only leave you. He'll use you to hurt me, and then vanish as though he had never known you.*

It fed the small voice in her mind that insisted that whatever he was, her father was the only one who actually loved her, who even *could* love her. That despite what Raum had insisted, a fallen angel could retain the capacity to feel such a thing. She was Mammon's child, after all. He had watched her grow up from her dreams. Would he really have done that if he didn't care?

And if he really didn't love her, could anyone?

Dru was watching her intently, and Ember had a sudden, terrible feeling that even her friend knew more about Raum than she did.

"What is it?" she managed to ask.

"He hasn't told you." It was a statement, not a question.

Ember looked at her for a moment, then shook her head slowly. "Whatever it is, if it put that look on your face, I doubt it."

She didn't want to know. She had to know.

Dru looked down, chewed nervously at her lip for a moment. "You know what? I think he should tell you himself. It might not mean anything. I thought it was pretty strange when I found out that he was the one watching over you, but this isn't—"

"Oh, no, you don't," Ember said, that anger flashing brightly again as she grabbed a hold of Dru's slim hand and refused to let go. "You'd better tell me, Dru. Because he's not going to. And this is important, because I *am* in love with him. So much it hurts. He's it for me."

Dru's beautiful face transformed into a mask of grief. "Oh, Ember..."

"Tell me." She heard the growl in her voice, knew she was heading for some strong emotion she wouldn't be able to control. Still, she needed to know.

Dru seemed torn, and Ember thought she was going to have to demand it again, but at length, she spoke in a voice quiet and apologetic and not at all like the brash, amusing vampire Ember had come to know. "I thought... or maybe I just hoped...that you knew. Especially since you just told him how Mammon was keeping track of you, in your dreams. Did...did things change between you two after that?"

"I don't know," Ember said, not understanding. "I don't think so." Had he clammed up on her more after that? He might have seemed more tired since then, but beyond that... Why couldn't she *think?*

"Why, Dru? Why would that have made a difference? He knew who my father was already."

"Yeah, he did," Dru said, a strange, unpleasant look

on her face. "But he didn't have such an easy way to get at him." When Ember only stared at her, utterly confused, Dru sighed and continued. "Raum and your father are the bitterest of enemies, Ember. Mammon is the reason Raum had to run from Hell. They've hated one another for as long as they've drawn breath. I don't know the details, but I do know that Mammon wants Raum's blood."

"And vice versa," Ember breathed, feeling as if all the air had gone out of her. Was that all she really was to him? A way to destroy his enemy?

"Pretty much," Dru agreed, but there was no sense of pleasure in her voice. "Their feud was legendary even before Raum went AWOL. It might mean nothing, or it might mean everything, Ember. I don't know, but this is what I mean about being careful with him, and all of the Fallen. Things are so often not what they seem."

"He was right," Ember murmured through lips that seemed to have gone suddenly numb. "He's just using me to hurt him... It's why he saved me... He was right."

Dru's brows drew together. "Who was right, Ember? What are you talking about?"

Ember shook her head. The hurt and betrayal welled up within her until she wanted to scream it. Instead, all she could do was swallow it back until she nearly choked on it. If Raum had explained it, if there had been any kind of reassurance that it hadn't mattered to him. But he'd kept it from her. They all had. What Mammon had been telling her fit so well. And now that Raum knew how to get at Mammon...

Her eyes widened in horror as she realized that

Kendra Leigh Castle 231

her dreams of Raum had likely been just as real as her dreams of Mammon. Had he been trying to draw Mammon in, as well, hoping for a final fight? Then she realized that if he'd been in her head, Raum already knew her secret: he knew she loved him.

And he'd still walked away without a word.

Ember closed her eyes and drank in a bolstering breath, trying not to let the pain of the truth cloud the facts. They had both used her. And she was done.

Ember pushed back her chair and stood up quickly. She felt slightly dizzy, her mind reeling from so much revelation. Dru stood, as well, her concern obvious.

"I'm so sorry, Ember. I shouldn't have told you."

Ember laughed, a strange, hollow sound. "Why not? No one else was going to. He probably would have waited, and then when the time was right, pulled me out as the secret weapon—"

Dru crossed her arms over her chest and shifted worriedly. "I don't know if that's what it is. He should have told you what the situation was, definitely. But, I mean, it's not for sure the worst-case scenario, Ember. You know I don't like them much, but you should really talk to Raum personally if you feel so strongly about him. Get it from him, not me. Kick his ass, if you need to! I just…I didn't want you to get hurt—"

"A little late for that," Ember said with a hard, mirthless smile. But Dru's crestfallen look had her softening a little. She came around the table and embraced her friend. "Dru. I needed to know. Either way, this is important. One of them is the man I love. One of them is my father. And at this point, I don't know if I should be within a mile of either of them."

"You need to stay away from Mammon, at least," Dru replied, eyes darkening. "He's nothing like these Fallen, Ember. I've met him. You don't want to."

"My first priority is finding Raum," Ember replied, dodging the advice. She needed to find him, confront him. The need to finally know the truth, all of it, from him was overwhelming. She knew he would never love her the way she loved him. One thing she'd learned was that Raum was a creature incredibly resistant to change, and he would never let the daughter of a mortal enemy into his heart, if he even had one. Still, he'd seemed to at least care for her. She clung to that, even though it was still going to have to be over between them. She couldn't put herself through the pain of having only part of him anymore.

But if it turned out he had only been using her, if he really felt nothing, Ember knew she would see it. And if that was the case, she was leaving Terra Noctem altogether. She couldn't return to Johnstown for long, but she'd get what she could together and figure out something else, far away. She'd take her chances on her own. Because having protectors seemed to have gotten her nothing but hurt. They'd come after her...but she had a few tricks up her sleeve that she hadn't shared with anyone.

Right now, she was glad she'd kept that small bit of information to herself.

"Please help me, Dru," she said. "I have to find him."

"Now?"

Ember nodded. "I have to talk to him. I have to know."

Dru looked at her so long, and so intensely, that Ember began to worry she wasn't going to find help even here. But finally, Dru nodded. "Okay. But just a look in Amphora, Ember, and I'm coming up right behind you. If he's not there, I want your word you'll come right back down here. You should be safe there, but I don't really blame Raum for telling you to stay put."

"I promise," Ember said, hoping she didn't have to break her word to the only real girlfriend she'd ever had. "And thank you, Dru. This means everything."

"You're reminding me why I swore off falling in love years ago." Dru sighed. Then she slid a sidelong glance over to Meresin, still looking both bored and ornery only a few feet away.

"I think we need a diversion," Ember murmured. She'd forgotten about Meresin, who could create deadly electricity out of thin air to threaten people with, and who was legendary for his incredibly nasty temperament.

Dru grinned then, baring her fangs and surprising Ember with the flash of humor. "No worries, babe. You leave it to me, and get your butt out of here as soon as he's preoccupied. Got it?"

She nodded.

Dru took a deep breath and stood. "Good luck, Ember. I'll be right behind you."

Then Ember watched as her friend tossed her pale, shimmering hair over her shoulders and didn't just walk, but prowled over to where Meresin was standing. At that point, she had a feeling about what was coming, but that didn't make it any less amazing to see Meresin finally realize he was about to have company, start to formulate some nasty comment or other, only to wind up with his mouth slightly open when Dru grabbed him by the shirtfront and hauled herself up to accost him with a kiss so scorching that Ember could actually feel the blast of heat where she was standing.

She had only a split second to be impressed, however. If she was going to vanish, it had to be now. She had only a glimpse of Meresin's hands fisting in the material at Dru's back before she ran. All she needed was the smallest head start before she could make it so Meresin would never find her.

She felt, just for an instant, the spark that was Meresin flare as she left him. She flashed through busy streets, trying to remember the twists and turns that led to the edges of the city. Her heart constricted painfully in her chest, fluttering wildly like a caged bird as she was gripped with renewed urgency: she had to find Raum, *now*. And just when it began to feel that it might burst free, she began to see the word that, to her, meant every-thing right this moment.

Amphora.

She found herself rushing upward, winding at a dizzying speed up twisting tunnels toward the world she had left behind. It was a wonder, Ember thought, the way she could navigate in the blink of an eye to avoid so much as touching another person. The vampires, the shifters, all moved with supernatural speed, but she surpassed them all.

A wonder. Or it would have been, Ember thought bitterly. But she couldn't take any joy in it, and even as the sweet scent of the fresh night air flooded her nostrils, the hair on the back of her neck prickled strangely. She passed through heavy doors, through an ornate archway, and stopped, at last, to find herself standing in the shadows of the club that was the gateway between the Above and Below.

She did not wait for Dru.

The light was low and violet, gleaming off the rich mahogany wood of the circular bar that dominated the center of the dining room. Ember strode through quickly, knowing her hair alone would attract unwanted attention in her direction. And indeed, the faces of the patrons, some human, some less so, turned to watch her pass.

She didn't see Raum. Worse, didn't *feel* him.

Damn it, I'm going to get caught.

But no one stopped her, so she could only assume no one who actually knew she was supposed to stay below was in attendance. She figured she could just go Warp Speed again if she had to, and by the time anyone would be asking about the renegade redhead, she'd be long gone.

Despite all her instructions, Ember breezed out the massive front doors, which were opened for her by two dark, lean men who acknowledged her passing with slight bows. Their eyes flickered reddish as she passed, and she knew they scented her blood. The confusion she saw let her know they also could scent that she was no ordinary human. She wondered, in passing, if there were other non-*nefari* half-breeds out there, children of the Fallen.

For the world's sake, she hoped not.

Raum, she thought, *where are you?*

He wasn't here. But someone else was.

She felt him before she heard him, that familiar voice that had always inspired both love and revulsion in her. Every hair on the back of her neck stood up, and her vision swam for a moment before returning to her.

"I'm glad you've finally come to your senses," he purred. "I've been waiting, my child."

Ember turned, and the turning seemed slow, endless. Finally, though, she laid eyes on him at last: her father. He leaned casually against the lamppost, his handsome face half in shadow. He was dressed casually, but smart: button-down shirt, khaki pants, a light jacket left unbuttoned. The light gleamed on the copper of his hair. He looked beautiful, and dangerous.

"Father," she said softly. The word felt unfamiliar on her tongue, but it seemed to please him. He shifted, catlike, away from the post and came toward her, looking exactly like what he was. A predator.

"Ember," he said, stopping only inches from her. His nearness was oppressive, suffocating, and yet she couldn't bring herself to move away. He lifted his hand to brush her hair away from her face, and the feel of his warm skin on her own made Ember shiver with distaste. *He's like Raum,* she thought. *The same. Not black, but gray... Whatever he is, I came from him, and he can't be all bad.*

But his eyes, glittering fathomlessly as they looked at her, were like looking into some terrible abyss.

"I don't want to hurt anyone," she said, her voice sounding weak and pleading to her own ears. Even now, she could feel his power reaching inside her, throwing open every dark door that she had locked against her most wicked impulses. And now she scented more on the night air. She smelled the promise of burning, and blood. And though she fought it, it made her quiver. This time, with desire.

"Oh, my sweet, naive child," Mammon crooned, his eyes filling her vision until they seemed to encompass the world. "It's not about what you want. It never has been. It's about what I want, what I need. And if I say you'll bathe in the blood of your lover, if I tell you to lead my legions to set fire to all the world, you'll do it, and gladly. I will make you the most terrifying demon of your kind. Because you're mine."

Then he spoke the words she had always longed to hear. But falling from Mammon's lips, they were only a twisted mockery of all she had dreamed.

"I love you, Ember."

Chapter 16

Raum stirred back to awareness slowly, groaning with the bright burst of pain that accompanied the movement. He wasn't sure where he was, only that he hurt. It was against his better judgment to open his eyes, when drifting back downward into silent darkness was so much more comfortable. But then a voice cut through the unpleasant haze of his discomfort, and he had no choice to but to rejoin the present.

"I warned you, Raum."

Justin. Raum's eyes flickered open, and he saw several things at once: that he was in a small, cell-like room, that his wrists and ankles were encircled by manacles made of a sort of stone he'd hoped never to encounter, and that the vampire king looked more furious than he had even thought him capable of, which was saying something.

Furious, but that wasn't even the worst of it. He looked crushingly disappointed.

That was when Raum knew something had happened. And though not a word had been said to explain, he knew what that something must have been.

"Where is Ember?" he asked, his voice sounding hoarse and strange to his own ears. The flash of violence in Justin's eyes only confirmed his suspicions. She was gone. He had failed.

Hello, brother.

"Mammon," he growled, memory flooding back to him. "Damn it, Justin, why am I chained up? Mammon found me. Does he have her? I have to find Ember...."

"Oh, you've done enough, demon," Justin snarled. "I don't suppose you remember the *nefari* who dragged your worthless carcass back here, since you were indisposed at the time, so I'll just remind you of the message that was sent along with you. *Hell doesn't deal with traitors.*" Justin's glittering red eyes dropped to Raum's torso. "I suppose that'll heal in time, but I wish it wouldn't. You have no honor, Raum. I'd hoped that had changed, but I was wrong."

Raum sucked in a breath when he struggled into a position where he could look down at himself, though the manacles were on short chains and tugged at skin that felt raw. He felt weak, his strength sapped by the onyx wrapped around his limbs. Scrawled across his chest was the word *Traitor,* formed of long red slices that oozed as he moved.

Something had been rubbed into the wounds so they would heal more slowly. Raum could feel the burning of it nestled deep in his skin. Still, he could barely spare a thought for it. His muscles bunched and flexed, and he gave the chains as hard a yank as he could manage.

The effort left his muscles shaking, but he was determined not to show it.

"Damn it, Justin, where is Ember?"

"Gone," Justin said flatly. "Went to find you, as a matter of fact, so you can at least be proud that you're responsible for getting her into her father's hands. It's my understanding that she walked right into them. Probably ran into them, once he told her how you'd tried to exchange her for your old title and position."

It was sinking in now, what he was accused of, and Raum thrashed harder against the chains, arching when the pain now ripped through him.

"Don't be an ass, Justin!" he snarled through gritted teeth, beginning to sweat with the effort he was expending. "I've done no such thing! Now unchain me. If Mammon's got her, there's no time!"

Justin, however, made no move. There was a sinking feeling in the pit of Raum's stomach then, and he realized that this time, Mammon had managed to get him into a position he couldn't get out of, couldn't just run from, in more ways than one.

"You've done enough," Justin said. "Those *nefari* came from Lucifer himself. You went right to the top, I'll give you credit for that. But then, you never did anything half-assed. That was always the problem with you."

Raum struggled to control the bellow that wanted to tear from his throat. Rage would do him no good now: Justin was a cool, analytical creature, and he'd be expecting a guilty temper tantrum from him. He would have to stay focused if he wanted any hope of getting out of this.

"Justin," he tried again. "I met with Uriel tonight at Amphora. You can check this. As I was leaving, Mammon got me from behind. I wasn't expecting it, I should have been looking, but I wasn't. I thought it was safe, and that was stupid of me. But I give you my word, no meeting between any aspect of Hell and myself took place except in the most involuntary sense."

The vampire shook his head slowly. "You disgust me, Raum. A demon's word is worthless. Always has been, always will be. All anyone saw was you meeting with someone who matches Lucifer's description." His lip curled. "Though I'm sure Uriel would be thrilled to know you were using him as an excuse."

"Did you forget that Lucifer and Uriel have the same coloring?" Raum snapped, furious that he'd played so easily into this setup without even realizing it. Few of the vampires knew any angel or Fallen by name. There had been no contact for too long. So of course no one would have known it was Uriel he was sitting with. Just a huge, intimidating blond with an ethereal air about him.

And Lucifer had never lost the look of the light-bearer, no matter how dark he got.

Now Raum did give a growl, pulling with all his might against the chains that bound him to the wall and ignoring the fire that shot through his body. "Hellfire, Justinian! I am no traitor! And I would think that you'd at least consider my word against theirs... I may be a demon, but I don't have a monopoly on lying!"

Something flickered briefly in Justin's eyes that gave Raum an instant of hope, but that was quickly dashed.

"Maybe you're right, Raum. Likely you're lying through your teeth. And either way, you're now responsible for whatever happens when Mammon uses Ember to blow the Nexus wide-open," he said, his voice turning bitter. "She was seen speaking with a red-haired man right outside Amphora, and then she was gone. She followed your pathetic, unworthy ass because she has feelings for you."

The thought of it, the mental image of it, was a body blow that took the wind out of him. He'd been gone too long, and the stubborn little she-demon had come to find him. Because she loved him, and was probably worried when he hadn't returned...

He made a noise—a soft, pained noise—when he thought of it. She was an innocent, and he had inadvertently placed her in hands that were very capable of twisting even that into something dark and terrible. She loved him, and it had destroyed her.

"I've been a fool," he rasped.

"That's something we can agree on," Justin said. "But if it makes you feel any better, Raum, I've been a fool, as well."

He started to turn away, but Raum couldn't let it happen. He had too many questions, and a now desperate need to make Justin believe him, to get out of here.

"Wait!" he growled. "What about Meresin? He was

supposed to be watching her! How did she even get away?"

The vampire's shoulders stiffened, and though he didn't turn around, he did answer, after a moment. "Drusilla thought she was helping. She...distracted Meresin. To his credit, he's completely enraged about what happened. And my sister will be punished, though she meant well enough. Provided she survives the next few days, that is."

Raum frowned, not understanding. "Why wouldn't she?" he asked, stunned that anyone could have distracted Meresin from anything. He was both angry and frighteningly single-minded.

"We won't pay for your sins this time, demon," Justin said, and it was then that Raum realized the vampire had refused even to use his name. He had ceased to exist as an individual in his eyes. He was only the word that was scrawled upon his chest. He was a traitor.

"We will make a stand against Hell, and hope that the angels find adequate proof that we don't harbor their enemies. I won't have my people picked off the way they were the last time. I won't have this city destroyed, and lives lost, for you. Not again. And when, and if, this is over, and we survive, your kind will be banned from this place for the rest of time. I swear it. I take this betrayal on my own shoulders, and it's enough."

Then he did walk away, leaving Raum chained to the wall and staring after him in disbelieving horror.

He had only one choice now, and he wasn't even sure he had the strength to manage it. He cursed whoever had discovered that onyx, among all the stones, had the power to weaken and hold a demon. But for him, there was one way out. Justin must have known, and hoped he would save him the trouble of tossing him out himself. Otherwise, he would have used a great deal more onyx. As it was, Raum thought he had enough strength to return to the one place he was tied to. Even if it would mean his death, to stay here meant worse.

And, Raum thought, he was beginning to understand that there were things worse than death. Even for a soulless creature like him.

His eyes slipped shut, and he focused every fiber of his iron will on a single point in space. And though no one was there to see, his figure faded slowly away, out of the halls of Terra Noctem.

And into another, darker plane of existence altogether.

Ember stared out the high arched window that looked out upon the Infernal City, her elbow propped on the marble sill. A hot wind ruffled her hair, carrying with it the faintest breath of brimstone. She wrinkled her nose against it, and wondered how anyone ever got used to that, to the faint stench about this place.

The city was opulent, decadent. Beautiful, even. But Ember's sensitive ears could still pick up the faint cries of the human souls from the vast wasteland that surrounded this desert metropolis. From this high up, locked away in her tower like a faerie-tale princess in a worst-case scenario, she could see all the unnerving landscape that Hell had to offer, depending on which window she chose: the strange rivers she'd seen in her dreams, the broken paths winding away toward foreboding cliffs, a dead-looking ruin of a forest and endless desert fading away to mist.

Her father was a monster. All of them were, in this place, Ember thought, recalling the beautiful, courtly creatures who had welcomed her with shining eyes and biting smiles. Their appearances were nothing more than pretty masks that covered up untold horrors beneath. Whatever darkness lurked within her, she didn't belong here.

But Mammon seemed to understand how to rouse the demon in her, and Ember was terrified that somehow, he would kill all she had that was human, and good, and twist her into a thing like he was. Was it possible? She didn't know. But there was no question in her mind that he would try.

"Raum," she whispered, mentally reaching out for him, wishing she could feel even the faintest hint of him. Mammon had done something to him, though he wouldn't quite say what; only that the traitor was finally getting what he deserved, and that she wouldn't need to worry about him anymore.

The possibilities made her sick. And anytime now, she was going to be trotted up to the surface and expected to...

Ember shoved away from the window to resume pacing in the small chamber. She didn't want to think about it.

A soft flapping noise caught her attention then, and for a moment, she was swept back to the night Raum had appeared at her bedroom window. Of course, he hadn't looked quite himself, but that had changed soon enough. She wished she could turn into something else, even a spider, so she could scoot out through a crack or something. As it was, she was pretty sure she wouldn't weather hurling herself out the window very well.

"Ember?"

She couldn't turn, couldn't move. It couldn't be real. Either she was losing it, or Mammon had decided to torment her as part of this whole package.

But then it sounded again, and it was hard to believe that even Mammon would be able to fake the sound of emotional pain so convincingly.

"Are you all right? Has he hurt you?"

It was him. Ember whirled around, and the sight of him, big and battered, with his beautiful black wings spread behind him, was almost her undoing. Then she saw his eyes, glowing faintly, and the worry and pain that were so clearly written in them.

She'd looked into a true demon's eyes, and they were nothing like what looked back at her now, reflecting all the things he'd denied being able to feel. Maybe it wasn't love, Ember thought. Maybe he'd been right, that he wasn't capable of loving her. But for right now, that Raum felt for her at all was enough.

He was the sweetest sight she'd ever beheld.

Ember made a sound, some sort of strangled whimper, before stumbling forward, her arms desperate to convince herself that he was really there, that she wasn't dreaming.

He met her halfway, and then her arms were wrapped around him as he lifted her off her feet, crushing her to him. Ember clung to him, breathing him in as though she'd been suffocating. Incredibly, she could feel him trembling against her as he buried his face in her hair.

"I thought I wouldn't find you," he said roughly, pulling back to cover her face in kisses that she matched with her own. "I thought I was too late."

"And I thought he'd killed you," Ember returned, winding herself around him tightly, terrified that he'd vanish as soon as she let him go. "I'm so sorry, Raum. I was pissed off and worried, and he was just waiting for me to do something stupid."

"No," Raum said, shaking his head. "He was ready to make his move, Ember. We all got too comfortable." He stroked her hair, and the tenderness in it was nearly the undoing of her poor, misguided heart. "If it's anyone's fault, it's mine. I shouldn't have said the things I did. Just tell me he hasn't hurt you."

The admission startled her, but she didn't want to make it into something it wasn't. She shook her head.

"No, but…I don't like how he makes me feel, Raum. Less controlled. Like he's got a better handle on my demon half than I do. So I hope you're planning to get me out of here, because I don't think we have much time before Project Nexus gets underway."

Slowly, gently, Raum unwound himself from her and lowered her feet back to the floor. But, Ember realized with wonder, he kept tight hold of her hand, as though he was just as worried as she that one of them would suddenly vanish.

Something had changed, she realized. Something fundamental in Raum seemed to have shifted. But what it was, and what it meant, were things that couldn't be explored here, in this awful place.

It was then that she noticed the angry red lines etched into Raum's chest, and realized what they spelled. She hesitated at first, but unable to resist, she reached out to brush her hand against the wounded skin. He didn't flinch, but the strain showed in his face.

"He hurt you." As she said it, her voice devoid of inflection, a terrible, black rage began to boil within her. It was like how she'd felt the night she'd been attacked, but worse. Because this was someone she loved, and she hadn't been able to stop it from happening. Violent images began to cascade through her mind, horrible thoughts of what she would do to Mammon when she got her hands on him.

He had hurt what was hers. No one hurt what was hers.

She felt Raum's pulse leap beneath her fingers before she let her hand fall away.

"What did he do to you?" she asked, and her voice was almost unrecognizable.

"It doesn't matter," Raum said. "Lock it down, Ember. You've got to, if we're going to get out of here. Inciting a bloodbath is only going to end badly for us. It's two against legions, remember. You can't win on their ground."

"I can't lock it down!" she hissed, unable to see anything but that word cut into his skin. *Traitor.* Traitor to what, to monsters like her father and his buddies? "They need to be stopped, Raum! I hadn't realized how horrible they were. This place," she said, her voice beginning to break as the reality of it came crashing down around her. "How did you live here for so long?"

He took a step away, and even that small distancing sliced through her like the blade of a knife.

"I was what they are, Ember. I'm not anymore, you were right about that. But I was, for a very long time. I was dark and selfish and cruel. Even when I had to run, I wasn't so different. Disillusioned, maybe. Then...I met you," he said softly. "The daughter of my enemy. The last thing I expected."

Her heart sank at his words. "Why are you saving me if that's how you see me?" she asked, willing him to say the one thing that could make it all right. The only thing she yearned to hear from him.

Raum shook his head. "Not here," he said. "I have things to say, but not in this place."

Things to say. Whatever that meant, Ember doubted it would be what she wanted. But she would take it. She had to, Ember thought defiantly, even as a hole opened inside of her she wasn't sure would ever be filled. And when they got out of here, she had a few things to say, as well. She was going to tell Raum how she felt about him. She knew she would never forgive herself if she didn't, come what may. Then...well, then they'd just see.

Escape, however, was first.

"We have to—"

"Hellfire," Raum said, then thrust her behind his back as the door swung open. "Do as they say. And trust me."

Chapter 17

She'd tried to do as Raum asked, to trust that he knew what he was doing even when the horned guards had dragged him from her room. To hang on to hope even when her father had arrived not long after, almost dancing with his glee as he escorted her out, promising a spectacle he was sure she wouldn't want to miss.

But by the time she had been seated in preparation for Raum's very public execution, that fragile hope had all but evaporated.

Ember watched from the Council's private box in the Coliseum Inferi, every inch of her body screaming in pain from the thin silver cords that she had been bound with. Not only did they bite into her skin, but from the moments her father's *nefari* lackeys had begun to wrap them around her, she'd been possessed of an ache so deep it seemed to come from deep within her bones.

All around her, Fallen and *nefari* alike screamed their approval as Raum was marched into the massive structure so much like the one in Rome she'd seen photos of. This one, however, was shining and intact, and the red stains on the walls around the dirt floor left no doubt as to what sort of entertainments this place was used for.

They were going to kill him, Ember had been assured. But first, they were going to hurt him. And she was expected to watch, even if her eyelids had to be sewn open.

Trust me. She wanted to, even on this. But how was Raum sacrificing himself to the whims of the Infernal Council going to solve anything? She slid her eyes to her left, where her father was watching the scene unfold with undisguised glee. On her right sat a *nefari* guard, whose face seemed to consist of mostly very long, very sharp teeth set below a pair of tiny black eyes that gleamed with ratlike intelligence.

Beside her father, a row of the Fallen sat upon thrones fashioned of precious gems and human bones. They were all as beautiful as angels, but their eyes, Ember had seen, were as dead as Mammon's. She had been introduced, with great fanfare, upon her arrival in Hell, and their names were so odd that they were easy to remember. There was her own father, the Prince of Avarice. Then came Belial, Prince of Sloth, Moloch, Prince of Anger, Beelzebub, Prince of Envy. And in the middle of all of them, his throne grander than the rest, with the bones of his throne dipped in platinum and gold, was Lucifer.

His beauty was almost too blinding to look at, with

his golden curls and wide, expressive blue eyes, his porcelain skin that glowed with good health. But his wings were as black as his heart, and instead of being feathered, as those of the other Fallen were, his were leathery like a bat's. Or a dragon's. And the pupils of those wide eyes were almost completely jet black, rimmed only faintly with a ring of purest blue.

All of them were frightening. But Lucifer was absolutely terrifying. Especially when he smiled, as he did now.

"Well, Raum. I hadn't really expected to see you here again so soon," Lucifer said, his voice like music. "I can't say we've all missed your charming company. But since we have it again, might as well have a little fun, don't you think?"

The crowd erupted into more raucous cheering at his words, and the King of Hell seemed pleased.

Ember tried to catch Raum's eye, if only so he knew she was there, if that could lend any comfort. But Raum stood proudly, naked from the waist up and clad in only the same leather pants that she'd seen him wear in her dreams. He carried his wings high behind his back, looking every inch the fallen angel as he glared defiantly up at the King of Hell.

"So," Lucifer continued smoothly. "What shall we do with you, hmm? We've had a number of interesting ideas from the others, but we'd really like to hear some input from you. It'll be so much more satisfying that way. But make it good, Raum. How would you deal with a filthy traitor like yourself? I like the artwork, by the way," he added, turning to Mammon. "Nice touch."

Ember felt herself leaning forward to catch his answer, and saw that the rest of the audience had done the same, silence falling like a stone over the Coliseum. She needn't have, though: when Raum spoke, his sonorous voice echoed easily throughout the structure.

"Brother King," he said, inclining his head and bowing slightly from the waist. "I submit that I am no traitor. And I would like a chance to settle things once and for all between myself and Mammon."

Lucifer pursed his rosebud lips, obviously displeased. "There is nothing to settle. He presented evidence that you meant to infiltrate the Council by pushing him from it, that you meant to influence the others to derail the important work that Hell has before it. You would have been the ruin of us all. Your dissatisfaction was not unknown to us before, Raum the Destroyer. But worse still is your association with the *seraphim*." Lucifer nearly spat the word. "How can you deny that you've joined with them to work against us? How is that not the lowest treachery?"

Raum looked up, and Ember was stunned at how calm he seemed. Especially because she knew how much his blood must be boiling just beneath the surface. The letters on his chest had barely begun to fade, and they still seemed to glow in the odd red light of this place.

"With all due respect, your highness, I was given no choice but to deal with the angels."

Lucifer snorted. "There is always a choice. Better to die than serve Heaven again."

"Better to live, to regroup and to plot another day,"

Raum replied. "Death is a stupid thing to invite when you have no soul. We've always done what was needed to survive. You taught us to."

Lucifer's lip curled. "I did not mean you should kiss Uriel's sandals. And if you thought so, you are the stupid one. However," he continued, "there is a small kernel of sense in what you say. Continue."

Over the discontented murmurs of the Council, Raum did just that. "The Prince of Avarice would not have gotten where he is if he were not one of Hell's most adept liars. I ask what I'm due for my many years of service to you, Lucifer, and for what I've been lowered to since I left here. The right to draw Mammon's blood is mine."

Lucifer bared his teeth. "Are you insinuating that he could possibly have fooled us?"

"I'm saying," Raum said, his voice smooth and soothing, "that he may have taken great advantage of his close relationship with you to destroy a political enemy. But he's not worth the price of what he destroys. I submit that Mammon is the one who has been seeking influence. I care not for my own life, but for your perception, and the glory of the Infernal, of the Fallen. He has destroyed me just to see if he could. I was an asset to Hell. What will he choose to destroy on a whim next, at cost to you? I would not see you Mammon's puppet, sire."

Mammon's face went as red as his hair. "Lies!" he bellowed, his fangs bared. "Miserable traitor, he has no shame! Let the Behemoth tear him to pieces, and then we'll throw them into the Phlegethon!"

The crowd erupted again along much the same lines, but Lucifer's shout was deafening and silenced them all. "Enough! Shut up, all of you!" He looked speculatively at Mammon, and Ember heard him say, in a soft, contemplative voice, "You *have* always hated him. And maybe I have given you too much influence over my decisions."

Mammon paled. "I…I never wanted anything that was not for the good of Hell, my king. Raum is a traitor, he—"

Lucifer waved away the words, silencing Mammon with a quick motion of his hand. A small smile played about the corners of his lips, and Ember shuddered at the dark promise in his eyes.

"Yes, yes. He's a demon through and through. Hard to argue with that. And hard not to appreciate it. You know," he said conversationally, "you have been a bit insufferable about having been the one to sire the next Breaker. And it *has* been quite a while since we had a proper grudge match for entertainment."

Ember listened, amazed. Raum had played so easily on Lucifer's inherent bloodlust and enormous pride. And she was pretty sure he was about to get what he wanted. Unfortunately, that had nothing to do with escape and everything to do with revenging himself at last on her father.

Doubt tried to creep in, then, when she remembered what Dru had said: *They're takers. And they've always had their own agenda.*

TRUST ME.

The words pushed into her head, as loudly as a shout.

She flinched, and stared closely at Raum, trying to see if there was any indication he had done that, or if it had just been wishful thinking on her part. She saw nothing, but his voice, heard in such an intimate way, left her with renewed hope that he knew what he was doing. The doubt was banished, at least for now.

If they started tearing him limb from limb, though, maintaining that hope was going to be a problem.

"What would your choice of weapon be, then, Raum? And make it good, or you'll lose our interest."

Raum's answer was automatic. "Fire sword."

A murmur ran through the crowd then, and Ember gathered that this was a weapon that the denizens of Hell could get behind. Which worried her immensely. Lucifer's brows winged upward.

"Well. That is a good one, if a bit expedient for my taste." Then he grinned. "I know, why don't we put it to your lovely daughter, Mammon? The one you've got all wrapped up for us over there. You've told us often enough how brilliant, how utterly advanced she is. And of course, how *devoted* to her dear father," he added, his grin widening as his gaze shifted to connect with Ember's. She only barely stifled the scream that welled in her throat.

"Tell us, dear girl, how would you like to see these two off one another?"

"She's unreliable in this matter, your highness!" Mammon yelped. "He came down here to steal her, he's been *touching* her, and you know that's the one thing that clouds a she-demon's mind!"

"You disgusting pig," Ember snarled, finally finding her voice through her anger. "What am I, then? A princess or a whore? So much for *my dearest* and *sweetheart,* huh?"

"It's possible to be all of the above, you know." Lucifer chuckled. "But we think Mammon may have exaggerated your devotion to him somewhat, hmm?" He looked thoughtfully at Raum. "He does have a point, though. Why would you want to steal her, unless everything he's accused you of is true?"

Raum shrugged then, and Ember felt a chill crawl over her skin at his cold smile. She hadn't seen him smile like that before, ever. It was a reminder of what he was. What he *had been,* Ember amended. He was no demon any longer. That, at least, was something she knew to be true, perhaps the only thing that was true in this horrible place.

Raum shrugged and shot a knowing smirk in her direction.

"Look at her, sire. Wouldn't you consider a she-demon like that an added bonus?"

Lucifer erupted into delighted laughter, and the crowd followed suit. All, that was, except Mammon. He turned his head to glare at her with dark promise. "You'll need to be taught a lesson after this, dearest, about obeying your father."

Ember smiled sweetly, and then spit directly into his face.

The blow he gave her then rocked her head back and made her see stars, but it had been worth it to see the astonishment that she would dare to do such a thing.

"Damn you, Mammon," snarled another voice, one

of the other Council members. "Keep your hands off her! Or were you planning on breaking the Nexus yourself?"

"You fool," Lucifer hissed at Mammon. "I've had enough of you for today, I think." In a louder voice, he shouted, "We hereby command a fight to the death between Mammon, Prince of Avarice, and Raum, Destroyer of Dignities and Robber of Kings! The winner shall sit on our Council, and the loser will suffer immolation by fire sword! So we have spoken, and we are Hell!"

A cheer went up at the announcement, a great wave of deafening sound that was an unmistakable cry for blood. No one appeared to care much whose blood it was, only that it was shed. Ember felt her heart sink as Mammon rose, gave a stiff bow to his liege and leaped from the box, wings spread, to land gently on the dirt of the arena floor.

Two squat, red-skinned *nefari* rushed out carrying a large chest between them, while another went about releasing Raum from his bonds. Raum rubbed his wrists, and then he did look at her, raising his head to lock eyes with her. Ember sucked in a breath as raw emotion blew through her with a surge of heat that had her toes curling.

She could barely bring herself to hope it…but maybe, just maybe there was hope for the two of them after all…

"Come now, this won't do," said Lucifer in her ear, and he sliced neatly through her bonds with one elongated claw. "You really are a lovely little thing, in spite of your parentage. Come and sit by me, sweet. We can watch the blood run together."

She had no choice but to follow, but at least the cords sliding to the floor gave her some much-needed relief. She looked for someone to get up and give her a seat, but when Lucifer resituated himself and patted his lap, she realized he had something else in mind.

"Come now, my little demoness. I doubt you're always so shy. Let's watch the show, shall we?"

Raum watched Ember gingerly settle herself on Lucifer's lap, and forced himself to tear his gaze away and concentrate on the matter at hand. It was an added distraction he didn't need, and Lucifer no doubt knew it. Both of them shared a fairly violent possessive streak. But Ember could take care of herself. He had to remember that, even though he would much rather be taking care of the job himself.

He only hoped the hurried missives he'd sent upon his arrival in Hell hadn't somehow gotten lost in the ether between worlds. Or even worse, that they'd arrived, and been ignored by all concerned. It was a deadly game he was playing now, but what choice did he have? If he'd attempted to leave with her outright, they would have been chased, and likely caught at the gates. And Mammon would never let her alone, even if the Nexus was somehow sealed. Raum knew that for certain now. Mammon considered her his property, his prize, and Raum knew the demon would chase them to the ends of the Earth. They would never have any peace.

Not until Mammon was dead. A thing he intended

to take care of presently. And by then, hopefully, the cavalry would be where he needed them to be. Or at least some part of it.

If not…well, he'd cross that bridge when he came to it.

"I'll choose first," Mammon snapped as the *nefari* opened the heavy chest they'd carried out. He was still overly pale, Raum thought, pleased that the demon was afraid. Mammon hadn't expected that his king would throw him to the wolves so easily. But then, years of influence and essential laziness, of wallowing in the decadence of the Infernal Court, had blinded him to what Lucifer really was. Raum remembered, and it had played out just as he'd hoped.

All but Lucifer's interest in Ember. But then, with luck, she wouldn't have to tolerate his hands on her much longer.

"Be my guest," Raum said blandly, moving to examine the four fire swords carefully laid within. To the casual observer, they would look like long, slim, finely crafted rapiers honed of a metal that shone like pale silver. But in the hands of one of angelic blood, dark or light, these were instruments of death. And one of the most effective methods of demonic fratricide available.

The wounds inflicted by fire would be much slower to heal. And a flaming sword through the heart would be the end.

After deliberating for a moment, Mammon selected the most ornate one, whose handle was made to look as though it had been fashioned of human beings in various attitudes of torment. With a faint smile, he whipped the blade through the air a few times, swinging his arm, warming up. The blade began to glow, brighter and brighter, until it was encased in a sheath of blue-white flame.

He looked as if he'd practiced recently, Raum noted, and felt a prickle of unease. He himself had often practiced with the blade as an outlet for his fury, but it had been a while. And seeing how easily Mammon handled it, he wondered, for the first time, if he could lose.

"Come on, traitor," Mammon said, flashing his fangs at him. "Hurry it up. I have things to do, worlds to invade. And you, as usual, are right in my way."

"Well, this should take care of that problem one way or another," Raum murmured, eyeing his choices. At last, he selected the simplest of them, though it was, in his opinion, of an even finer quality than the others. Deceptive.

He'd always been quite good at deception. Hopefully, this would be no exception.

Mammon snorted. "You can't beat me, Raum. I wish you'd give it up. Did you really think I was going to sit around and let you take my place? You're weak," he sneered. "You wouldn't have the stomach for what's coming, and I knew it. You're a disgrace to the Fallen. And you've touched my daughter for the last time."

"Keep dreaming," Raum replied, testing the blade, getting a feel for its weight. He felt warmth ripple up his sword arm as the precious metal tapped into his elemental power. The blade changed, and was soon alight.

"Oh, I will," Mammon purred. "See how Lucifer

fawns over her, my Ember? I had hardly dared to hope it, but she will undoubtedly become one of his consorts. If I play my cards right, his *favorite* consort. And when there is Hell on Earth—"

"That really is a dream, Mammon," Raum growled, blocking out the wild grunts and catcalls from the stands. "How many thousands of years will it take for you to see that?"

"Hmm. Which one of us has the access to know such things? I wonder," Mammon said, tipping his head with a smirk. "A few little Fallen traitors aren't going to change anything." He rolled his head around to loosen his neck, and then lifted his blade to point directly at Raum's heart.

"Now why don't we get this over with?"

The *nefari* closed the chest and skittered out of the way, and the door through which they'd come in was shut with a heavy slam. The crowd roared, knowing the fun had finally begun.

They circled each other warily, giving one another a wide berth as the cries of their brethren urged them on. Raum heard his name shouted in encouragement, and heard it cursed. None of it mattered.

Only winning mattered.

At last, Mammon's impatience got the better of him. With an animalistic shriek, he rushed him, the bright fiery blade slicing dangerously close to Raum before he could parry. Then the swords met, and sang, as fire and metal collided for the first time.

Once the fight was engaged, Mammon was relentless. The blade flashed through the air so quickly it was a blur, over and over again. But Raum found, to his relief, that his skills returned quickly. He blocked each thrust, and then, when the moment was right, went on the offensive, driving a stunned Mammon back toward the box where the Council was seated. About to be cornered, he did what Raum had been waiting for him to do: he flapped his great wings and took to the air.

In a split second, Raum was up after him, and the two of them spun in a dizzying ballet, each trying to draw first blood. When Mammon left him the smallest opening, Raum was ready: he lashed out with a movement so quick it was hardly seen, but Mammon's shriek, pain and fury mingled, left no doubt as to who had finally been wounded.

Blood fountained into the air, spattering across the "artwork" carved into Raum's chest. A long red gash opened down the demon's biceps, and he glared at Raum with undisguised hatred as Lucifer roared his approval.

"This ends now," he snarled, and lunged, arrowing straight for Raum's heart. Raum dodged it, but Mammon's speed was incredible when he was riled, a thing Raum had nearly forgotten. He felt the tip of the sword graze his flesh along his side, and knew that both of them were now bleeding.

Mammon grinned. "Hurts, eh? That's nothing. I'm just getting warmed up."

The deadly dance continued, whirling, blades flying, higher into the air as the crowd's screams for blood became deafening. Raum looked for any sign that his opponent was flagging, but the blasted demon appeared to be thriving on finally having gotten his chance to take him out. Raum's side throbbed dully, and he hoped Mammon's wound pained him at least as much.

How long it went on became unclear to him, time warping as they fought. It was likely only minutes, but it felt like hours, until finally, Raum saw his opening. Mammon twisted slightly to the left, exposing vulnerable flesh on his torso, and Raum drove his blade inward and up, directly through whatever was left of the demon's twisted and blackened heart.

With an inhuman shriek, Mammon stiffened, eyes widening as they locked with Raum's. And then he plummeted like a stone from the sky, catching fire as he fell, until he hit the ground with a blinding flash of flame that had Raum throwing an arm over his eyes.

When he could look again, all that was left was some ash, rapidly scattering in the breeze from the impact.

Mammon was gone.

Raum's name rose up from the assembled, like a drumbeat, and he remembered, just for a moment, what it had been like in the days of his greatest glory.

"Raum! Raum! Raum!"

He could have it all back, he knew. All that glory, and the blood and pain that retaining it would require. And he would be as empty as he had ever been. More, because he would have thrown away a love that was the sweetest thing he had ever known.

The Reaper Jarrod had been right, that night Raum had healed Ember in the woods. He was still Raum. But he was no demon anymore.

He descended, hovering in the air before the

stunned members of the Council. He could see Ember's uncertainty as she watched him, knew how he must look, bloodstained and bleeding, fresh from the kill. Still they chanted his name.

"Well," Lucifer said, barely raising an eyebrow. "Welcome back to the family...*brother*."

"Ember," he said, ignoring him. "Come on. We don't have much time."

Belial, silent until now, rolled his eyes. "You're home now, Raum. There'll be plenty of time for *that*." The others chuckled, but Ember's eyes stayed on him, still wary.

Then he held out his arms. "Come with me."

"You got it." Her voice was weary, relieved as she scrambled off Lucifer's lap and launched herself into the air before the king of Hell had time to do more than snatch at the air where she'd been a half second before. Raum caught her easily, savoring the feel of her in his arms as he cradled her against him. Better was the look she gave him, full of more love than he'd ever imagined might be bestowed upon him.

"I'm finally free of him. Both of us are. Now let's blow this joint."

"Oh, no," Lucifer said softly. "No, I don't think so, Raum." His eyes began to change, darkening until they were a window into the soulless abyss he had become. "Not at all."

"Hang on tight," Raum said, and launched himself, and the woman he loved, upward into the acrid night air of the underworld.

There was a great rushing sound behind them, like a

flock of birds all taking flight at once, and Raum knew that if he and Ember succeeded, it would be with all of Hell nipping at their heels.

He soared faster than he ever had, his wings slicing through the air as he shot toward the place where he knew the legions were already massing, hidden in the murky mists of Hell's borderlands. The place where the worlds grew thin.

Ember clung to him, burying her head against his neck to keep the wind from her face. The warmth of her breath against his skin steadied him, gave him strength. Faster he flew, even as the murderous cries of the rest of demonkind grew louder behind him. And above it all, he heard Lucifer's infuriated battle cry, and knew that if he was caught now, his death would be neither quick nor easy.

"Listen to me," he said against her ear. "I need you to remember what Mammon taught you."

She stiffened. "What?"

"We're going to break through the Nexus from this side, Ember. And with luck, there'll be help waiting on the other side to seal it right back up again. But I need you to remember how to break it."

"I don't know what you're talking about!" she protested, her voice muffled against him. "I don't know what I'm *doing*, Raum!"

"He would have trained you well, Ember. It's what you were made for, to be a Breaker. And— Hellfire, this is worse than I'd thought. No, don't look."

The obstinate woman looked anyway. Raum didn't know exactly what she was thinking as she looked down upon the massed armies of Hell, miles of *nefari* soldiers all waiting in front of a distant and gleaming patch of mist that sometimes, depending on how it shifted and swirled, looked almost like the view into a peaceful little town.

No, he didn't know. But he could guess.

"You've got to remember, Ember. It's in there. I'm sure of it."

"Oh, God," she moaned as a flying demon shouted an obscenity not far behind them. "I'm not supposed to do this, remember?"

Never breaking his speed, Raum pressed his lips against her ear again, trying to let her feel all his love for her, all his faith in her ability. "It's the only way now. You can do this. Close your eyes, love. Feel it calling to you. And then do what you're meant to do."

She fell silent and still against him, though the shimmering Nexus rushed toward them at an ever-increasing rate. He waited, and waited, worry beginning to gnaw at him. Didn't she remember? Would Mammon have left her so unprepared, for all that?

Then he realized that Ember wasn't just silent. She was concentrating.

She was…*glowing*.

Her face was knotted with intense concentration as Ember let the song of the Nexus take her. And indeed, she began to glow as brightly as the fire sword as he carried her, rushing headlong into the breach. After a moment, he realized her lips were forming words he could not hear. And at the same time, the mists surrounding the Nexus began to clear, and the view of

Ember's neighborhood in Johnstown became so real that Raum could hear, above the din, a roll of thunder in the bloody, bruised sky as the last of the sunset tried to slip away.

"Now!" he roared.

Ember's eyes flew open, full of Hellish red light.

"Patefacio via!" she cried, her voice carrying through the darkness. Then there was a sound like tearing, like screaming, as the fabric that separated two worlds was ripped in two, and a single fallen angel and his woman slipped easily from one plane of reality to another.

As, soon, would those chasing behind.

Chapter 18

Ember clung blindly to Raum as power rocketed through her. It was both beautiful and terrible, the sure knowledge that she held the power to rend the fabric of whole realms of existence, that as some creatures had been made to create, so she had been given the power to destroy.

Hear its song, Raum had said, and the Nexus *had* sung to her, a singular, strange melody that had rippled through her and brought forth the memory, at last, of what she must do. Then the words had come, slowly at first, then in a great rush, ending with the command to open the way.

Familiar voices reached her ears, shouting things she couldn't quite make out as air, real air, flooded her lungs. It was hard to concentrate, hard to feel anything but the reverberations of what she had just done. Her father might be dead, but she had wound up doing his bidding nonetheless. She had opened the Nexus.

And she hoped to God Raum knew how to close it again.

The shouts grew louder as Raum touched down, and Ember managed to open her eyes, incredibly drained as the power at last began to ebb from her.

She was home.

Her eyes widened as she realized exactly where the Nexus had opened. She and Raum had landed in her front yard. Except…where her house had once been, there was now a jagged rip in the air itself, casting a red glow in the deepening twilight. Beyond it, there was a terrifyingly clear view of the massed armies of Hell. Above the din, Ember could even now hear the orders being screamed, to march, to destroy.

They were the voices of the Fallen, all the lords of Hell. And at their forefront, blue eyes gleaming like windows to madness, soared Lucifer.

Ember struggled to sit up, but her limbs didn't seem to want to cooperate. A quick look around, however, even from her vantage point, was stunning. Around her waited a sea of pale-faced warriors, male and female, and though they were nowhere near the numbers of *nefari* marching on them, the vampires' numbers were impressive. Among them were plenty of shifters, werewolves mainly, but also others she didn't recognize in their various and more exotic animal forms. She saw Justin and Dru moving among them, shouting encouragement, and commands. Other members of the

Necromancium joined them, readying their army for attack.

All Raum's brethren, the exiled Fallen, were gathered all around her in a tight circle. Their faces were grim.

"Where is Uriel?" asked Raum, his tone urgent. "They have to heal the breach, or they're all coming through!"

"They should be here," Gadreel said, sounding more somber than she'd ever heard him. "But I don't know if your message will have reached him in time, Raum. We only just got it."

"But there are so many," Raum replied, sounding bewildered.

"Yeah, well, Justin thought better of chaining you up once we all had a word with him," Murmur said, and then there were a few smirks, which told Ember that more than just words had been exchanged. "When you were already gone, we got everyone ready to move on short notice. Just in case you did something stupid, like bring Hell back with you."

"Nice going on that, by the way," the red-haired demon called Phenex added. "Right on time and everything. Unlike some other celestial beings." He looked up and scanned the sky again, which was dark and full of stars. "Shit, Raum, we're going to have to fight without them."

The roars of the demon horde grew louder, and Ember felt Raum tensing against her.

"Let me stand," she said, wanting to stand and fight with the rest if that's what it came to. There were her friends, this was her world, and there was no way she was going to run and hide while everyone else defended it, and each other.

She knew it was bad when he didn't argue with her, but just quietly, gently, set her down. He gave her a moment to lean on him, to steady herself, and then rose. When he did, Ember could see he'd come to some sort of decision about what to do. His shoulders were thrown back, wings spread, his jaw set. That frightened her.

But it was the tender kiss he gave her that nearly broke her heart.

"Remember me," he said softly, touching his forehead to hers.

Then he was gone with a flash of midnight-black wings, leaving Ember to watch in mute horror as he headed straight for the Nexus.

"What is he doing? He can't fight them all himself!" she cried, turning to Gadreel. The demon looked back at her, his bright green eyes dull with resignation, and shook his head. She'd never seen him look sad. But they all did, she realized.

Every last damned one of them.

"He's not going to fight them," Gadreel said softly, as a rising wind carried Lucifer's enraged shriek to them, the sound painful. "He's going to try and heal the breach himself. I don't know if he can, but he's got balls, I'll give him that."

"I thought only an angel could do that!" Ember protested, not understanding anything but that he was leaving her, and that he didn't expect to be coming back.

"Because you have to channel the Light," Murmur

said, watching the unfolding scene with something like amazement. "We gave all that up a long time ago. It would burn us if we tried it...been part of the Dark for far too long. I doubt he'll even remember how. I don't."

But Ember realized, in a flash of horror, that he did know.

The burns. The burns on his hands.

He'd burned himself healing her, saving her life by channeling the Light. The realization of what he'd done, what he'd risked, before he'd even really known her, rocked her to her core. Whatever else he was, whatever else he'd been, he was a good man at heart.

But to heal the breach between worlds was going to be a thousand times more difficult than healing a single human being.

And he would never know that she loved him.

"Even the angels don't usually make it," she heard someone whisper. "He's done for."

There was a sudden commotion above them, and a murmur went through the crowd as one by one, heads tipped back to look for the source of the noise that echoed so gently, yet drowned out all the cacophony of the approaching demon horde. It was, Ember knew without a doubt, the silvery flutter of thousands upon thousands of wings, a sound of such heartbreaking beauty that even now, as she watched the only man she would ever love begin to pulse with deadly light, a single tear of pure joy slipped down her cheek.

"Raum! No!" Boomed a voice that was as sonorous

and majestic as an ocean wave from somewhere up above.

But it was too late, either because Raum couldn't hear, positioned as he was so perfectly between the two worlds, or because he had simply gone too far to make it stop. His arms outstretched, he glowed brighter, brighter until Ember had to throw up her arm and shield her eyes. But the hole had begun to shrink, filling in slowly from the edges as though mending itself back together.

The screaming from Hell grew louder, a chorus with all the fury such a place could possess.

There was a blinding flash, and Ember had a single glimpse, seared into her memory, of Raum's wings changing from deepest black to pure white. Then he burst into flames and fell from the sky, which was now nothing but a placid and unremarkable curtain of unbroken black.

And the only screaming left was her own.

He'd died.

That was the only outcome he'd been prepared for, and the only one that made any sense as Raum drifted in warm, peaceful darkness. It didn't explain why he could still think, of course. Or why he felt himself cradled in warm arms that stroked and caressed, smoothing his hair from his brow.

But there had to be an explanation, Raum reasoned. Maybe what he'd done had merited him a tiny taste of Heaven after all. Or maybe he just wasn't all the way dead yet. He'd definitely burst into flame, and it had hurt like a son of a bitch. So if that was the case, and he hadn't quite died, it shouldn't be long now.

Likely, he decided. But at least he couldn't feel the burns.

Raum sighed and decided to just enjoy the arms, scented faintly of cinnamon and clove, that held him.

"I think he's waking up."

That voice. He knew that voice, and it pulled him upward from the peaceful, floating depths into which he'd drifted. With that upward drift came pain, at first faint, then increasing to an itching, aching symphony of irritation that seemed to be just beneath his skin.

"Raum? Can you hear me?"

Ember. Suddenly he didn't care about the pain, didn't care about anything but getting back to her. In the murky depths of his memory he could still hear her screaming, the most singularly heart-wrenching sound he had ever heard. More, because he knew she had screamed for him, and for the heart he'd broken. He would never be able to fix it now.

But it had been the only way to save her. And that was the selfish truth, why Raum knew he must be only dying, and not drifting in some small patch of Heaven. He hadn't sacrificed himself to the breach to save Earth, or to stop Hell. He'd done it to save Ember.

Somehow, he opened his eyes, heavy though the lids were, and sore besides. The effort was well worth it, though, because he was treated to the sight of the most beautiful smile he had ever seen.

Her hair glowed in soft candlelight, and her honey-colored eyes were lit with a light of their own. She had his head cradled in her arm, he realized, as she stretched out beside him, warming him, soothing some of the places where his skin was so uncomfortable he wanted to scratch it off.

"Ember," he said, wincing at the sound of his voice. It sounded as if he'd been gargling with razor blades. He tried again, though, when he saw how pleased she was with the effort.

"Sorry I went and got myself killed."

She burst out laughing, even as a few shining tears spilled down her pale cheeks. "You idiot. If you were dead, you couldn't feel me do this," she said, pressing her lips to his cheek. It felt decidedly undeathlike, he decided.

"Or this," she continued, pressing another kiss to the corner of his mouth. Even better.

"Or this," he finished for her in a low growl, turning his head to meet her soft, warm mouth fully. It began innocently enough, but he couldn't resist the thoroughly more pleasant sort of heat he felt as her lips parted against his. Together, they indulged in a long, lazy exploration of exactly how close to death he was.

According to one particular barometer, Raum noted, he was about as alive as he could get. Ember's chuckle told him she'd noticed, as well.

She drew back and looked down at him, threading her fingers through his curls and brushing them away from his face. Concern turned her eyes to dark gold.

"I thought you'd left me. I didn't understand what you'd done for me, that night in my bedroom, until you went and threw yourself into the Nexus. Why didn't you just tell me, Raum?"

"Saving your life was new for me," he admitted. "You didn't need to know."

"Well, worrying about you losing your life is new for me," Ember replied. "Raum, there's something I need to tell you."

This was the part where she left him, Raum thought. Where she told him that loving a demon, or even an ex-demon, was too much for her. But there was no way he was going to let that happen. Even before he'd gone and burned himself up, he'd decided he was going to spend a great deal of time making damn sure Ember knew how much he loved her. The rest of her life, if necessary. Starting now.

"There's something I need to tell you first," he said, not missing the flash of irritation in her eyes when he cut her off. He might have smiled, if he'd wanted to prick that beautiful temper of hers further. Instead, he took her hand in his and stroked it gently, and her irritation turned to puzzlement.

"I've been an idiot," he said. "A complete and utter ass. You should probably toss me out and refuse to see me ever again."

Her lips curved into an inviting smile. "Yes, yes and the thought had crossed my mind," Ember said with a soft laugh.

"But I can't let you do that, even though you'll probably call me a high-handed jerk for it, and I'm probably going to keep acting like one from time to time."

Ember's eyes softened, shimmering a little in the

candlelight. The tenderness in her expression took his breath away. How had he been afraid of this? She was all he had ever wanted. She was everything.

"Because?" she asked softly.

"Because I love you, Ember Riddick. I love you with all my wretched heart, and if I had a soul I'd love you with all of that too. I don't ever want to be without you. Please stay with me. Be my wife. Just be *with* me."

She didn't say anything for a long moment, but she didn't have to. It was written all over her beautiful face, and whatever Raum had of a heart, he felt it soar.

"Raum," she murmured, "you know I'm yours. All you had to do was ask. Because I love you, too, with everything I've got."

Then, despite the pain, he pulled her to him for another kiss, losing himself in the magic of this incredible woman who had given him her love. He only wished it could be forever...but he would cherish every moment that she had. His own eternity would never seem so dark again, now that he had been given such a precious gift.

Finally, Ember drew back just a little, careful not to press too hard on the rest of him. She stroked his face, her touch like silk on his stinging skin.

"You look like you have a nasty sunburn," she said. "I was afraid it would be so much worse, but it still looks painful. Are you uncomfortable? He said you would be."

"It's miserable," he agreed, knowing he would feel anything but miserable as long as she was near him. Then he frowned. "Who said I would be?"

"I did," came a voice from the doorway. Raum lifted his head a little, despite the fact that his abused skin protested at the movement. There, incredibly, was Uriel, larger than life, dressed casually in a pullover and jeans and leaning against the doorframe. His eyes were serious, but he did crack a smile as he sauntered into the room.

"You look like you've been microwaved. Glad to see you awake, though."

Raum glanced around, and finally realized he was back in the apartment he and Ember had been sharing in Terra Noctem. Which made no sense, considering.

"Are you sure I'm not dead?" he asked Uriel. "I don't think I merit an angel's feet touching the sullied grounds of the City of Eternal Night."

"I've been thinking a lot since our evening at Amphora," Uriel replied. "The archangels may be ancient, but there are things that need to change. The people here were willing to risk their lives for the Balance, for Earth. We can't ignore that. Especially not now, when Hell's fury will be all the greater."

"Yeah, we did piss them off, didn't we?" Raum rumbled. He grinned even though it pained him, remembering the looks on the faces of the nobles, and of Lucifer as the way into Earth was shut.

"It won't be the end," Uriel warned. "There is no end. For a time, it may be quite a bit worse. He wants your blood now. All of you."

Seeing the way Ember flinched at Uriel's warning, Raum gingerly moved his hand to place it over hers. "He won't get it," he assured her. "Look what we did,

Ember. If we can make it through that, we can make it through anything. Speaking of which," he said, turning his attention back to Uriel with a frown, "why exactly am I not dust?"

Uriel tilted his head to the side. "Well. I'm not sure how you're going to feel about this, but it seems…you may have been forgiven."

The words settled strangely with him. He felt a rush of things: grateful, relieved, afraid of what that meant. "I didn't ask to be forgiven," he protested. "I can't go back, Uriel. I want what I have here." He looked at his woman. "I want Ember."

Uriel's smile was alight with warmth. "Of course. Without Ember's love, not to mention her incredible patience," he added with what Raum felt to be an un- necessary smirk, "you never would have come so far. You risked everything. Why would anyone want to take that away from you?"

He relaxed, but only slightly. "But…what am I, then? What do I do?"

Uriel, instead of saying anything, took one of Raum's hands, and one of Ember's, and folded them together on Raum's chest. For a moment, the feeling of the three of them joined thrummed through him like a rare and beautiful song. One he had heard long ago. And something slipped inside of him, a tiny spark that filled him with the thing he had felt when he had opened himself up and healed the woman who now lay beside him.

Light.

He knew what it meant, and was overwhelmed. Beside

him, Ember gave a soft gasp, and he knew something had also passed between her and the seraph.

"I have been asked to give you these gifts," Uriel said. "You're two halves of the same whole now. As it should be." His voice was suddenly gruff, and Raum's wonder was tempered with the blooming suspicion that his old mentor...his friend...was about to get girly on him.

"Don't you dare cry," he growled. "Just because I finally did something right doesn't mean I'm going to be any nicer to you. Or that I'm going to quit bitching about the white wings running everything."

Uriel shared a look with Ember that she seemed to find funny, then stood. "Raum, I don't think I'd know what to do with myself if I didn't have to listen to your mouth for the rest of eternity. Now rest. You'll heal, but it'll be a few days yet. Oh, and I believe there's a vampire lurking around here somewhere who wants to apologize to you, if you're up to it."

"I will be," Raum replied, distracted by the look Ember was giving him, which promised a very pleasant afternoon if he could figure out how to work around this blasted stinging and itching. "Later."

"Thank you," Ember said to the seraph. "Really."

"And thank you," Uriel said to her, giving a small bow of acknowledgment. "I do like him, you know, even if he is an awful pain in the ass. But then, he always was."

"Bite me," Raum grumbled, but he was grinning as Uriel gave a backward wave and headed out the door, shutting it behind him and leaving him and Ember alone in the gentle glow of the flickering candle.

"I appreciate the ambiance," he said, sliding his hand over her hip now that they were alone. She arched one brow.

"I hate to bust your bubble, but I'm not trying to seduce you. You're supposed to stay in as little light as possible until you're healed."

"We can both see in the dark," he pointed out. "And as for trying to seduce me…do I detect the scent of honey?"

Ember narrowed her eyes at him. "Well. Maybe I just like candlelight. And you've been out for two days. I missed you." A faint line creased her brow. "I worried you wouldn't wake up, even though Uriel promised me that you would."

"What did he give you?" Raum asked, curious, though he thought he already knew. That brought Ember's smile back, far brighter than any candle.

"Eternity. For me, and for us. You?"

Raum felt the light of his newfound soul flicker and dance inside of him, in the places that would never be dark again. One way or another, he and Ember would have forever. Whatever else came, whatever else was asked of him and the others, that was what mattered. He looked at their hands, intertwined, like the two of them.

"The same," he said.

Love never fails.

Damn if the overbearing seraph hadn't finally been right about something.

"I love you, Ember Riddick. Now and always."

"I love you, too, Raum. Forever." Ember leaned in for

a kiss, but then paused, a wicked twinkle in her eyes. "New wings and all."

He realized then, with no small amount of horror, exactly what she and Uriel had thought was so funny. Just wait until the others got a look at them. They probably even had those glittery gold tips....

Hellfire," Raum started to growl. "I'm never going to live this do—"

Then Ember, his mate, his love, silenced him with a kiss.

* * * * *

REQUEST YOUR FREE BOOKS!

2 FREE NOVELS PLUS 2 FREE GIFTS!

 HARLEQUIN®

nocturne™

Dramatic and Sensual Tales of Paranormal Romance.

YES! Please send me 2 FREE Harlequin® Nocturne™ novels and my 2 FREE gifts (gifts are worth about $10). After receiving them, if I don't wish to receive any more books, I can return the shipping statement marked "cancel." If I don't cancel, I will receive 4 brand-new novels every other month and be billed just $4.47 per book in the U.S. or $4.99 per book in Canada. That's a saving of at least 15% off the cover price! It's quite a bargain! Shipping and handling is just 50¢ per book.* I understand that accepting the 2 free books and gifts places me under no obligation to buy anything. I can always return a shipment and cancel at any time. Even if I never buy another book from Harlequin, the two free books and gifts are mine to keep forever.

238/338 HDN E9M2

Name _____ (PLEASE PRINT) _____

Address _____ Apt. # _____

City _____ State/Prov. _____ Zip/Postal Code _____

Signature (if under 18, a parent or guardian must sign) _____

Mail to the **Reader Service:**
IN U.S.A.: P.O. Box 1867, Buffalo, NY 14240-1867
IN CANADA: P.O. Box 609, Fort Erie, Ontario L2A 5X3

Not valid for current subscribers to Harlequin Nocturne books.

Want to try two free books from another line?
Call 1-800-873-8635 or visit www.ReaderService.com.

* Terms and prices subject to change without notice. Prices do not include applicable taxes. N.Y. residents add applicable sales tax. Canadian residents will be charged applicable provincial taxes and GST. Offer not valid in Quebec. This offer is limited to one order per household. All orders subject to approval. Credit or debit balances in a customer's account(s) may be offset by any other outstanding balance owed by or to the customer. Please allow 4 to 6 weeks for delivery. Offer available while quantities last.

Your Privacy: Harlequin Books is committed to protecting your privacy. Our Privacy Policy is available online at www.ReaderService.com or upon request from the Reader Service. From time to time we make our lists of customers available to reputable third parties who may have a product or service of interest to you. If you would prefer we not share your name and address, please check here. ☐

Help us get it right—We strive for accurate, respectful and relevant communications. To clarify or modify your communication preferences, visit us at www.ReaderService.com/consumerschoice.

See below for a sneak peek at
our inspirational line, Love Inspired®.
Introducing HIS HOLIDAY BRIDE
by bestselling author Jillian Hart

Autumn Granger gave her horse rein to slide toward the town's new sheriff.

"Hey, there." The man in a brand-new Stetson, black T-shirt, jeans and riding boots held up a hand in greeting. He stepped away from his four-wheel drive with "Sheriff" in black on the doors and waded through the grasses. "I'm new around here."

"I'm Autumn Granger."

"Nice to meet you, Miss Granger. I'm Ford Sherman, from Chicago." He knuckled back his hat, revealing the most handsome face she'd ever seen. Big blue eyes contrasted with his sun-tanned complexion.

"I'm guessing you haven't seen much open land. Out here, you've got to keep an eye on cows or they're going to tear your vehicle apart."

"What?" He whipped around. Sure enough, mammoth black-and-white creatures had started to gnaw on his four-wheel drive. They clustered like a mob, mouths and tongues and teeth bent on destruction. One cow tried to pry the wiper off the windshield, another chewed on the side mirror. Several leaned through the open window, licking the seats.

"Move along, little dogie." He didn't know the first thing about cattle.

The entire herd swiveled their heads to study him curiously. Not a single hoof shifted. The animals soon returned to chewing, licking, digging through his possessions.

Autumn laughed, a warm and wonderful sound. "Thanks,

SHLIEXP1010

I needed that." She then pulled a bag from behind her saddle and waved it at the cows. "Look what I have, guys. Cookies."

Cows swung in her direction, and dozens of liquid brown eyes brightened with cookie hopes. As she circled the car, the cattle bounded after her. The earth shook with the force of their powerful hooves.

"Next time, you're on your own, city boy." She tipped her hat. The cowgirl stayed on his mind, the sweetest thing he had ever seen.

Will Ford be able to stick it out in the country
to find out more about Autumn?
Find out in HIS HOLIDAY BRIDE
by bestselling author Jillian Hart,
available in October 2010
only from Love Inspired®.